I0593191

THE
PENDULUM

THE
PENDULUM

J. L. WHITTON

Copyrighted Material

The Pendulum

Copyright © 2023 by J. L. Whitton. All Rights Reserved.

No part of this publication may be reproduced, stored in a retrieval system or transmitted, in any form or by any means—electronic, mechanical, photocopying, recording, or otherwise—without prior written permission from the publisher, except for the inclusion of brief quotations in a review.

For information about this title or to order other books and/or electronic media, contact the publisher:

J. L. Whitton
Jaidenwhittonauthor@gmail.com

ISBNs:
978-0-6454713-0-4 (softcover)
978-0-6454713-1-1 (eBook)

Printed in the United States of America

Cover and Interior design: 1106 Design

Dedicated to my friends and family.
Without their love and continued support, this book
would have never been possible.

CONTENTS

Chapter One 1

Chapter Two 10

Chapter Three 19

Chapter Four 29

Chapter Five 37

Chapter Six 48

Chapter Seven 53

Chapter Eight 62

Chapter Nine 72

Chapter Ten 81

Chapter Eleven 91

Chapter Twelve 100

Chapter Thirteen 111

Chapter Fourteen 120

Chapter Fifteen 129

Chapter Sixteen 139

Chapter Seventeen 151

Chapter Eighteen 158

Chapter Nineteen 168

Chapter Twenty 176

Chapter Twenty-One 186

Chapter Twenty-Two 195

Chapter Twenty-Three 204

Chapter Twenty-Four 212

Chapter Twenty-Five 221

Chapter Twenty-Six 231

Chapter Twenty-Seven 240

Chapter Twenty-Eight 251

Chapter Twenty-Nine 260

Chapter Thirty 269

Chapter Thirty-One 281

CHAPTER ONE

At the start of the twenty-first century, the world's fears about unchecked population growth were realised. There were widespread food, water, and energy shortages, the conflict over which caused mass migration on every continent. As a steep global recession developed, countries watched their currency become worthless. It was one of the worst series of crises the modern world had ever experienced. A war for territory and control of assets erupted between the Australian military and a group of renegades known as the "Militia for Severance."

The civil war ravaged the continent, and victory—for either side—relied on funding. Most of the Militia's money came from their large-scale criminal activities; the remainder was provided by sympathetic breakaway groups all across the world. The Australian government had no financial reserves and had to rely on profits generated from their domestic market and exports. Other friendly nations were involved in their own conflicts; they were able to contribute only limited, sporadic funding and aid. The Australian government finally agreed to a cease-fire and began peace talks with the Militia.

The rebels had several non-negotiables. The most drastic was the division of the Australian continent into an eastern and a western sector. The rebels demanded complete forfeiture of the eastern sector, and they named it "The United Republic of The Southern Continent" (U.R.S.C.). With more existing infrastructure and better resources, the potential for growth and prosperity made the eastern sector far superior. Having won this concession, the Militia set about the unenviable task of building their new country from the ground up. Eventually, the U.R.S.C. government took the shape of a loosely defined, benign collective dictatorship.

The rebel agenda was to create a place where all types of lifestyles and diversity were encouraged, where all ideologies and cultures were embraced and an ethos of art and expression was promoted. There were no laws that banned or restricted personal freedoms, and laws relating to immigration were so relaxed that almost anyone could gain entry into the country. These ideals were supported by a rewritten Constitution and the passage of many laws that were much more lenient than the former Australian regime's. After much discussion, a modified type of Capitalism was chosen as the commerce system. There were many wealthy and powerful individuals in the new government, who ensured that the U.R.S.C. became a tax haven, with essentially no regulation on business. The atmosphere appealed to industrialists and businesses alike, and they flocked to the region.

The new country, unfortunately, also became a sanctuary for criminals from all over the world, fleeing their own countries to start again in the U.R.S.C. "Starting Over" became a popular catchphrase in the U.R.S.C.—and it was quickly seized upon by advertising agencies to entice people to move there. It worked, and people—on both sides of the law—streamed into the new country in unprecedented numbers.

By the beginning of the second decade of the twenty-first century, the U.R.S.C. had become a global economic superpower.

Ally Rose (a name of her own making) operated under many aliases; remaining anonymous was part of her profession. She had lived under this identity for so long, she felt that's who she had legitimately become. In reality, she was an alienated French immigrant. After being separated from her family during the massive conflict and unrest in Europe, she migrated to the U.R.S.C. in search of a better life. She missed her family terribly and had never fully healed from losing them.

Ally Rose was a Facilitator.

That was the informal title describing any one of a large number of mercenaries to whom citizens with elite connections would come when they were desperate for something. The criminal nature of the methods sometimes employed by Facilitators was no secret. Her clients had tried many other ways to get what they were seeking, but it was common knowledge that *Facilitators got things done.*

Facilitating had made her fabulously wealthy, but she had witnessed and done terrible things and was forced to associate with society's worst people. She struggled to justify her lifestyle and profession, as it conflicted with her overall generous, accommodating persona. She was a mercenary caught in an incompatible, unfulfilling existence.

She had scheduled a meeting with her client at midnight in the Rose Garden of the sprawling Corinth Park. She had arrived moments before he did.

"If you have the connections to even locate me and the finances to afford my services, then surely you can pay for the transplant. So why are you not going through legal channels? Are you that desperate?" she asked.

"I wouldn't have come to you unless it was a last resort. I've got no other options—the system has failed me. I can afford the procedure, but they're having difficulty finding a donor. Ever since the majority of the health system was privatised, the waiting lists are extensive. The insurance company won't help with the surgery. My daughter needs this procedure as soon as possible. I need your help. I'll do whatever it takes to save her—money isn't a question," he said frantically.

"Before we continue any further, who was your connection for finding me?"

"I told an associate of mine—a previous client of yours, whom I won't identify—how dire my situation was, and they referred me to you. They said you were one of the best Facilitators on the market."

"While I appreciate their recommendation and your enquiry, this is an extremely high-risk operation, and I need to know that I can trust you. I can facilitate your request, although I'm going to need some type of remuneration—a bond or collateral," she said.

"Of course, anything. I'll give you whatever you want," the man said, sliding off his expensive gold watch and offering it to her.

"I don't want your possessions. Like I was saying, I can facilitate your request, but the organ trade is something I strive to avoid. There are other people I can contact who have more expertise in that area, though it would take longer and would require money."

"No, it can't wait! My daughter can't wait—she needs this operation urgently. If your other sources can organise the surgery more swiftly, could you refer me to them?"

"Even if I did, I would require some type of payment. I'm not going to refer a person they don't know to do a transaction of this nature. That's the dynamic—you don't know my identity, and I don't know yours. That's how it works. I don't want any type of paper trail, written correspondence, or telephone contact—meeting in this park is dangerous enough. Nevertheless, you will meet me here at the same time tomorrow night with half of the transaction fee. Only after this is done will you receive further instructions. Do you understand?"

"Yes, I understand," he replied.

"And you're fine with someone else's son or daughter being harvested?"

"No—that's why I'm so conflicted, but I don't know what else to do for my family. Just the fact that I'm meeting with you should demonstrate what I'm willing to do."

"Anything for family. Don't arrive here with any type of recording device or anyone accompanying you—hidden or otherwise—as I'll find out. Then you won't have any family to worry about anymore."

"How do I get my daughter out of hospital and when?" he asked.

"I repeat: I'll give you further instructions tomorrow night, *after receiving the money*, because that's not a part of the process I'm facilitating. It's your responsibility to coordinate that part of it," she said. With that, they began walking in opposite directions. They were located on the fringe of the "Marketplace," a collection of boroughs in Clarion, a city in the U.R.S.C. renowned for the illicit services offered there. Corinth Park was relatively empty at that early-morning hour; in the distance were a few indistinguishable figures, and, along the pathways, lantern light pierced the tree branches, which swayed gently amidst the hot gusts of wind. Regardless of the time, the Marketplace would invariably be a hive of activity, pulsing with a devious energy and people indulging in revelry.

She exited the Park onto the long grid-like streets.

She was meeting her friend Portia D'Amico, a corrupt detective in the Major Crimes Division of law enforcement. They had to discuss an upcoming robbery plan before she went to a billiard hall to contact an associate about the organ transplant. Ally had walked several blocks among the skyward-soaring buildings. As she came toward the meeting point, an empty lane between office blocks, she removed a handgun from her shoulder holster. A menacing black vehicle was approaching at a rapid pace.

It was Portia.

She came to a sudden stop next to Ally. "Get in the car! Get in! Get in now!" she said frantically.

"What's going on? You look terrible," Ally said as she got into the passenger seat.

"It's really bad—this is really bad—I need your help; somebody's put a fucking hit out on me, Ally. I discovered only a few hours ago from an informant that a Facilitator has been paid to do it. I need your help to find out who it is. We have to find out everything we can about this—who put the contract out and why. Then tell them to call it off, or we fucking kill 'em all." Portia said as she accelerated aggressively. She was visibly distressed and high on drugs. "I've been searching all through the Marketplace. Here—I've got some cocaine if you want some." She placed a bag containing two kilograms in Ally's lap.

"Thank you. This is just really unexpected. I'm sorry—this is a lot to process. Do you have any evidence or indication at all who put out the hit on you and why?" Ally asked.

"No. I don't know. I've been out of control lately—you know that. I've been furiously searching my brain and thinking, *Who could have done this?* and *What did I do to deserve this?* Even the stuff we've done together—like a few weeks ago, when I gave you that badge, and we raided that drug dealer and stole their supply. I've been extorting people, helping certain drug racquets and sabotaging others. It could be anything—and I'm falling apart right now because of it." Portia was driving erratically, swerving between lanes.

"Why are you driving so recklessly? We don't want to draw any extra attention to ourselves."

"Because I'm a fucking detective in the Major Crimes Division, Ally! I can run around this city with impunity! I'm the hand that feeds! I pull the strings! I've got free rein! You and I don't have to worry about anything, but we've got to stay on the move. I'm driving so wildly because I'm paranoid and stressed. I'm sorry, Ally. I'm not angry at you. I'm just on edge because my life is in jeopardy, and I'm trying to work out the next move and stay alive."

"Do you know exactly where we're going?" Ally asked after sniffing some cocaine and feeling an intense rush.

"Not just yet. That's why I need your help. All I know is we're going to find out some information." Portia almost had an accident with another vehicle—she veered around it wildly.

"This is insane. You're a detective! If they can't help *you*, then who *can* they help? I mean, why come to me?"

"Because I'm under suspicion by some of my superiors for taking firearms from the evidence locker. And if they find out about *a plot to murder me*, they're going to ask questions. They'll be looking for a link between the murder plot and someone that I've done wrong to. Then, it'll be much worse. The superiors in the bureau receive a certain amount of money, power, and other benefits from helping criminal connections," Portia said.

"You said that an informant conveyed this information to you recently. How can you trust them? What did they say? It seems to be scarce on details."

"It was a reliable source, a reliable informant. They didn't know very much, unfortunately, and I was very fucking hostile toward them. I extracted everything I could. I interrogated them right where you're sitting. All they knew was that there was talk circulating around the Marketplace and the Red-Light District that a contract with an enormous reward had been placed on a detective in the Major Crimes Division. The informant confirmed that I'm the target, but he hadn't ascertained who authorised the contract. They said that some Facilitator had taken up the job, and they mainly congregate in the Marketplace."

"We're going to figure this out. I'm going to help you, but I need something," Ally said. They had a strong relationship, an interdependent alliance, but, ultimately, they were friends. Their first encounter had been when Portia investigated her for fraud. After some negotiation, they got into business together and unexpectedly developed a friendship.

"What do you need?"

"After I met with you, I was going to a venue to conduct some business of my own. I can utilise my contacts, and we'll be able to resolve your situation. What I need is your help to organise an organ transplant."

"Yeah—sure, sure, that's no problem. When this ordeal is over, I can help you with that. I know some excellent surgeons, some discreet locations, and it's all very hygienic. No questions asked, no records."

"It's an eight-year-old child, though."

"Really? Fuck! Ally! Fuck! That complicates things. That makes the whole procedure more difficult. All right—I said I would help you, but this is risky; you have to be careful. There's been some intel going around the office about the black-market organ trade. Some of my colleagues have been investigating and shutting down a lot of racquets. We're going to have to exercise caution. Anyway, where were you going after I saw you?"

"I was going to a billiard hall, 'The Shark Tank,' on West Forty-Second Street, near the Laurent Highway. There are a few people I can ask about this contract on your life, but we're a considerable distance from there now," Ally said. They had driven the opposite direction, to a borough comprising massive housing-project buildings for the socially downtrodden.

"Thank you for your help. I know the place—don't worry. We'll go down Liberty Avenue Thoroughfare and get onto the Laurent Highway—we'll arrive there in no time," Portia said, maintaining her ferocious pace. They journeyed to the billiard hall. Portia brought the car to a screeching halt in a dingy alleyway that ran behind the building. "Get your weapons ready," Portia said before snorting more cocaine.

"Whoa! We are *not* going in there aggressively. I come here quite often, for business and pleasure. I can't have my reputation here ruined; we need to approach this the correct way."

"I'm sorry, Ally, but we have to go in there on the offensive; we have to be uncompromising." Portia reached behind her seat, produced an automatic shotgun, and loaded a drum magazine.

"Portia, you can't go in with that. You don't understand! We can't go in all guns blazing! Ideally, you shouldn't even go in there. If they realise that you're a law enforcement officer, or if anyone recognises you from all our wild exploits, you're dead—and so am I for associating with you. I'm not excited about being seen with you in this venue. Sorry—I'm just being honest. You're my friend, but it's bad for both of our reputations. Besides, if the Facilitator who has been paid to kill you is in there, they won't hesitate to murder you. Now I know you're distressed and upset, but you've got to follow my lead on this. You've got to come in with me and be silent. I'll do the talking and ask the questions—just don't go crazy in there! Don't shoot or kill anyone; don't brandish any weapons or shout at anybody. Please let me take control."

Portia reluctantly agreed. Each armed with two handguns, they entered the billiard hall. The tension in the air was palpable; it ran high as they made their way through the haze of smoke, the place humming with indecipherable chatter and the sound of colliding billiard balls. Any new arrival into the club would attract looks. Ally and Portia could feel the attention focused on them, but they continued with confidence. Ally spoke to many individuals and played several billiard matches in exchange for information. She was a highly skilled player, but so were the other patrons. Portia lingered in the background while Ally conversed between matches. She had a very subtle way of extracting what she needed without seeming deliberate. Eventually, she gathered enough details to assist Portia, and they left shortly after 2 a.m.

CHAPTER TWO

They knew of some people and had the names of others who might know about the hit on Portia, but they were unsure of their exact locations. To find their first target, a human trafficker, they had to contend with the city's murky sex industry. Prowling the seedy parlours and markets frequented by their suspect, they stalked through dim corridors and soiled boudoirs, searching for the target, a man who wrongly blamed Portia for his business partner's murder.

One destination took the pair through a grizzly slave auction held in an underground facility, where they witnessed the gross exploitation of individuals in the depressing trade. When that yielded no results, they moved on to the next place the target was known to frequent: a sex and fetish club that was a front for criminal activity. Going in alone, Portia negotiated past the security guarding the door by posing as a patron. The darkness of the club was punctuated by vast arrays of lasers and strobe lights.

Portia wove her way past revellers in elaborate fetish costumes of leather straps and masks, lingerie and latex bodysuits. In an exclusive room on the club's top floor, she encountered the target. She was in tactical mode, conducting herself without showing anger or eliciting a response from the suspect or the security. He recognised her as she approached and told her to leave immediately. She began amiably with her questioning and behaviour towards him. He was infuriated by the mere sight of her; a confrontation simmered as Portia balanced her approach to avoid further disruption. The security was hovering around them, but, with a signal of his hand, he put them at ease.

"Before you say anything, I know you despise me, but you must understand—I did not kill your associate. I've already told you we were doing a standard search of the vehicle, and he pulled a gun. Wardrop shot him—I didn't. Anyway, I've been hearing some disturbing reports about a contract on my life, and I've come to say it ends tonight. Call off this contract on my life before you end up like your friend and partner," Portia shouted over the pulsing rhythm of the music.

"I don't know what you're talking about. I'm not part of any plan to kill you—I haven't heard anything about it," the target replied loudly. He continued to deny any knowledge of the plot.

"Why should I believe you? You'd say anything to make me believe you're not in on this and leave you alone. I've got enough on you already to arrest you; I could just as easily plant some evidence on you and have a small army of detectives sniffing around here before you even know what you're being arrested for," she yelled. The person's entourage stood by, looking on coldly.

"Look—I'll prove it to you if you'll fuck off and leave me alone," the target replied. He contacted his new business partners and proved he was not part of the murder plan. Bleeding from injuries inflicted by the club's security on her way out, she returned to the car and Ally.

She continued speeding through the streets with an adrenaline surge coursing through her.

Ally knew of an exclusive party on the roof of a high-rise building where some people of interest were in attendance. They surveilled the building and concluded that the security was too extensive and that they would not be able to gain entry. That meant they had to refine their methods and try again later, when the circumstances were better. Portia glared despondently at the top of the building; the answers she sought were, cruelly, out of her reach.

They braved a slew of other locations, looking for other targets; at every turn, they were outnumbered and could not approach them. Time after time, they inserted themselves into dangerous settings and situations, storming through sinister locations in the city with no regard for life or law, interacting with crime-hardened gangsters. After tearing through dingy drug dens, loitering in dive bars, and scoping out gambling venues, the only thing Portia could do was interrogate informants and lower-level employees of the people she was after. Under Portia's direction throughout the night, Ally was forced to hurt—and kill—many people she didn't even know. Portia was at the end of her fraying rope and turned on Ally, questioning her closely while they waited for an informant at a deserted underpass. Enraged, Ally firmly denied any connection to the contract on Portia's life. An intense argument ensued between them that ceased only when the informant arrived with some useful information.

They'd lost all sense of time and were surprised to see dawn breaking. They couldn't continue to interrogate and murder people in broad daylight, and, so, slowly, they wound down their rampage. They were both badly injured from altercations. Both of Ally's eyes and cheeks were bruised, and her lips were swollen. Their clothing was covered in coagulated blood, a mixture of theirs and others.

They sheltered at Ally's hotel room, a spacious penthouse suite on the top floor of Serendipity Fair, a luxury beachfront hotel. They smoked marijuana and silently pondered their night of carnage. They had a panoramic, 360-degree view of the ocean and the city framed in the soft morning light, the sun splashing colour across the water as it rose. They had gained much of the information they had been seeking, but neither of them were prepared to learn of the contract on Portia's life—or that it was a small piece of a wider mosaic of corruption, blackmail, and murder.

But now they knew that the plot against Portia had been devised by some of her superiors in the police force who were enraged by her behaviour. Not only had she been disrupting the criminal enterprises they were invested in, but she was also seizing weapons and drugs to resell for her own profit or personal use, killing their associates, and assisting their competition. The officers had outsourced the contract to their criminal allies to avoid being implicated in the scandal. In turn, the criminals found a ruthless Facilitator to carry out the job. These revelations had left them stunned, and Portia was nervously pacing by the floor-to-ceiling windows.

"I can't believe this," she said repeatedly under her breath.

"I'm struggling to comprehend this whole conspiracy *and* how intense last night was," Ally said.

"I know, I know—I'm astounded. I never would've expected that this was an inside job and that it goes right up to the very top. But, while it may defy belief, we've got to evaluate the situation realistically. We're in a better position than we were mere hours ago. We've gained a lot of traction. We managed to locate some of the criminals involved but not the particular people we need to call off the hit. We know their identities, but we haven't been successful in hunting them down. We also failed to identify the Facilitator. This is still a whole web of deceit, betrayal, and greed." Portia gazed out at the ocean, tears rolling down her bruised cheeks.

"What are you going to do?" Ally asked, breaking a tense silence.

"I'm not entirely sure. I didn't want this, Ally. Now I'm far out of my depth. I never wanted the corruption that seems to come with being a detective. I dreamed of being a good detective . . . fuck. I aspired to help the disadvantaged people of society. Now, I'm feasting on them like a vulture." She went silent, leaning her forehead on the glass while breathing deeply. She was disgusted because she had been forced into oppressive child labour herself.

"I'll stand by you, Portia, whatever course of action you decide to take," Ally said reassuringly.

"I appreciate that. I'm aware of the terrible things I've done to a lot of people—both innocent and guilty—and I've got to live with those consequences and take responsibility for my actions. All that I've done here is commit crimes against people who were already poisoned by greed. I know what I must do. I've amassed an extensive dossier on the people involved in this murder conspiracy. It could bring them all down."

"That would be even more dangerous for you. There is a piece of Greek Wisdom that says, 'Danger can never be overcome without danger.' There's no easy way out of this predicament. The life that we lead is constantly overshadowed by danger, violence, and regret. I can't even tell people what I do—I can't disclose that I'm a Facilitator. I have to lie and say I'm a financier. Only a few weeks ago, I witnessed an enemy being fed to a tiger. The growling, the sight of his intestines, and his screams still resonate in my mind. Yet we continue this way of life," Ally explained.

"You're correct, though. Everything you just said describes how I feel and the conflict raging inside of me—like I'm morally bankrupt and numb. Condemning them for their crimes doesn't excuse what I've done," Portia mused.

"My intention was not to upset you any further. I'm sorry. What are you going to do with this dossier?"

"That's where it gets complicated. I need to do this right. I think this was meant to happen; some type of wider reason has set these events into motion. I'm going to confront my colleagues with the information I have on them. I won't release it now, but I'll let them know I have it in my possession. In exchange for keeping it confidential, I'm going to force them to call off the hit on my life. Then, I'm leaving the Major Crimes Division. I've been wanting to leave this line of work and this way of life behind—this pit of despair that I've fallen into. That's why I believe that fate is playing a role in this." Portia walked away from the window, sat next to Ally, took her hand, and stared intently into her eyes. "I want to thank you, Ally. I'm so grateful for your help and your friendship. I never would've been able to solve this crazy riddle if it weren't for you. I don't think I can ever fully repay you, but I'll try."

"Of course, darling. It's my pleasure to be able to help you through this ordeal, because I care about you, Portia. You don't have to repay me." They hugged tenderly, and Portia got to her feet.

"I've got so many things to do. I need to go now and see if I can resolve this mess."

"I need to go to sleep; I've been awake for days. But, first, I need to wash this blood out of my hair and clean up these wounds," Ally replied, examining the extent of her injuries in a mirror.

"What are you doing later?" Portia asked.

"I'm meeting a client at midnight in the Corinth Park Rose Garden, to discuss this organ transplant," Ally replied.

"Excellent. I'll meet you afterwards, and, from there, we'll go to a different location and start the preparation for the procedure. I haven't forgotten about it," Portia exclaimed.

"Thank you. I appreciate that."

"Where will I meet you, though?" Portia inquired.

"Meet me at 1 a.m. at the Hyperion Nightclub. I know it's unsafe, but there may be people there who can help."

"I'll be there. Goodbye, Ally."

"*Au revoir*," Ally responded. She treated her wounds and washed the blood from her hair and face. She soaked her bruised body in a soothing bath. One of her coping mechanisms was drinking alcohol and using drugs; she felt it helped her process the deplorable things she had just done and witnessed. She knew it was just a short-term fix, but it made her feel less despicable about herself and her actions. She was exhausted after being awake for so long. With great care, she got onto the bed, the pure silk sheets luxurious on her skin.

It was well into the evening when she awoke to the sound of her alarm clock. She looked outside; the city skyline was stark against the backdrop of night, the skyscrapers were dotted with squares of light, and the full moon was looming above. Always punctual, she had left herself an adequate amount of time to bathe and refresh before her rendezvous with the client. Travelling around the city was chaotic, so she preferred to walk. She was not afraid of being unaccompanied; always heavily armed, she was proficient with a variety of weapons. It was a requirement for the profession she had chosen.

"What happened to you?" the client asked as he first approached Ally.

"I received these injuries while I was out Facilitating your request." She noticed he was carrying a large briefcase. "Does that contain my money?"

"Yes, it's here—half of the transaction fee. One and a half million in $500 bills, all unmarked and non-sequential." He was obviously nervous; Ally produced her handgun.

"Open it," she said with a stern tone.

He placed it on the park bench between them, lifting the lid to reveal the bundles of money.

"If there is any sort of tracking device in this suitcase or any type of listening device, I'll find it—and I'll kill you."

"No, no. There's nothing at all like that in there. I wouldn't do that," he replied as she inspected the briefcase.

"An update on your request: I have managed to get some assistance, so we can go ahead with the procedure," she said, satisfied with her inspection.

"Thank you so much—thank you."

"Some unforeseen circumstances came up last night. I was fulfilling your request when another issue presented itself. So, I apologise. I had to attend to this problem, and, as a result, I have not gathered as much information about the logistics and some other aspects of the surgery. Like I said, I apologise. That was unprofessional of me. After you and I are finished, I'm meeting with the associate who is assisting me. Hopefully, they will be able to provide more details about when we can actually do this transplant. It was arranged by chance, so I'm reluctant to schedule another meeting, but we must meet again, and then, I promise I'll have everything figured out and ready to go."

He gave Ally a puzzled look. "But my daughter is running out of time; the more time that is wasted, the closer she comes to dying."

"I said I apologise. I almost died several times last night in pursuit of your request. So, I've got to look out for my own interests. Even if you wanted to look elsewhere and seek out the service of another, you can't, I'm afraid. There's no going back now; you've already given me the deposit, and it's not refundable. Besides, this isn't the simplest operation to bring together; something of this magnitude takes time and expertise. That's why you sought my help—because you can't do this alone. Let me do my job. I'm trying to expedite it. I don't need this money. I've already got millions more than this. If you want to run away right now, you'd better run fast or be bulletproof because you have no choice. I need to leave to maintain my schedule. Meet me here the same time again tomorrow evening, and I'll have all the information you need."

"I'll be here," he said.

With that, Ally abruptly left and made her way toward the Hyperion Nightclub. It was a high-class establishment; a dress code was enforced. Ally had all of her footwear and clothing custom-made. She looked stylish in a black silk suit, long pants, and a jacket she wore over a black long-sleeved satin blouse. A rose embroidered onto the blouse collar meant only certain people could identify her as a Facilitator. Unable to wear high heels due to the restrictions it placed on her movement, she was sporting a pair of black combat boots. They were not usually allowed in the club, but they made an exception, as Ally was a respected and well-regarded patron.

CHAPTER THREE

As she approached the club, loud screams from a woman caught Ally's attention. With her handgun drawn, she followed the source of the noise, her concern increasing. The screams seemed to become more urgent. In a clearing off a path, she could see two silhouettes in a struggle. She sprinted through the darkness to approach them from behind, maintaining the element of surprise. Going down an embankment at high speed, carefully avoiding tree roots and rocks, she got closer to the commotion. A man was on top of the woman, attacking her. She had her weapon trained on him before he even noticed her presence.

"Help me! He's trying to rape me! Help me—please!" she yelled when she saw Ally.

"How dare you! Get off of her, before I fill you with bullets!"

The man was also wielding a gun, and, right now, he had it pointed at the woman. It was a tense moment; motionless, he stared at Ally.

"Get off of her!" Ally ordered, aware that he was planning how to kill her. The standoff continued; in the moonlight, Ally could only faintly see their outlines.

Without warning, he moved violently, discharging his weapon toward Ally. The round lodged in the embankment. The woman screamed again as Ally fired three rounds into the man, the second proving fatal. Ally came toward the woman and knelt next to her, helping her to sit up and rubbing her back.

"I'm sorry you had to witness that, but he won't hurt you anymore."

"Thank you—thank you so much," the woman repeated between sobs.

"Sweetheart, do you have a mobile phone? I'll call an ambulance for you; come with me. We'll wait for the paramedics on the street. I'm not going to leave you until they arrive." Ally put her arm around the woman's shoulder and escorted her onto the street. "How old are you, darling?"

"Nineteen."

"So young. I'm sorry. I felt like there was no other option."

"No, you had to do that to help me. That guy just dragged me off the street."

Ally called the ambulance and stood by, protecting the distressed young woman. She'd felt compelled to help, but the incident had put her behind schedule. She started obsessively checking her watch while they waited outside the park. Strangers walked past, oblivious to their presence, continuing on without offering any assistance. Before the paramedics took her away, the woman asked, "What's your name?"

"My name's Ally, darling,"

"*What*?! That's *my* name. That's amazing. Thank you for saving me."

"No problem. I hope you get better soon. Here—take this. I don't need it. It's a gift, to help with your future." She handed the young woman the briefcase with the money. "Goodbye, Ally. I hope you have a fast recovery and a good life." The ambulance pulled away and disappeared into the flow of the late-night traffic.

After greeting the doorman and tipping him several thousand dollars to allow her to keep her weapons on her, she went to the bar as she scanned the premises for Portia. She ordered a martini and continued to look around the venue, which always radiated an air of sophistication and elegance. She never became too intoxicated in public; she constantly had to be on edge, forever vigilant of her surroundings. She noticed some individuals who were watching her very intently—two men were seated at a booth, and a third man and a woman were alone at separate tables. They were scattered throughout the nightclub but were focused on her.

She was growing apprehensive about the situation; out of the corner of her eye, she noticed a tuxedoed man moving slowly toward her. Ally was an extremely attractive woman; she garnered a lot of attention from men, often unwanted. She turned her head in acknowledgement, realising who it was.

"Ally."

She hugged him, and he kissed her on the back of her hand.

"Osiris, it's so good to see you."

"Likewise. What are the chances of us meeting here unexpectedly?"

"I know what you mean—of all the places we could be. What brings you here?" Ally asked.

"Multiple reasons. I'm here mainly for enjoyment. I like coming to this venue, although I see that business matters are creeping in. Unfortunately, we're not alone here this evening."

Ally glanced at one of the people in the booth who had been keeping watch on her. Taken by surprise, the man picked up a drink menu; in his haste, he had picked it up the wrong way around. He pretended to browse the menu, but Ally could see that it was upside-down. She knew that these people presented a threat, but she needed to ascertain who they were.

"They followed me here. They've been watching me since I arrived," Osiris said.

"Until I saw you, I was under the assumption they were here for me. They have that menacing presence of undercover police. Are you certain they followed you here?"

"Yes, I'm certain. I've been up to a lot of bad things lately, and, obviously, one or more has demanded their attention," Osiris said. He was another Facilitator operating in Clarion. Originally from Australia, he was formerly a soldier; he was unwillingly caught in the U.R.S.C. conflicts as a young man. The chaos had set his life on a depressing path of military service, violence, mental trauma, and conflict. Despite the fact they were competitors, Osiris and Ally had an amicable bond, an affinity—they would trade playful insults and attempt to outdo one another. They had a history of flirtation and innuendo, creating a strong undercurrent of sexual tension. Enamoured with each other, their attraction was undeniable, however, the nature of the relationship had rendered them both unwilling to admit it first. A type of unspoken romantic impasse.

Osiris said, "I wasn't sure if I should ask. I don't mean to be rude, but are you in danger? How did you get those injuries on your face? Looks like something extreme happened."

"I know I look horrendous," Ally said.

"No, not at all. That's not what I meant. Please don't interpret it in that manner. Beauty is only skin deep; your beauty runs much deeper, and you always look really flattering in black."

Despite Ally's nervousness about the situation, his compliment made her feel slightly happier.

"Black mirrors the colour of my soul . . . I was just out Facilitating, helping a friend, and it got quite intense. You know what it's like in the profession."

Osiris nodded. "Yeah, of course, I know what it's like. If I didn't, I wouldn't have these vultures following me."

"What are you going to do about them?"

"I'm not sure, but they're getting under my skin. I'm about to go over there and confront them."

"No—please don't do that." Ally said; she had noticed Portia had finally arrived; Osiris had also noticed her presence. He began to inspect a photograph he'd slyly produced from his tuxedo pocket, Ally looked at the photograph and saw that it was Portia, the same one used on her law enforcement identification record. Like a nauseating flash, the realisations hit Ally.

"Holy shit—it's her," Osiris said quietly. Ally gave Portia a very concerned look as she came closer, and then she swiftly turned to Osiris.

"Osiris, you can't do this. She's a friend of mine, and, as you know, she's a detective. As you're likely aware, other detectives were involved in the plan to murder her. It's a trap. If you kill her, you will incur the full wrath of law enforcement, and those involved will offer you as a sacrifice, a scapegoat, left to face the consequences. She may even be able to help you with your situation. Please . . . for me."

"Hello, darling." Portia came up and hugged Ally, who had been thrust into a life-threatening predicament. "Have you heard any updates on our situation?" Portia asked.

"Not necessarily. It's difficult to explain. I'm not sure if you two have met. Portia, this is Osiris."

"Nice to meet you," Osiris said as he kissed the back of her hand.

"Osiris, do you mind if I speak with my friend in private?" Ally asked nervously.

"No, not at all." Ally grabbed Portia and pulled her away to an area over by the bar, where there were no patrons. "Listen to me. Don't make it obvious—but look around. We are being watched as we speak," Ally whispered.

"I know. I noticed them when I got here," Portia said.

"Who are they? Please tell me you're not delusional; please tell me you did not bring any agents here to watch the place."

"Of course not, Ally. I would have to be delusional or idiotic to do that. I know who they are—they're detectives, colleagues from the Major Crimes Division, although I don't recognise one of the men sitting in the booth. Anyway, if they're tracking your friend, chances are he's doing some seriously illegal shit. Now we're in an even-worse mess because I've recognised them, and they've definitely recognised me."

"What are we going to do?"

"I'm going to handle it; this may actually work to our advantage."

"I also have to tell you that Osiris is the Facilitator—the Facilitator hired to kill you. I apologise, but I have just discovered this," Ally explained.

"Are you fucking joking with me right now? And you just casually introduced him to me, like nothing was wrong? What the fuck is the matter with you?"

"I've been put into a very difficult situation. I didn't know he was going to be here; we encountered each other by chance. I think I've convinced him to abandon the contract. I told him it was a trap."

"*You think you've convinced him,*" Portia said with a tone of sarcasm and disbelief.

"He'll do it for me. It wouldn't be a waste of money, however, to offer him more than he is being paid, to incentivise our deal."

"I might be able to help him in exchange for sparing my life. I could deter these agents from following him—or, at the very least, find out why. That's how we can work this to our advantage. I'm going to go over there and talk to them," Portia said.

"No . . . don't tempt fate."

"I have to if we want to get out of this situation. Let's go back and inform him of what's happening." Portia walked aggressively up to Osiris. "It's come to my attention that you've been given the task of ending my life, but it looks like your life is in jeopardy, too. So, that gives us something in common. Now, as I'm sure you're aware, those detectives are following you, and I'm sure you'd like to know why. Evidently, you've done something serious for them to be scrutinising you. Correct me if I'm wrong, but one of those men at the booth is an operative of the A.C.E. intelligence agency. If this is true, then you're in serious trouble. If I can discover why they're after you, and if I can potentially help you with this problem, will you agree to spare my life?"

Osiris frowned, uncertainty etched onto his face as he contemplated his next choice.

"Please do it for me, Osiris," Ally interjected. "Please."

"If you can get these police to stop watching me, then you have a deal. Ally informed me that if I killed you, the police force would betray me, putting all the blame on me. Is this correct?"

"Undoubtedly. Whatever they told you was a lie; any protection or deal they offered you was completely fabricated. If you had carried out this hit, you would have been utterly betrayed by the people who arranged it. I won't hold a grudge against you for being involved in this. You're merely a pawn, an expendable victim to them. You guys keep conversing. I'm going to confront these slimy officers who managed to sneak in with the humans."

Ally and Osiris talked about their dire straits as Portia accosted the two men in the booth. "What the fuck are you doing here, Trent? You're jeopardising my investigation—an *active* investigation—which, as you're aware, is a crime," Portia remarked.

"Fuck off. I'm not aware of any investigation involving you. I don't trust you or anything that you say. Besides, *you're* actually interfering with *our* case. Now piss off," Detective Trent Wardrop replied.

"I'm undercover, keeping surveillance on those two individuals, and you're making them suspicious. What are you doing watching them as well?"

"I can't discuss that, as it's part of our ongoing investigation. I'm not aware of any other active investigation, certainly none relating to you. I know you're a liar, Portia. Why would they have two separate cases on the same individuals without any communication or collaboration? It doesn't make any sense . . . "

"Look—I need you and your unit to disperse and leave these targets alone. They're getting increasingly nervous about your presence, and you're threatening to blow my cover," Portia argued.

"If anything, whatever little game or trick you're trying to play here is endangering us, why are you talking to me right now? This is the worst possible time—it's risking the whole investigation. Would you like me to call our supervisor and ask him? He should be able to clarify why these investigations have overlapped."

"Who are you?" Portia asked the anonymous man. She looked at him intensely, trying to glean any information about who he was. "Who is he, Trent? Tell me."

"I'm not at liberty to disclose that information, I'm afraid, as that's part of an ongoing case," Trent said as the unknown man stared at her blankly.

"You're, you're a fucking federal agent, aren't you? He's a federal agent, isn't he, Trent? Now who's the one keeping secrets? There's been no mention around the office of a case in conjunction with federal agents. I know you and other detectives from the Major Crimes Division are up to something covert, covering up your *own* major crimes. Well, be careful throwing stones, Detective Wardrop, because that glass house can come crashing down around you—we can all be exposed." Portia leaned over the table, almost whispering, "Then I'll write your obituary in the dirt . . . so the rain can erase any memory of you."

"All hearsay, D'Amico, merely speculation and idle threats."

"Maybe that's what I want you to believe." After an intimidating look, she left them alone. Remaining composed on the outside, inwardly, she'd been shaken by the developments. It meant their circumstances were much worse and were rapidly spiralling out of their control. If the rival detectives were working with another federal agency, then there was now very little she could do. She had a lot of authority and influence, but those agencies had much more jurisdiction.

Ally could tell by Portia's demeanour that the encounter hadn't gone well. She walked toward them with a brisk stride, hanging her head. She looked up at Osiris. "You have to start being honest with me, or I'm seriously considering letting them arrest you now. I thought that may have been an intelligence operative, but now I suspect he's a federal agent, which is just as serious. What have you been doing to attract federal attention? They don't deal with matters related to Facilitating, and they're doing some combined operation with the Major Crimes Division. Something enormous is happening, with serious complications for us all. I can't have them here prying and interfering with my affairs. We've been seen together, so we're all caught up in this now. We have to co-operate, but you need to tell me what you've done."

"I don't want to discuss it here, in case anyone is listening. Can I tell you once we've left this place? I promise I'll tell you everything, but first, we all have to get out of here," Osiris said.

"Fine, but you have to tell me when it's safe to do so. Otherwise, any agreement we have is void. Right now, we've got to figure out how we're going to get out of this place. I don't know what's going to happen to us when we go outside. They're going to have backup out there, keeping surveillance, in case things go awry. As soon as we leave, they're going to follow us. Do you have a vehicle, Osiris? Because we cannot use mine."

"No, I'm afraid, but I have access to one that's relatively close. I've got a plan, but you've got to trust me, and you've got to do everything I say. I know you've got a lot of power as a detective, but this is beyond our ability to control without some external assistance. I've got some insiders working here in the club who can help. I also know the floor plan and an escape route. From there, we're going to a discreet location." He took a pen from his tuxedo pocket and wrote the location onto a cocktail napkin, showing both of them. "Remember that location in case we get separated—don't forget it," he said, scrunching and placing it into his pocket. "We have to quickly move to the Europa Lounge Area. I know the employees working at the entrance. They can get us through, and they'll be able to stall the detectives, but not for very long. From there, we have to go through a series of corridors and areas used only by the employees. We can get away; when we're a safe distance away from anyone who may be watching, I can organise our transport to the location."

Portia said, "You two go. I'm going to stay here and hopefully distract them. I need to see if I can get any more information about this, about everything—I have to. You guys go ahead. I know where to meet you." She glanced at her watch. "It's one thirty. If I'm not there by 5 a.m., you know something has happened to me. Just leave me—and leave Clarion, too."

Osiris said, "If that's what you need to do, Ally, we need to go; start following me now—now!" He stepped back from the bar and started walking in the direction away from their pursuers.

"Goodbye, Portia," Ally said as she followed directly behind Osiris. She took a sly glance at the people watching them. The sudden action had caused a noticeable disturbance amongst them; their heads darted around, looking at each other in surprise and mouthing words. They traversed the enormous room, and, with a look from Osiris, they walked straight past the two employees at the door of the Europa Lounge. With his floor plan, they navigated the labyrinth of passages and rooms before escaping through a hidden door unknown to law enforcement leading to an adjacent property.

CHAPTER FOUR

They emerged into a dimly lit and isolated area behind the building. It was now a frantic mission to reach safety, both rapidly drawing weapons. "This way," Osiris said while running in a northeasterly direction, toward an alleyway.

"Where are we going?" Ally asked between sharp breaths.

"There is a car parked in a warehouse near the Seventy-Seventh Avenue Bridge, in the industrial area of the Harbour District."

"That's blocks away, and we have to go through Bolter Central-Gardens. We're never going to make it without being seen."

"I know it's a long distance. I apologise—that's the closest vehicle we have access to. I've been unable to contact anyone who can help."

Bolter Central-Gardens was a collection of boroughs that housed thousands of gang members, one of the most impoverished, high-crime areas of the city. They fled through a network of deserted alleyways and backstreets, stopping to assess the scene before exposing themselves and moving to the next available cover. The police were already hunting them, mobilising every available unit, issuing a bulletin to be on the lookout for ". . . a Caucasian male and female, both approximately 190 centimetres tall, both aged roughly in their late twenties or early thirties. The male had short dark hair and was wearing a tuxedo. The female had long blond hair and was wearing a black suit. . . ." They even issued a search-and-destroy notice, giving any officer the authority to shoot them on sight. That prospect was on both their minds, and they were now running for their lives.

They had to roll the dice and run through the treacherous, gang-controlled Orion Park; they had their weapons drawn the entire way. A police helicopter lurked overhead; its churning blades created a harrowing noise. It shined a blinding halo of light that swept across the ground as it probed for them. It was pointless to hide in the thick vegetation of the park, as the helicopter was equipped with thermal- and infrared-imaging cameras. They had no choice but to cautiously make their perilous way through the park. They could see that the helicopter had deterred many others who were also fleeing. Ally and Osiris could see them scattering in every direction to avoid unwanted interaction. Police helicopters were always a target for indiscriminate gunfire. They could hear many shots fired from different areas, and they could occasionally see the tracer rounds disappearing into the darkness or hitting the underside of the helicopter.

After clearing the park, they continued weaving through the urban grid. The journey wasn't without incident; they suffered many close encounters with gang members, who were harassing them under the impression that they were a rich couple who had gotten lost—an easy target for robbery. Ally and Osiris had to set them straight by killing three of them in two separate confrontations.

In a neighbourhood notorious for unsanctioned justice, Ally and Osiris happened upon a large gathering of gang members, who began following them. They had heard about the escaped fugitives and were convinced it was them. They wanted the couple out of their neighbour-hood, so that they didn't attract any police attention. It was a difficult situation; in a loud conversation, Ally and Osiris tried to convince them that this was a case of mistaken identity. They continued the conver-sation as they tried to get away. The gang were insistent on following them and were becoming more aggressive, arguing that, whoever they were, their presence and trespassing angered them. Without wanting to exchange bullets, at the first opportunity, they sprinted away. Massively outnumbered and realising they needed to cover more ground to stay on schedule, Ally and Osiris descended into the subway system.

They decided to board a train for a short section of the journey in order to escape both the police and the gang. They crossed over sev-eral lines of track to reach the platform. A few brave commuters were spread throughout the filthy, graffiti-riddled coffin-on-rails. Ally held onto both handguns under her jacket. They had to sit in forced silence while jarring noises echoed through the rattling carriage. The lights would cut off to pitch black and then flicker back to life and bathe the interior with a sickly yellow glow. In the tense environment, no one made eye contact or spoke; they watched each other closely, without making it noticeable.

The public-transport network could be an extremely dangerous place, and many crimes were committed aboard trains and in stations. Normally, Ally and Osiris would avoid exposing themselves like this to law enforcement and criminals, but, today, they had no choice. Within minutes and without incident, they arrived at their destina-tion: Dockland-Quay Station. After many challenges, the pair had successfully negotiated their escape.

The Harbour District was a secluded place at night, and it attracted a lot of unsavoury characters. Alert and on edge, Ally and Osiris walked down a deathly quiet street lined with decaying industrial warehouses; the streetlamps saturated everything with a grimy orange light.

"Wait right here," Osiris said as he quietly disappeared into an alleyway along the side of the warehouse. Ally pressed her back against the wall, scanning the area with her weapons ready. Some prostitutes were congregating much farther down the street but presented no threat. Minutes later, Osiris emerged in an anonymous, black four-wheel-drive vehicle.

Ally climbed into the large, armoured high-end vehicle, and Osiris continued in the direction they had been walking. Osiris drove with extreme caution through an intricate web of secluded streets, avoiding any major roads. The method was time consuming but effective. He was extremely alert, paying very close attention to the surroundings.

Ally had grown increasingly dismayed with the situation and was very confused. She asked Osiris to explain why those federal agents were after him. Initially he was reluctant and changed the subject. He mentioned how beautiful her accent was; she became angered and raised her voice, demanding that Osiris give her an explanation.

He eventually agreed and informed her they were after him because he had gotten involved with the Militia and was participating in their grandest plan since forming the country: a military coup to overthrow the increasingly tyrannical United Republic government. Nobody was sure how the government had found them out, as they had only recently begun investigating the plan. He had become connected with the Militia through his Facilitating work. By assisting some clients, he gradually got exposed to more elements of their operations and was introduced to more facets of the organisation. He described how he was unsatisfied with his life and as a Facilitator. He was trying to fill a void with drugs and alcohol after a lifetime of combat had left him psychologically scarred but forged him into the person he was—a person who protected and looked after the rights of others. He wanted to be a part of something greater than himself, or, at least, make an effort, as he saw the rewards outweighing the risk.

Their cautious approach and route to the meeting point had paid off as they arrived without incident. Their destination was an abandoned factory on the city's northern limits, damaged during the conflicts in the past and never repaired. Warily, Osiris approached the factory, driving at a very slow pace and checking around for any signs of danger. He manoeuvred the vehicle into a shadowy vantage point that obscured them yet allowed them to see the potential entry and exit points.

Ally asked if he was worried what could potentially happen to him.

He admitted it would be a lie if he said he never thought about what might happen to him. He was aware that he had contributed to much of the misery, suffering, and negativity in the world and that, if a sacrifice of that enormity was required of him, he would accept it. Osiris looked straight ahead in solemn reflection.

In the silence, Ally stared at him with surprise. She had been exposed to his altruism and caring nature before but was touched by this admission. She held his hand. "I don't want anything to happen to you, though you seem very determined that this is something you must do. You must come out of this unharmed. What about all the disruption? What about the displacement, misery, and destruction? I understand your motives and reasoning, but does this justify all the inevitable carnage that a coup like this will bring?"

"Yes, I'm conflicted about that—whether it's justifiable to cause destruction in the pursuit of change. I feel uneasy about every aspect of this. I've thought seriously about the points you raised and the questions you asked—whether any of this is the correct thing to do or if it's a mistake. What if we just replace one evil, unjust system with another or an even worse one? What happens when the next group of people want to stage a coup against that government and that system? When I see the pain and agony that already exists within this country, to do nothing and let it continue is the biggest mistake I could make."

What Osiris said resonated through them both; they remained silent in a tacit state of introspection. Finally, Ally broke the silence:

"Remember a few months ago, when we were having dinner at *La Petite Soleil*? Do you remember I was talking about moving back to France, or to the Seychelles, and you said you wanted to join me?"

"Yes, I remember."

"Then please join me. I want you to come with me. We don't have to live a luxurious existence. I agree that this place is not the role model for living or ideology that it appears to be. It's like a star that shines bright with promise—yet you can't get close to it or embrace it. I don't want to say that we'll have a perfect life if we move. It won't be the solution to all of our problems. I want to support you in what you're doing. Much to my dismay, I don't think I can stop you. Can we compromise?"

"Compromise," he repeated. "What do you mean?"

"What if I join you in this coup? Honestly, I'm not excited about the idea. I don't want to, but if that's what's needed to support you, then I'll do it. Just like you expressed to me, even after everything that's happened, I still want to help people. If I do this with you, after the objectives are accomplished, would you leave this place with me?"

"I'm thankful beyond words that you would want me to move with you. I can't describe what that means. To usher in a revolution and then flee in the aftermath defeats the purpose; it feels wrong," Osiris said.

Ally replied, "I can understand why you would feel like that. If we proceed with this coup and survive, once we've overseen the changes, will you stand by me?"

Osiris said, "The fact you would offer to participate in such a dangerous undertaking to assist a friend is so honourable. Because you're willing to do this, yes—I will move with you when this is done, Ally. I guess we have a mutual dependence on each other now. I don't want you to get hurt or killed, certainly not by helping me in something like this. It wouldn't be right of me to stop you from doing *anything* when I'm so certain and so unwavering in my views. We've come to a stalemate, an impasse."

"I'm glad you can see it in that context. If I can't change your mind or sway you into a different direction, then you can't stop me from being there with you. I feel a deeper connection to you than I've ever felt with anyone. That's why I agreed to do this and why I want you to join me," Ally declared.

"That's how I feel. I've had only a few opportunities to discuss it with you in such a raw sense. You know the requirements of the business we chose to get into. Relationships are so fleeting and shallow in this lifestyle. I feel a profound connection to you, and I hope I haven't given you the wrong impression. I wasn't fully aware of exactly what our relationship was."

They leaned in to kiss. She was self-conscious that her lips were swollen, yet that dissolved immediately as she fluttered into ecstasy, and pleasure reverberated throughout her body. They shared the passionate, tender moment until the gravity of the situation sank back in again. They wanted the spontaneous display of affection to continue, both so desperate for connection. Unfortunately, they had to focus on what was currently happening. Osiris looked at his watch. "It's twenty minutes past four. She should be here soon."

"I'm growing worried about her. You heard what she said: we have to leave if she fails to appear by 5 a.m. and get out of Clarion. Where're we going to go?"

They talked about where they would go. Osiris suggested the Lawless Zone. The country had within its borders a sprawling Lawless Zone that comprised roughly ten percent of the country's area, which was divided into twenty-four subzones, each assigned a letter from the Greek alphabet. Entry to the Zone was rarely without difficulty. Osiris suggested they relocate to the city of San Lola, where he had

Militia connections. Ally mentioned that her father lived there and was involved with criminal enterprises. She coldly said she would prefer not to acknowledge his existence. She explained how her father had left for the U.R.S.C. by himself, leaving Ally abandoned as a young teenager in France during conflict and instability. He had never told her the truth about what had happened to her mother. Ally firmly believed that she'd been killed and that her father had had something to do with her murder. He had given changing excuses and alibis throughout her life.

She thought they should wait for Portia and see how the situation developed. Osiris started to respond, but they both noticed a vehicle coming toward the factory. They tensed up again, watching as the person driving the vehicle chose a discreet location to obscure their presence. Even in the reduced lighting, Ally was certain that it was Portia. "That's her," she said.

"How can you be sure?"

"It's her. Who else could it be? I'm going to investigate."

"No, not alone. I'm going with you," Osiris said.

CHAPTER FIVE

While they were talking, the occupant emerged from the vehicle, a silhouette that hovered in the darkness. Osiris and Ally exited the vehicle and slowly went toward the factory, taking a path that kept them hidden as they moved toward the unidentified person, taking shelter behind various items. The suspense mounted as they came into close proximity. Osiris stayed behind while Ally advanced further, taking cover behind a large pile of debris. The tension was high as Ally nervously waited until she had confirmed the person's identity. The person stayed in the shadows for what seemed like hours and finally moved into a dimly lit spot. Ally aimed her weapon at the person. She lowered it when she confirmed that it was Portia. Quietly, Ally called out her name, repeating it several times until she noticed her presence. "It's Ally."

"Where are you?" she called out quietly in response, looking in the wrong direction.

"Over here," she replied, revealing her hand.

Portia crouched down and slowly moved toward her, a highly modified machine gun slung over her shoulder. When she got closer, Ally saw that she was covered in blood, and she was certain that some of it was her own. The area around her nose and mouth was smeared.

"What happened?" Ally asked.

"I'll tell you after we've discussed what just happened. Where's Osiris?" Portia replied, breathing heavily and clearly intoxicated on drugs. Together they carefully walked over to where Osiris was waiting, as Portia talked briefly about her ordeal. It was a reunion of unreserved sadness. They all mournfully acknowledged each other.

"Can you tell me what happened?" Ally requested.

In a flash and to their shock, Portia pointed her weapon at Osiris. Ally immediately went to intervene to prevent a tragedy from unfolding.

"Drop the gun," Portia said. He complied and let it fall to the ground. She kicked the gun away, bouncing along with a grinding noise. She advanced on him with an overwhelming urgency.

"Hey! Hey! What's the matter? I thought we'd come to an agreement!" Osiris asked before she delivered a forceful punch, hitting him on the nose. He wasn't knocked unconscious, but he staggered back in a daze. Blood began streaming from his nostrils.

Portia took one hand off the weapon, unholstered a handgun, and placed the barrel under his chin, digging it in with fierce pressure.

"We did have an agreement. That was before I discovered the truth about you—about what you did to attract the attention of those federal agents."

"Please don't do this," Ally pleaded, trying to get between them.

"Stay out of this, Ally," Portia shouted.

"Ally, I don't want you to get hurt," Osiris said sternly. His voice was muffled from holding his nose.

"You shut the fuck up. You don't know what I went through for you. After you two left the nightclub, those detectives wanted to kill me for interfering with their operation and for letting their target get away—and now I know why. They're after you because of your affiliation with the Militia and a plan to overthrow the government. I went through the worst ordeal to get here. I had to hurt a lot of people. Now I've been implicated in helping a felon escape, and my career is ruined. If I didn't have sensitive information on those detectives involved, I'd be completely ruined. I almost became a fugitive because I was helping you, and you didn't even disclose the nature of your crime or the reason why they were hunting you. *That's* why I'm angry."

"I'm sorry, Portia. I couldn't tell you there in case someone was listening. I had to protect my own interests. I'm sorry that you were in danger and got harmed because of me, but I was worried about my own survival. I'm sorry if that sounds selfish, but I don't care—it's the truth. I wasn't at that nightclub for any reason relating to you. I was not there to kill you."

"It's true. We encountered each other by chance," Ally exclaimed.

"There's no room for *chance* here. I don't believe you were at that nightclub for some other purpose."

"I was—you've got to believe me. I was at the Hyperion Nightclub to speak with an associate about settling a dispute. When that was mediated, I saw Ally there; she and I are friends, so I was enjoying her company. I had no possible way of knowing you were going to be there," Osiris pleaded.

"Listen to him, Portia—it's true. When you arrived, he was taken by surprise. He even looked at a picture to confirm it was you. He had no idea you were going to be there, and I didn't mention anything. You *know* that I wouldn't," Ally said, still trying to get between them.

"You have a picture of me?" Portia asked with a searing tone.

"It was for the job," Osiris explained. "I needed to be able to identify you if I saw you. I'm sorry, but that's just part of the process."

"Tear it up," she said.

"Okay, I will. I'm just going to get it out of my pocket. Don't do anything irrational." He very methodically reached into his pocket, took out the photo, and tore it into many pieces that he scattered in the breeze.

"Why are you part of a plan to overthrow the government?" Portia asked.

"Osiris and I have been through this, Portia. He wants to be on the right side of history and bring about change."

"We all do," Portia said.

"I'm joining him; we have already had a discussion about this while we were waiting for you," Ally said.

"So, you're getting involved in this now? Do you understand the severity of what you're getting into?"

"I'm not pleased about being a part of it."

"Then why do it?"

"I want to be a part of bringing about change as well. I want to create a better life for people. We have all become corrupted and strayed from our original dreams and desires. You can understand that, right, Portia?" Ally asked.

"Yes, I can. I've already recounted to you my deep disappointment with myself at how my life turned out, how it progressed. How I gradually became an amoral criminal, the type I set out to put in cages. I have to reconcile with that. But why do it like this? Why destroy and kill when there are other ways?"

"What other ways?" Osiris asked.

"I don't know. I don't mean to say that I have all the answers right in this moment, but aren't there other ways?" Portia responded.

Osiris admitted, "Agreed. There are other ways, but, sometimes, a little disruption like this is the only way, the only solution. We've been repressed for so long that this is the only way to fight back. I want to channel my aggression properly, but I know there's going to be casualties. You weren't here for the discussion that I had with Ally. I don't like the fact that violence is sometimes a side-effect of change, but it can't be avoided. Some of the biggest changes throughout history have come about through upheaval, disobedience, and protest. Like the French and Russian Revolutions."

"Why don't you learn from their mistakes? You'll become the tyrants you set out to destroy."

"Perhaps, but I've got to try. Yes, it's ultimately subjective that the changes we want to implement are best for everyone. We can debate them to death, but, eventually, someone has to *take action*. It isn't going to be perfect; it isn't going to be the panacea to every problem, but that's something I'm willing to accept. I have to be open to the idea of change because it would be unethical of me to deny any alteration to what has already been done. I know it's going to cause a lot of pain and change a lot of people's lives; we'll have to live with a different 'normal' for a while. I realize that I may sound like a martyr to you or some brainwashed Manchurian candidate."

"Yeah, you do. You sound like somebody who's been indoctrinated, who's been fed lies and been manipulated. I should kill you and save a lot of lives for doing it." She shoved the gun into his throat harder.

"Please, Portia—don't kill him. Please don't do this. He means a lot to me. I'm the one who convinced him *not* to kill you. If it weren't for me, Portia, you would have been dead as soon as you left that nightclub. I've done so much for you in the past few hours. I've bled for you, killed for you, cried for you. I was focused on my own business, my own problems when you came rushing into my life with *your* problem. I'm your friend, so I helped you, but it wasn't an ordinary problem, and the response I gave you was no ordinary effort. I killed an entire room full of people for you last night with that automatic shotgun. I counted five bodies turned to pulp. And that wasn't even *all* I did for you last night; I risked my life multiple times."

"I understand. . . . We've got to get out of here. If you get caught for this, you're both going to be executed."

"I know. I'm not happy about this, but I was compromising with Osiris, and we came to an agreement. There's a lot to explain, and it's hard to do so while you're so erratic and unpredictable. I'm not playing a huge role in this coup. I'm supporting Osiris, and, yes, I'm aware of the consequences if we should get found out. But if that's what it takes, then I'm ready to make that sacrifice. We're going to be a part of this coup, and, once it has been successful in bringing about the change that's needed, Osiris and I are leaving this country. There'll be nothing left for us here then but empty promises and wind."

"That's if you make it out alive. Because of Osiris, all of our lives are in jeopardy, because he refused to tell us what was really happening. I will spare your life. Ally has convinced me otherwise and saved your life like she did mine."

"Thank you, Ally," Osiris said.

"You're probably going to get killed anyway during this coup or before it if you get caught. Ally, I really don't think you should do this. There's more constructive ways to do what you're intending."

"No, they haven't worked . . . " Osiris started.

Interrupting him, Portia said, "Be quiet. I was talking to Ally. She's the only one who saved you from getting a bullet in the head."

"I know, Portia. It's hard to convey a point to you when you're like this. We need to defuse the situation; we need to relax and have a proper discussion, like civilised adults, not waving guns at each other like savages. We're better than this, and you two both know it, so can we put down the weapons please, and have some sense, some humanity? Can we have some resolve and peace and understanding instead of this violent conflict? Surely, it's not beyond you? We're capable of much greater things, so why are we doing this? Why are we so focused on destruction?" Ally reasoned.

"Then why are you doing this, Ally, if you're talking about all of those things?" Portia said, still firmly holding her gun to Osiris's neck.

"I don't have the answer, Portia. I don't know. What do you want me to tell you? It's such a conflicting thing. Whether we are contributing to an activist dilemma and deterring people from our cause. I get that. We are simply trying to do what we think is right. I'm sorry if that makes me a hypocrite or whatever you want to label me. Go ahead—judge me all you like, but I've done a lot of favours for you, and some understanding and reciprocation would be appreciated right now."

"Ally, I realise that this is a complex issue, but I also realise that I'm not acting as I normally would under the circumstances, and the drugs certainly don't help. I do understand the reason why you both feel the need to do this, to combat the wrong and injustice in this world—I want to do that, too. It was difficult for me to accept there's issues outside of my control that I can't change or worry about . . . The reason I'm upset and angry is because, without regard, you endangered Ally and myself. You claim to be so noble, and yet you've hidden this information at such a vital point. It's wrong to get Ally and me sucked into your situation to become victims."

Osiris responded, "Like I said, this was all thrust upon us, each of us. You just spoke about fate, and that's what happened. I'm struggling to define it as well, but I apologise. I'm really sorry about what happened, but our lives just intersected. There was a degree of separation involved because we both know Ally, but we were all thrown into that situation. I tried to navigate it as best I could. Again, I'm sorry that you got hurt, but I offered for you to come with us when we made our escape, but you wanted to stay behind."

"I had to. If I didn't, we'd probably all be dead now," Portia responded angrily.

"All right. So that was required, but I didn't anticipate that. I didn't expect things to develop like this. Ally and I were desperate to get out of there and get to safety. Because you were helping me, I didn't want to leave you behind. There was nothing personal about accepting the contract to kill you. It's part of my business. We've had a turbulent introduction, but you're a good person, Portia. I can see that, judging by what you've done this evening for all of us."

After hearing Osiris say that, Portia, slowly and unwillingly, took her gun away from his neck and concealed it. He rubbed the area where she had pressed the barrel in as she stepped back, the machine gun now aimed at him. Ally stood in front of Osiris defiantly, ensuring Portia couldn't shoot him.

"Get out of the way," Osiris said.

Ally's and Portia's eyes met, locked in a deep stare. After a prolonged period, Ally glanced down at the gun. Portia stood down and rested the machine gun on her shoulder, the barrel pointed to the sky.

"Can we please talk about this in more detail now?" Ally exclaimed. She stepped aside and looked at them both.

Osiris looked at Portia. "I'm willing. Are you?"

"Yes, I am," replied Portia.

"You haven't explained what happened after you found out why the detectives were there—after we left," Osiris inquired.

"They seized my vehicle and were going to ambush me outside; the venue staff alerted me, and I escaped. From there, it was a desperate race to reach a safe-house. They came after me furiously, putting a reward out for my capture, appealing to any criminal willing to collect the bounty. I had to kill quite a few people who attempted to stop me from getting here. I was able to equip myself with more weapons and another vehicle. It was a struggle I didn't have to be in. Our lives have changed. The events of tonight will be irreversible."

"What are we going to do, Portia?" Ally asked.

"I'm glad we've de-escalated the tensions because I don't really know what we're going to do. I'm not going to be a part of this coup.

I agree with a lot of the things you've said, but I'm not interested. I want to make a difference with a different approach. It seems you're both certain about this, and it appears I can't convince you otherwise. So we're all going to work together to get out of this. Because I have those files on the other detectives, they won't be able to do anything for now, but that's only temporary. We're going to have to gather our possessions and get out of Clarion if you want this plan to be successful."

"Where are we going to go?" Osiris asked.

"I think it's best if the two of you go somewhere together and I go on my separate path."

"Portia—no! You must come with us!" Ally said.

"It's the safest option. You told me that you weren't excited about this coup, but I don't have any attachment to anyone. You told me your motives for doing this. It's indicative of the person you are, Ally— you're caring. It makes sense, but this isn't my fight, my destiny. I'm sorry—we have to split up—"

She abruptly stopped talking and closed her eyes; she began swaying and dropped her weapons. With a moan but still conscious, she fell to the ground.

They both went to help her; Ally lifted Portia's shirt and saw the massive bruising on her abdomen. She was disoriented, a vacant look in her eyes. "Portia, when was the last time you slept or ate something?"

"I can't remember—days ago," she slowly replied. "Can you get me some water please? There's a bottle of water in my car."

"Of course. Osiris, can you carry her to our vehicle, please?"

"Sure."

"No, I'm fine. . . ." She started to get up.

"Portia, don't get up. You're in no state to leave here by yourself. The drugs and adrenaline have worn off, and you need rest."

Portia coughed profusely and spat out some blood, Ally went to retrieve the water while Osiris carefully picked up Portia and carried her to their vehicle, her body limp. "Thank you, Osiris," she slurred quietly.

"That's fine."

"I'm sorry I punched you."

"That's fine, too. It was an excellent punch—it felt amazing," he said ironically.

"It was a good punch," Portia responded in a delirium.

Ally came back with the water and held the bottle to Portia's lips; she slowly sipped it, with Ally's hand on the back of her neck to support her as she drank.

"Thank you, Ally," she said, water trickling from her mouth. "Please don't take me to hospital; I'll be an easy target there. I know other doctors, professional doctors who will help me; they don't ask any questions. If you're going to take me anywhere, then take me there. . . . Actually, I'd prefer if you didn't do that, either."

"If you won't go and get medical attention, will you come to where I'm staying—at the very least? So that I can look after you?"

"Yes. Thank you, Ally,"

"Before we go there, I need to go to where I'm staying and get some important possessions," Osiris said.

Portia cautioned, "No—it's too dangerous. If they're keeping watch on the place, then they could start following you again. Assume that they have already seized those possessions. Someone must burn the vehicle I arrived in. There is a mass of evidence inside that can be traced back to me."

After fulfiling Portia's request, Osiris started the remaining vehicle, and they left the area. Ally sat in the back seat with Portia, her head resting on Ally's shoulder. Ally tried to clean some of the blood off Portia's face with the water, wiping it with her jacket.

"Do you have any cigarettes, Ally?" Portia asked.

"Yes, here you go." Ally took an antique cigarette case from her jacket pocket and gave her a cigarette. With a groan, Portia slowly lifted her head and lit it. Ally lit one as well. "You've got a bad cut on the back of your head," Ally said.

"Yeah. I think I hit my head on the ground when I was assaulted by those gang members. I know that they kicked me in the head a few times. I feel quite dizzy."

"I'm going to get you something to eat, okay? Then you should get some sleep."

"That's sounds like a good idea; that's what I need," she said, exhaling smoke.

"Where are you staying, Ally? Are you still at the Autumn Plaza on North Electra Avenue?" Osiris asked.

"Serendipity Fair on Ocean-View Boulevard."

"Good. I know where that is. We'll be there shortly."

"We will discuss our plans to a greater extent when we're all in a more coherent state. I need to rest. After everything that has happened, after everything we have been through, my body aches, and my mind's racing," Ally said. They made it safely to Serendipity Fair, and Ally put her arm around Portia as they walked through the underground parking lot. They got into the elevator and went straight up to the fiftieth floor. Ally felt so relieved to walk through the door to comfort and safety. Even though it was only temporary, the place felt like home to Ally, whose life was anything but certain or permanent.

CHAPTER SIX

The Penthouse Suite was fully equipped with beautiful antique furniture of the highest quality. Ally
and Osiris helped Portia onto a chaise lounge. Osiris sat on a lounge as
Ally went to the kitchen, which was incorporated into the open floor
plan of the enormous main room.

"I'm sorry, Portia. I don't have much food here; I don't eat here very
often. I have some fruit, or I can call up room service; the kitchen is
open at all hours. I could get them to make whatever you want. When
I do eat here, the food's unbelievably good. They make these beautiful
pea timbales garnished with mint and tarragon leaves and a saffron
spiced tomato coulis on the side. It's delicious."

"No, I don't want you to call them. I don't trust anyone coming
up here. You don't know who they are. They could be undercover or
something. No—I don't want to do that," Portia mumbled.

"You don't have to be paranoid. We're safe here."

"I just don't feel comfortable with the idea."

"If that's what you want to do, I understand."

"I'll have some fruit."

Ally, a strict vegetarian, ate a very healthy diet. She came over to Portia with a bowl filled with a variety of fruit. After she had eaten, Ally helped her to undress and put her into the shower. "Sit down, Portia; I don't want you to fall." Ally stayed close to the shower in case anything happened.

Portia sat hunched over. She tucked her knees in close to her chest, crossed her legs, at the ankles, and slumped her head. The water cascading through her gorgeous dark hair and, dripping from her body, had small traces of blood swirling through it. She was weeping hysterically.

"Everything is fine, Portia," Ally reassured her. "You're in a safe place now. I'm not going to let anything happen to you." There was a halt to the conversation as Portia continued crying. Ally tried her best to cheer her up.

"*Ex nihilo nihil fit*," Ally said.

"Pardon?"

"I was just reading your tattoo: 'Nothing comes from nothing.'" Portia had the Latin maxim tattooed near her collarbone.

"Originally, I got that to remind me of where I came from and my upbringing. Nothing was going to come out of that life. Recently, though, it applies to my life in general," she said between sobs.

"Now, I don't know, Ally. I don't know about anything anymore. All my beliefs and principles have been shaken. Do I have control over any part of my life? Or am I just on a trajectory where everything's already been decided and I'm just a spectator to it all unfolding? I just feel like everything has been erased, and I simply don't know . . . what I should do."

"You're not alone. I had a similar conversation with Osiris. We went into detail regarding the same type of questions you were raising. I've wondered about all that; I've stayed up late into the night, unable to sleep. For me, this is an existential crisis—struggling to think what meaning I can extract from my life. I want to know the answer, too, especially with everything that has happened over the past few hours. I've also thought through the whole "determinism" question: Can anyone make any type of difference, or has it already been determined, and we're just going through the motions? Is there some far-reaching design or plan, or is everything fate, or destiny, or chance? Have I ever told you about my theory, Portia?"

"No. I'm interested in hearing it, though."

"My personal philosophy is that the universe is like a Pendulum, a Pendulum that's a conglomerate of karma as I understand it—the cyclical consequences of all our actions, serendipity, and fate. I know that sounds strange, but I believe everything happens for a reason, yet there's a distinct element of randomness to life; paths intersect every day all over the world. Chance encounters happen; I don't believe in coincidence.

"So, the universe swings like a Pendulum, it swings high and low. As it periodically traverses through our lives, it inevitably brings with it a series of changes, consequences, potential outcomes, possibilities, opportunities, and providence. Each swing resets the things the previous one established and alters our lives. It can be viewed as a positive or negative thing, but, really, it's indifferent and gives us direction. Without it coming through our lives, we wouldn't move forward or backward—we'd simply stagnate.

"So as comfortable as we may get in our routines, we need the swing of the Pendulum to progress our lives, to nudge them along further, to more definitely illuminate the trajectory of our life's arc. Sure, I'd love to be young again, to be innocent and unfettered by obligation. I can't, unfortunately. I'd love to spend all my days here on the beach, drinking and fornicating in a paradise, but that's ultimately a charade. As appealing as it is to live in a perfect place, we need to grow and flourish. We can't change what happens, but we can change how we react and adapt to what happens.

"We all need to evolve and grow in the face of adversity. People become so involved in their own ambitions—I'm guilty of this, too—that they lose sight of the bigger picture, for reasons that range from societal conformity, to the expectations of peers, to the fear of failure, or other outside pressures. Their ambitions and dreams become clouded, and they become unclear as to what they want or how to achieve it. They don't realise that they must take a step back and let the inevitable working of the universe run its course, though they can't just abandon all initiative in their life.

"Trusting in something as vague and ambiguous as 'The Universe' is too difficult for most people. Yet, by doing this, the fog will be lifted, and their hopes will become clear again. The Pendulum has a plan for everybody. When it comes hurtling back into our lives, energy and momentum thrust us to the next stage. Life is a mixture of chance and predetermination. I know that sounds contradictory, but we just have to relinquish some control and let the natural order of things happen. Then it will all fall into place," Ally stated.

For a few moments, both Ally and Portia were engrossed in their own thoughts.

Portia replied, "That is interesting to consider. We may not always be aware of it, but it can't be stopped from having an influence on our lives. What I've been thinking about lately is . . . maybe there's a scheme or a plan—and chance and luck occur either way. It's an anomaly that can't be avoided—it's part of the system. We try to eliminate it, but it inevitably occurs."

Ally inquired further. "So, you think that the universe is kind of like a conscious entity, making choices, influencing, and guiding our lives? But you're saying we can have an impression upon it, that we can choose how we utilise it and choose how to react to the circumstances it provides. Is that the theoretical and elusive *free will* we all have?"

"Yes. Maybe they're like universal constants, all tuned to a fine ratio of interaction. All working in unity. Everything is just an interplay or combination of these constants. It's like a formula, and all of these phenomena we have terminology for are just glitches in the system. We think the glitches are something to be eliminated, but they surface regardless, and the more we try to fix them, the more glitches are created."

Portia stayed in the shower for about an hour. Ally didn't mind being there by her side, if it's what it took to console her friend and make her feel better. She said to Portia, "You can't put that bloodied, dirty clothing back on." Ally looked at the pile of clothing on the bathroom floor. "I'll get you something to wear." Portia stood there soaking wet until Ally dried her with a towel.

"It must take you forever to dry your hair," Portia observed.

"It certainly does," Ally answered. She had light ash-blond hair that went down past her buttocks, and she was much taller than Portia. "In this light, you look like a young Hedy Lamarr."

"Thank you, Ally. That made me feel really good about myself. You've always reminded me of Marilyn Monroe."

"That's very flattering—you're too kind. Here, dry your hair, and come with me." She treated some of Portia's wounds. After that, Portia followed Ally into her bedroom to her wardrobe. "I'm sorry. I don't own many items of clothing—as you know—but, here—sleep in this." Ally gave her a silk camisole to wear. After Portia slipped it on, Ally showed her to one of the other six bedrooms. "You can sleep here now; it looks like you need it."

Portia awkwardly fell onto the bed. "Oh, this bed is so comfortable." She struggled around, tangled in the silk sheets until Ally helped her into a comfortable position. "Goodnight, Ally."

"Goodnight," Ally said softly. She turned out the light and walked down the corridor to the living area.

CHAPTER SEVEN

She saw Osiris standing on the terrace, staring out over the ocean as it started sparkling with the onset of the rising sun. Osiris was deep in reflection, bearing witness to the beginning of a beautiful morning. The open space gave the feeling they were one with the sky. A refreshing breeze would occasionally meander through, making it even more pleasant. He was still deep in thought when she came and stood next to him, admiring the peaceful setting—so different from the chaos of the night.

"Our whole reality has shifted. Nothing will be the same now, will it, Osiris?"

"I don't think it can be now—not after what's happened—which is why we should savour this moment; we may not be fortunate enough to have another. Which is why I wanted to come out here, have some whiskey, smoke a bit of marijuana, look at the ocean, relax, and temporarily escape the chaos of last night."

"I understand," Ally said.

"It's pretty high-quality."

"I'm all too aware of that from experience and, shall we say, overindulgence. I got it from this great cannabis dispensary in the Marketplace. I'm going to take a bath now. You're most welcome to join me."

"Sharing a bath with a beautiful woman—that sounds awful." They both smiled, relieved to have a minor moment of happiness.

"What's the matter, darling? Are you afraid that you won't be able to control yourself or your arousal if you see me naked?"

"I might not be able to, no."

"Come on. After last night, we should probably set about planning our escape, but I need to just forget that, even for a fleeting moment. Please join me." She held out her hand.

Instead of taking it, Osiris picked her up, cradling her in his arms.

She smiled, as it took her by surprise. She put her arm around his neck and kissed him on the cheek as he walked toward the *en suite* in Ally's bedroom.

"Is Portia better now?" he inquired.

"Yeah, she's asleep at the moment, but she's much better," she said.

The room was elegantly modelled after a Roman bathhouse, complete with carved pillars, marble tiles featuring luxurious reliefs of goddesses, and mirrors with ornate gilding. The enormous rectangular bath measured five metres long and three metres wide. Built into the floor, it was the centrepiece, situated in the middle of the room. It was constantly refilled by the hotel's water system and heated, a deluxe feature of the Penthouse Suite. Ally lowered the tinted blinds. The early-morning sun filtered through, gradually becoming brighter, casting a fabulous golden-coloured hue on the marble-tiled walls. They lit some candles, rendering the atmosphere even more sensuous. They enjoyed each other's company in this tender moment. A radio placed next to the bath was tuned to her favourite station. The likes of The Rolling Stones, Led Zeppelin, and The Beatles carried melodically through the bathroom. The ether was soothingly placid as they soaked in the water, drinking whiskey, smoking, telling stories, and laughing.

"This is really beautiful right here," Osiris said. "This lovely view, this serene setting, and your company."

"I agree. This is so tranquil, I don't want to get out."

"Neither do I."

"Although I'm tired after that horrible evening, I'm not going to sleep just yet. I'm enjoying this far too much."

"Would you like another drink?" he asked.

"Yes, please."

Osiris reached for the crystal decanter beside him and refilled Ally's matching tumbler.

While listening to a Pink Floyd song, Ally watched the hypnotic water reflection rippling on the wall and drew a pleasure-filled sigh. She said, "My actual name is Alexandrine."

"What?" Osiris had been looking out the window but was now focused on her as their eyes locked. In their world, a person disclosing their actual name was a sign of enduring trust and respect. The importance of the gesture was impossible to underestimate.

"Alexandrine Chevalier."

"It's befitting for such a beautiful lady. I'm just a little surprised."

"Nobody—not even Portia—knows that."

"I feel privileged that you would tell me that. It's bizarre that we have to keep them secret. My real name is Memphis Jackson . . . hence the moniker 'Osiris.'"

"Memphis. I'm fascinated by ancient Egypt. Like a part of the Egyptian death ritual, where the heart of the deceased was weighed on scales against the goddess Mayet or her likeness, an ostrich feather, symbolising Truth. If the heart was innocent, it would be of equal weight to Truth, and the deceased would then be granted passage to the afterlife. Unfortunately, I don't believe that my heart would be innocent. Rather, it would be a totem, a beacon of darkness, to be devoured by the hybrid monster Ammut."

"You're too harsh on yourself."

"Not with all the atrocities I have gotten away with. I'll have to face some punishment for them one day. I'm not a religious person. I know people like me don't go to their graves without facing consequences for their actions. If not, then the world seems so wrong, foreign to me."

"What made you come to the U.R.S.C.?"

"I came here as a teenager. I think I had just turned sixteen or seventeen. After losing contact with everyone I knew during the conflict in France, I was drifting around alone and terrified. After I fled to the Seychelles, I wanted a better life and more opportunity. I vowed that I would travel to the U.R.S.C. to improve my situation. I arrived with idealistic dreams of contributing to the collective culture, improving my situation and taking control of my future. I wanted to make an impact in the arts, cinema, and in the theatre, creating thought-provoking, boundary-pushing material that also entertained. I was part of a thriving scene, enjoying success up north in Boheme, because it's the entertainment capital, and I was attending a prestigious university on a full scholarship. Before I graduated, I was struggling to survive financially. There were a few art exhibitions where I was selling pieces, and some of my plays were being performed in theatres, but it was not enough income to survive on. I had developed quite an expensive drug habit."

"Is that how you were introduced to such a different world? I'm curious, as it seems so far removed from *this* way of life."

"Yes, all my aspirations were overtaken by the criminal underworld of the U.R.S.C., which is never far from the surface. I was almost completely broke and bankrupt. I witnessed how much money some people I knew were making from investing in large companies and enterprises as the wealth of the United Republic exploded. I took it seriously and changed my university subjects to study finance and economics. After graduating, using their connections, I began acquainting myself with certain people, and I handled finances for a rolodex of prestigious clients. This was all legitimate at first—I was doing business and everything the correct way. My big mistake came when I got involved in financial management for illegal organisations and clients; it was then that the embezzling began. I started a shell company, registered it, went through all the rigmarole to make it appear real, and took money from investors and the organisations.

"Things were going exceedingly well for a while; I lived a life of excess. Yet it started to deteriorate when some of the clients began to ask questions about discrepancies in their figures. Other investors from whom I had stolen large amounts of money gave information about me in exchange for lesser sentences on other crimes they were caught for. Acquaintances in powerful positions warned me: My company and I were under investigation by the Major Crimes Division. The offices in my building were raided, and so was my apartment. I had a few associates working for me who were subsequently investigated. It was a terrible situation, but the detectives couldn't find anything on me or anyone else. My acquaintances got the investigation stalled long enough so that I could leave before any serious repercussions developed. The company was temporarily banned from trading during the investigation. When that expired, I listed the company on the market and sold all my shares. Then it was purchased by a larger firm and amalgamated. I fled Boheme in a rush, with no possessions—but with millions of dollars made from deception."

"That's when you relocated and came to Clarion?"

"I heard of its Marketplace district and the enterprising prospects here, as well as the fact that Clarion was emerging as the financial capital of the U.R.S.C. I thought the anonymity and the country's most populated city would be able to give me shelter. The alluring prospects attracted me here, and I fell back into the throes of greed and manipulation."

"If you're anything like me, what you found in this city was not what you hoped for."

"Exactly. I haven't been able to get into any type of professional career or honest living here; all I was doing was bouncing aimlessly between places. This is also why I'm staying in this hotel; I have been looking for a permanent property, but because everything has been so crazy, I haven't done anything about it. For the last two years, I've been living out of my suitcase. Fortunately, I have a great lease contract with the hotel management and the owners. I can stay here indefinitely if I want. When I relocated, I had amassed quite a fortune, and, to protect it and ensure its growth, I established another company to cover up my crimes. I made another mistake by going into Facilitating and working by myself. I was more selective with my clientele, handling only my own money, and not brokering so many deals, The financial world was enormously stressful for me. What about you?"

"I was born here when this was still Australia. I was only a kid when the war erupted. Fighting, slaughter and brutality were my mentors. Because everything was taken from me I mistakenly thought there was nothing else to learn from or inherit. I witnessed things then that probably explain my penchant for the Facilitating lifestyle—or instilled in me a hatred of it. I'm unsure which. I'm horrified by it, yet I participate in this lifestyle in an implicit manner. This existence isn't easy to get into or out of. I guess I was like you, in a way, when I was younger, wanting to change the world through design and innovation, allowing everyone in the world access to fundamental things for life. When everything settled, I drifted around for a while smuggling drugs and weapons before I joined the military and did a few tours of duty overseas. I was more involved with combat engineering and mechanics, but, again, I just saw what we were doing, how we were destroying another country under the guise of whatever lie they were telling us. I left the military and became a mercenary, performing operations and private security contracts around the world. I came back here to work for myself, to be the master of my own universe. We've got a lot in common."

"Cheers to that," Ally announced. They gently clinked their tumblers together and finished the contents.

"Another drink, *mademoiselle*?"

"*Oui, monsieur*," Ally said.

Wading over, Osiris refilled her tumbler, and she took another sip.

"So, 'Alexandrine,' 'Ally'—what do I call you now?"

"Whatever you like."

"Alexa?"

"Yeah, I like that," she smiled.

"Anyway, how did you meet Portia?"

"She was investigating the legitimacy of my company, looking for financial fraud and embezzlement. She started following me around everywhere and keeping constant surveillance on me. I couldn't take it anymore, and I bribed her to leave me alone and forget the investigation. I told her that I could provide her with ongoing financial assistance, drugs, whatever she needed. She almost arrested me one night in the Marketplace. I was so nervous, I thought I was going to be imprisoned for the rest of my life. But I bribed her with two kilograms of heroin, and she told me she was this crazy adrenaline junkie who went around on drug-fuelled escapades, robbing criminals but helping out others. She would give me all of these expensive items she'd seized from people. I didn't know what to think of her—she seemed crazy at the time. She asked me to join forces with her and said we could share our knowledge. She would give me inside intel on the movements of law enforcement.

"She would notify me if certain things were going to happen so I could avoid them, and I assisted her where I could with intel on the illegal, criminal element of things. At first, that's what it was. She would share all the things she had confiscated with me, and I'd help her. We both found targets to extort or steal from. It was not good for my reputation as a Facilitator, but it was great to know that your ally had so much power. You could go around with this almost invincible feeling—we could do whatever we wanted. You might say we were co-dependent, but we developed a close connection and became real friends. For a while there I didn't care about the possibility that either one of us could be killed. There were some seriously intense times; I don't know how we survived. On one occasion, she passed out from sedatives and crashed an undercover law enforcement vehicle full of stolen drugs and money into a department store. I was in the passenger seat and had to get her out. I'm not sure how she got away with that. Lucky? Maybe. Maybe not."

"Luck is a pretty abstract concept. Was it luck that we ran into each other at the nightclub and because of that we're here now and our futures, including Portia's, have become intertwined?" Osiris remarked.

Ally replied, "If we hadn't met at the nightclub, would we have encountered each other in a different location? I think we would have. It is a swing of the Pendulum—that's my metaphor. I have explained it to you before concerning the workings of the universe. I think it helps me rationalise an otherwise chaotic world."

"I see what you mean. I like it—it's an interesting analysis. Arthur Schopenhauer said that 'Fate shuffles the cards, and we play.' So we sit at the table, distracted by playing, under the hypothesis that we can have some control over the game, when all the while, more profound forces are at work around us. Fate may shuffle the cards, but what we do with them is up to us. Is that where luck comes in?" Osiris reasoned.

"I would be lucky to know—I told you this was good-quality marijuana!" They both laughed. "It's humorous," Ally continued. "We're trying to work out the whole universe and everything—and I can't even get my life together . . . Osiris." Ally's tone shifted, and her voice was now tinged with sadness. "With everything that has happened, I don't know when we'll be able to enjoy another moment like this. Like I said, the trajectory of our lives has shifted. As much as I dislike the idea, we must talk about how we're going to get out of Clarion and where to go."

Osiris responded, "Luck happens when preparation meets opportunity. Whether we're responsible or it's decided by something greater, we have to welcome whatever may come. If we do everything we possibly can and still lose our lives, then it was destined to be."

CHAPTER EIGHT

They stayed in the spacious bath for much longer, devoted to a conversation they needed to have. Both of them wanted to stay there forever, forget the outside world, and luxuriate in each other's divine company—like an Elysian field of eternal fantasy. They kept putting off getting out, drying off, and going to sleep. But they knew that, inevitably, they had to confront reality and face the question of sleeping together and sex.

Ally said, "I gave Portia my camisole to wear, so I guess I'll just have to sleep naked."

Osiris knelt in front of her and gently dried her statuesque body with a towel. He looked up, and their eyes met.

"And you can't sleep in those bloodstained clothes, so I guess we will have to sleep naked . . . together," Ally said, giving Osiris a frisky smile.

"Perhaps we could cuddle for warmth."

"Yes, please," she said seductively. He had finished drying her, and she used another towel to dry him. He couldn't hide his arousal as she wiped the towel over his body. They moved from the *en-suite* to the bedroom, and Ally sat down on the spacious four-poster bed.

"This suite is amazing. The furniture's all so luxurious—this is the nicest bedroom I've ever been in," Osiris said.

"It's a glorious room to sleep in. I absolutely love that the bed faces the ocean, so that, when you wake up, beauty's the first thing you see."

A teardrop-shaped piece of crystal suspended over by the window had caught the sun and cast little rainbows around the room. Ally pointed to it. "That crystal is so lovely, so peaceful. It really adds a nice aesthetic to the room. Here, come and lie down next to me."

After swinging the crystal back and forth like a pendulum, Osiris joined Ally on the bed, and their eyes met again. They tried to continue the façade of competition they'd started, each silently daring the other to act upon their impulses, but their desire was irresistible, and they began to make love. They caressed each other softly, in pure indulgence. It was the most passionate, tender lovemaking either of them had ever experienced. To both, it felt surreal to share a romantic liaison after dreaming and fantasising about it for such a long time.

In afterglow, they lay and cherished the tranquillity of the moment. They tried to re-start their earlier serious conversation, but slowly, they fell asleep in each other's arms.

They were still unsure about their on-again/off-again relationship. They were realistic about their lifestyles and business. The reality of their work and what they did were not conducive to a steady, permanent relationship, and they were the first to admit it. They enjoyed the flexibility and freedom of a casual arrangement. It was a difficult time when they first met, and they both felt they had to be careful about what they revealed. It was an apprehensive period that took on the appearance of an elaborate dance, circling silently while withholding the love they were feeling.

Ally awoke first; she lifted her head off Osiris's chest and looked at the ocean, now fully shimmering in the early-afternoon sun. Her head was still reeling with thoughts about the previous evening and the wonderful experience they had just shared. She sat up, and Osiris stirred, his eyes slowly opening with a few weary blinks.

"Hello, darling," Ally said.

"How are you?"

"After what happened last night, I'm feeling great. That was amazing, so nice. I can't remember ever feeling that kind of affection between us."

"It was definitely intense."

"'Intense' is an understatement. 'Intense' doesn't even come close to describing it. Why did we wait such a long time to reawaken our physical relationship like that?"

"I'm really not sure, but I'm glad we could enjoy an encounter like that before we have to deal with this dilemma surrounding the coup." He paused. "Let's make love again."

"Yes, please. That sounds delicious," she purred, an excited look on her face, a frisky look in her eyes. She put on a bold red-satin neckerchief before they made love again.

Portia slept for many hours; her body was thoroughly exhausted. She woke up well into the evening, lathered in a thick coating of sweat that had soaked onto the bed in a large stain around her. Her body was desperately trying to get rid of toxins. In some areas, it was mixed with blood. She was in a state of confusion, her head swooning. For a moment, she looked around, unsure of where she was, before everything came bearing down upon her again. Even though she was injured, she was annoyed at wasting valuable time by sleeping so long. She clambered out of the bed and went to find Ally and Osiris. She was struggling to remember the layout of the suite. She found them on the terrace, stargazing and talking in a lap-pool, in each other's arms, and their clothing scattered beside the pool. Portia walked out onto the terrace, and they turned to look at her.

"Good to see you. You're looking much better," Ally said.

"Yeah, all things considered. Thanks for all your help," she replied with a raspy voice; her eyes were almost swollen shut from being assaulted. She stood there with her arms crossed, looking very uncomfortable.

"Come sit down." Osiris gestured to a chair by the side of the pool, into which she slowly eased herself, wincing occasionally from pain.

"While you were sleeping, Osiris and I began formulating a plan to make our escape."

"Excellent. I have to apologise for consuming so much of our time the way I did, but, as chaotic as the events of last night were, they were also kind of cathartic. There were so many things revealed. I can help you with the preparations."

"We have made some decisions about how we're going to get out of Clarion and where we're going to go," Osiris said, looking at Ally.

"What exactly did you decide on while I was asleep?"

"I tried to secure all of the documents required for a new identity and to gain access through any part of the country unchallenged. Ally has everything she needs—although how I'm going to get everything *I* need and our exact strategy is still something we have to debate."

"So, at the moment, both you and I don't have all of our forged documents prepared—right?" Portia asked.

"I had them all where I was staying. I can't go back there to access them. You said it's too hazardous to return there. I had some reserve documents stored at another location, which is also now inaccessible, but I can get more created without much difficulty."

"How long will that take?" Portia asked.

"A few hours at the maximum, but that's still an inconvenience. Many things can happen in that amount of time. From there, we need to schedule a private jet and a flight out of Haltana Airport to the Lawless Zone. There's a runway there controlled by the Militia."

"That could be a disaster. The air space above that is restricted, and, if you don't have the right clearance, you'll get shot down."

"I can get us the correct security clearances from the Militia, and there aren't many other places we can go, given who's after us. Anywhere we go outside of there would be a problem. Some locations would be comparatively less dangerous, however, on balance, it's the best place for us. The majority of the Militia forces are there, and the main attraction is that there's protection from prosecution," Osiris explained.

"What will you do, Portia?" Ally asked.

Portia was silent for a moment.

"I'm leaving the Major Crimes Division—I know that for sure. I can't even go back to my office or my apartment to retrieve any of my personal items. I have to go totally rogue, which means they're going to hunt me. After that, I don't know whether to hand the information I have to a journalist or to someone in the broadcast media."

"Don't do that. The media outlets in this country have become so monopolised now, controlled by a few tycoons working with a hidden agenda, assisting their powerful allies. They regurgitate false information as part of an agenda to incite division and weaponise fear. You can't trust them to report your information truthfully," Osiris argued.

"That thought has crossed my mind. There are a few remaining independent sources with integrity that I could offer it to, a few sources that I can trust. I'm still deciding whether or not to do that. I'm unsure of where to go. I have to leave this fiasco. I don't think I should stay in the country. There's not a lot of opportunity for me here. I can sympathise with what's motivating you to topple the existing regime. This country's become so tyrannical. Aggravating division, crippling debt, rights and civil liberties diminishing, surveillance and dominance increasing. I might move back to Italia; I was almost a teenager when I sought refuge here, and I have not been back to see my family."

"Why don't you come to the Lawless Zone with Ally and me? If you choose not to move overseas, there's a lot of danger in this area for you. I don't believe you would be able to live a comfortable life with that worry eating away at you. You would always be looking over your shoulder, and that insecurity would increase extensively if you ever disclosed that information. If done correctly, the knowledge you have could go toward repairing this nation. You voiced some of the issues it's facing. You could have a role to play in addressing them."

"I can't go into hiding in the Lawless Zone for the remainder of my life. You're correct when you say nowhere outside of that area is completely safe and free from harm. But I can't go there with you just yet; and now that we have the cover of night, we must go into the city and get everything we need to disappear. I must go to a safe house to retrieve some documentation and weapons, among other things."

"Do you need money? Because Osiris and I could give you as much as you need."

"I'm grateful for the offer—that's also something I need to get from the safe house. But we're going to need some heavier weaponry if we encounter anything while we're out there."

"I have some powerful guns available here, and Osiris stockpiled more in the back of that vehicle."

"I need to go to the Marketplace to get my documents and papers, but the time it will take depends on how many other clients they currently have," Osiris stated.

"We know what we need to do, then. Ally, do you have some clothing I could wear temporarily?"

"Yes, come with me."

She got out of the pool and dried herself. She got dressed and gave Portia another outfit to wear before placing her possessions into a single suitcase. She had learnt to travel lightly. With a swift pace, they gathered large suitcases of weapons, explosives, and ammunition to smuggle through the hotel. Ally was a wealthy, esteemed guest, and her suite was in a private section of the hotel. She had access to areas that were restricted to other guests, allowing them to move through without causing suspicion.

They descended into the subterranean parking lot. The mood was sombre as they got into the vehicle, surfacing in a flash onto the pulsing city streets. They were sure of their direction but unsure of what was going to happen along the journey. It was the end of the week, so the streets were particularly active. There was some argument over how they should complete the series of objectives. Portia insisted they travel to her destination before anywhere else; she maintained that, once she got the false credentials and papers, she could more easily help them progress their exit strategy.

"I don't understand why you're insisting on doing all of your business before we attend to any of our matters, Portia," Osiris argued.

"Because I have the insider position, the knowledge that can help us gather everything we need to assure the best chance of making a successful getaway. When we have those papers, we can become *whoever*. I can manipulate what we need and give us the best possible chance for escape."

Osiris agreed, and they travelled to Alhambra Beach, where Portia's safe house was located. They made it there quickly, but, as the vehicle crept down an uneven, narrow alleyway with collapsed fences and overhanging trees, closer to the unassuming house in a quiet back street, they realised it had very recently been the target of an arson attack. There was police tape, undulating in the wind, around the house. "Fuck . . . This can't be happening. No—this is a nightmare! Those bastards are trying to cut off all our avenues of escape. They're forcing us to resurface; what are we going to do?" she shouted.

"It's all right, Portia. Now we just need to go to another location. What other places do you have available? There was an apartment there in Beau Monde we were using recently, where we held that financier's wife hostage."

"You're right, but we have to go to another location—we can't use that apartment. I almost got caught for that and had to stop using that place. Just let me think for a moment. Osiris, take me to Ariadne Fair. There's a safe house there belonging to an organisation I'm helping. I had to store some contraband there, and we're going to retrieve it."

Their destination was an affluent borough in the city's South. The streets were lined with leafy trees and luxury buildings. Portia directed them to a driveway beside an ornate residential building. The seven-story tenement was purchased and controlled by a criminal organisation Portia had given protection to; she made sure the building was safe from raids and surveillance. Ally had her weapons hidden under a trenchcoat, gripping onto a fully automatic handgun as Portia had a tense conversation over an intercom with the people inside, who were watching them through a network of cameras.

Ally heard Portia reply to a muffled voice: "I need your help; you know I wouldn't come here unannounced if I wasn't desperate. . . . You know the telephone lines are crawling with surveillance. . . . They're with me. They're not police. I wouldn't bring anyone here I don't trust. . . . They're Facilitators—The Rose and Osiris."

After the heated exchange, they were eventually granted entry to the building. Ally's fear heightened, as they were now in a vulnerable position. They trailed behind Portia as she found the people in charge of the safe house and continued the argument. Ally and Osiris waited outside the room, several people with machine guns watching their every move. It was a painstaking scenario. They could hear her talking about how she had done so many favours for them and was demanding a favour in return. After a prolonged period, Portia persuaded those in command of the safe house to help her. With no warning, she burst into the corridor. "Come with me—they haven't given us much time," she said as she pushed past them. She walked down the corridor, entering a code onto a keypad on the wall that unlocked a heavy steel door.

It was a large room, littered with a wealth of different items: firearms, bundles of money, drug-manufacturing machines, counterfeit luxury goods—the list was extensive. They stood in the doorway as Portia filled another suitcase with what she needed, throwing in bundles of money, clothing, various drugs, weapons, and ammunition. She grabbed a key off a table and talked them into giving her one of their high-end four-wheel drives. "Let's go, now," Portia said, walking towards the door with the full suitcase. They were escorted from the building; she went to get the car, which was parked in a garage farther along the street.

They followed her to an all-hours document-storage facility near a deserted commercial district, out of the city, and waited for her outside. In her storage room, she rummaged through a filing cabinet and found her collection of false passports and a hoard of other fake identity documents. The Marketplace was their next location. They stayed close together and drove cautiously on the roads, trying to avoid suspicion. Osiris had numerous connections for document forgers from Facilitating and the Militia, some of the highest-quality work in the whole country. The originally lax laws regarding identification documents for travel and immigration had been completely changed. It was becoming more difficult to prevent being tracked. Osiris went to his preferred people, who worked out of an office in the Olympia building, which was owned by corrupt property developers and the same entity that owned the Hyperion Nightclub. They had to leave their weapons in a special area of the foyer. Ally deposited three handguns, a trench knife, and knuckledusters into a metal tray given to her by an employee and was instructed to remove her satin headscarf.

Now unprotected, they entered the building. The office was located on the upper floors, which looked over the Neon Circuit area of the Marketplace, the signs outside like fireworks, in a strange synchronicity, as they gave off an unnatural glow. Alone, Osiris took the elevator to the office. Ally and Portia waited for him in an exclusive area for wealthy patrons; they drank alcohol and conversed with associates, but that couldn't disarm the situation or take the edge off. Osiris returned after a short consultation to join them. The swarm of activity and distracting lights made the stress unbearable for Ally. The documents were delivered surprisingly fast, but their perception of time was warped, and it felt like much longer. It was the early hours of the morning, and the sun would be rising soon.

From another floor, Osiris used a secure telephone line to contact certain people from the Militia who could arrange an aircraft and pilots for them. Osiris was instructed that, without successfully gaining clearance, they would be unable to leave without drawing attention, or to approach the Lawless Zone without being shot down in flames by the military. What arose next was one of the most challenging parts of their plan.

They had to contact the Civil Aviation Agency, a government body regulating all air travel within the country, and, using their false documents and clearances, schedule a legitimate flight plan and get permissions to fly out of Haltana Airport and over the Lawless Zone airspace. Portia took the lead, posing as a wealthy film producer; she used her false-company details to fill out the form that the operator administered to her over the telephone, which was rigorous—manipulating details about the aircraft, cargo, destination, the passengers, and the reason for the flight which was to scout filming locations. Osiris contacted the people from the Militia again, and everything was finalised. Pilots were chosen, and a private jet was awaiting them in the hangar. It was an agonising wait, but the flight plan was accepted, and their exit from Clarion was assured.

CHAPTER NINE

The last objective was to meet the pilots at the airport, who were being escorted by several other Militia members also going to the Lawless Zone. "The time is five forty-five; we need to be at the airport before 7 a.m. to join up with the pilots and the other people travelling with us," Osiris said, looking around anxiously.

"We must go now, then—we can't leave anything to chance. I want to make sure we have an adequate amount of time to get there, in the event something happens. Besides, I can't stand this place," Ally said.

"We have to travel together. You must come with Ally and me so that we don't get separated. You can use our vehicle once we've reached the airport."

They descended to the main foyer and collected their weapons. The city was coming alive with the onset of morning; they noticed an increase in vehicles on the roads. Osiris was an excellent driver, hugging the road, and leaning sharply into corners. He immediately went in a northerly direction; his nerves were beginning to surface. Portia immediately knew where he was going. "Stay off the Orbital Highway, Osiris. There're too many police, and you're going to attract attention to us."

"It's the easiest way to the airport—it goes around the *whole city*. We can be there in a few minutes. We have to arrive there on time, or they're leaving without us, and we have to do this all again," Osiris argued.

"You don't want to sabotage yourself now, do you? Go through the Eighth Avenue Tunnel, take the Westview Overpass, and then get onto the Clarion Expressway."

"If there's been an accident or something on the Expressway and it's gridlocked, we're not going to make it. I have to take the Orbital."

"What about the Metro Arterial Road? That connects to all of the airports; it's riskier, though not as heavily used as the Expressway. The likelihood of a chokepoint there is low," Ally interjected.

"Actually, she's correct. If there's an accident or delay on the Metro, we could probably just divert onto an intersecting Avenue and find an alternate route . . . turn right here, drive along Agora Square, and then go another three blocks past it . . . go straight through this intersection and along East Sixty-Ninth Avenue," Portia directed.

"Are you sure? You're taking us closer to the city centre. If traffic is at a standstill, and if there's a lot of police activity around there, we could be arrested," Osiris said.

"This is the way we've been forced to take now. I'm nervous about going through the main part of the city, but I'm confident this is the best route. If any law enforcement tries to stop us, I'll take responsibility and kill them myself," Portia explained. Osiris adjusted his driving route and followed the directions Portia gave him until they reached the Arterial Road. From there, he knew the correct way. Haltana Airport was the smallest of the city's four airports; it handled mainly private jets, light aircraft, and flight training, as opposed to large commercial aircraft.

The Militia had planned to instruct the airport workers to allow them access through a restricted area, direct them to the correct hangar without having to pass through the security checks, and allow them to keep their weapons and other illegal paraphernalia. The insiders were waiting at a gate to let them through. After instructing them where to go, they drove behind a row of hangars until they reached Hangar Eighteen. They spotted the other passengers congregated around the aircraft and parked at the back of the hangar. They had ten minutes to spare until their scheduled departure. As they loaded their luggage on and prepared to board the aircraft, a crushing realisation dawned on Ally. She turned to Portia; "We're never going to see one another again, are we?"

"No, Ally. No, we won't. I'm sorry. This is our final goodbye. Who knows? With all our talk of fate and luck, our paths could cross again in this crazy world," she said, but Ally knew it wasn't true by the look on her face.

"We had a lot of good times, a lot of wild times together; I'll never forget those."

"Yeah, I'll always remember those," Ally said softly.

"I'm so thankful I had the privilege of meeting you. You did so much for me. I can't believe you're going. Nothing will ever be the same again. Goodbye, my friend."

"Goodbye, Portia."

"It was our destiny, for this to happen like it did. You take care of yourself, and have a good life. I love you, and I'll see you on the other side," Portia said as they embraced. They looked at each other for the last time, turned, and walked in opposite directions. Ally was crushed, as another person had gone out of her life forever, and it broke her inside. Osiris put his arm around her as they ascended the stairs into the cabin. "I hope I'm doing the right thing by going through with this. I've already made many sacrifices. This has cost me one of my only friends, one more relationship destroyed because of this horrible life I chose to lead. Becoming a Facilitator has ruined my life," Ally lamented.

Osiris reassured her, "If we do this and do it right, nobody else will have to make that choice—to live a life filled with regret and offering no opportunity. It's too late for us." They took their seats next to each other at the back of the aircraft. The aircraft roared to life; the pilot guided it out of the hangar and began to manoeuvre onto the runway.

Ally was gazing out the window, consumed with sadness over farewelling Portia when a series of movements and noise caught her attention. A fleet of police and military vehicles burst onto the runway, blocking it. She looked to the sky to witness helicopters descending on them. With an abrupt surge of movement, the force engaged the aircraft. To the distress of everyone aboard, they were surrounded with frightening speed. They were in total disbelief, as an arsenal of weapons were trained onto them.

Unknown to the occupants of the aircraft, the government had been intercepting codes the Militia had been using to relay information to strategic points. Government cryptographers deciphered these codes and discovered the plans for the coup. They were also spying on their encrypted frequencies by forcing captured Militia soldiers to become double agents, who continued the conversations while providing valuable secrets and information to the government. The search for Osiris had intensified after he'd escaped from the nightclub. Their entire correspondence regarding the aircraft had been monitored. They knew he was going to be there with other valuable Militia targets.

Portia watched helplessly from a distance, so far away the people appeared miniscule. The pilots were told over the radio to turn the engines off, and, so, they were forced to. A woman then spoke through a loudspeaker, informing them she was Victoria Ulrich, a Commander who belonged to Special Tactics and Training in Crisis, known as S.T.A.T.I.C., a ruthless agency feared for accepting nothing less than total destruction. She ordered everyone to exit the aircraft and surrender immediately. The consensus among those in the aircraft was to fight to the death. A woman named Fabia Reynard, known as "Fox," loaded a machine gun, ready for a confrontation.

"Don't go out there. You'll be shredded into pieces," Ally pleaded with her.

Fabia railed, "I'm not surrendering. Fuck that. I'll die on my own terms. They're going to execute us for treason, regardless. We're renegades now. If this is what I need to do, then so be it; I'm not falling into their hands to be humiliated and fucking paraded in front of the masses."

Ally tried to get Fabia to cool down. "Don't do anything irrational and heated in the moment. Think about this carefully—this is a volatile situation. If it's handled correctly, we may actually live long enough to be here when this coup begins. This could be where it begins instead of ending in disaster."

"Fuck you," Fabia hissed. "I'm going out there. You can stay behind and get held hostage by their justice and prison system—be their captive, for all I care. It doesn't change my mind."

Screaming, she opened the aircraft door and began firing as she revealed herself to the horde of law enforcement officers. A hail of gunfire tore through every part of her anatomy, and pieces of her body littered the doorway and toppled down the aircraft steps. The noise was deafening. Dozens of bullets ripped into the cabin, ricocheting around, forcing them to take shelter on the floor behind their chairs.

Ally turned to Osiris. "Osiris, I'm going out there and surrendering."

"No—Fabia was right. They're going to kill us no matter what we do. We have to fight."

"So, our lives are just expendable, anyway. Then you can remain here and fight, but I'm not going to engage in that. Listen to me: You need to surrender with me! You need to go out there with me and surrender, do you understand? I don't want to hear any argument whatsoever. We're going to concede this together, without a fight, without ending up like her. We're not dying today," Ally said, infuriated.

"We can't go back. We're cornered. We can fucking give them a last fight—go down fighting." They were both heated and shouting amidst the mayhem of other loud conversations and arguments, further compounded by the noise outside.

"So, our lives were just expendable. My life was merely a disposable element of your plan. How *dare* you insist on going through with this and then falter at the first sign of trouble? How can you be so opposed to a solution that does not involve getting shredded by bullets? You're no good to your cause or the Militia if you die, Osiris." Two more people took their chances and rushed toward the door. Taking cover, they opened fire, only to be met with a fusillade of bullets and the imminent demise that awaited them. Their argument was interrupted by the overpowering noise of shooting and the distressingly short screams of the dying.

"Don't you understand? It's the endgame now. This was an outcome we had to be ready for. We had to be prepared to die for this, even in a manner that's not to our liking. I'm ready to die and transcend fear," Osiris yelled.

"Now you truly sound like a maniac."

"Call it fanatical, but I'd rather die knowing that I strove for something meaningful. I don't live just for the sake of living. That's only *existing*! If we want to submit, then we are killing ourselves slower. I know it's not easy to accept. Death is confrontational."

"I call it naïve . . . Thank you so much. Now I'm going to be executed because of your greed. We were going to have such a fabulous life—well, we *could* have. But now, we're going to die, because you were so focused on your views, and whatever it took to achieve them. You were so caught up with this plan, so eager to adopt a cause, that you didn't care what it cost. I'd rather be with Portia. I want to go be with my friend, but now I'm never going to see her or you again. I'm never going to be able to do anything after this. I hope that you're satisfied with destroying everything. I wish I'd never crossed paths with you in that nightclub—none of this would've ever happened. I just need to be away from you, so I can think about what I'm going to do."

The siege had generated massive hype; the media outlets were covering the major incident unfolding. The details had been very scarce, the media only gradually learning more about who the people were and why the siege had begun. In preliminary reports, it was understood to be a domestic terrorist group or citizen revolt. The city was alive with talk of what was being reported was false, a perfect example of the police and government cracking down on its citizens. The citizens' rage rose to a breaking point, and then ignited. One of the Militia members antagonised the situation by contacting an illegal radio station and imploring citizens to take up arms and show their support by taking to the streets. Protestors swarmed the perimeters outside, the crowd growing tremendously. Their presence swelled so greatly that the focus became containing them before ending the siege. As the afternoon gave way to night, the atmosphere deteriorated. Ally and Osiris watched from the windows as the spectacle grew and then descended into a riot. Hangars and buildings were being set ablaze, and protestors were getting shot on the runway as they moved toward the aircraft.

Ally had distanced herself from Osiris, but it was difficult in the confined space. She joined with some of the others to talk about their options. The mood among them shifted frequently between living and dying, whether they were doing the right thing or making a mistake, and whether they should make a final stand together or all surrender. They had initiated contact with a negotiator, which caused a ferocious discussion as they formulated their demands and further broke the cohesion. Three Militia members took the lead and would moderate who talked. Their bargaining was interrupted when a loud explosion from outside the plane commanded their attention. They all scanned the windows and saw that an aircraft had been destroyed nearby. Floodlights allowed Ally to observe the condition deteriorate as a large group of the protestors responsible were shot. The survivors were mercilessly picked off one by one, while, behind them, flames and smoke leapt high. When a female Militia member unexpectedly committed a horrific suicide, Ally looked at Osiris in disgust. "Look at her. Is this what you wanted? Because now it's happening. Look out there at the carnage already unfolding," she yelled.

"Everyone here knew what they were getting into. They know what's involved, and so do you, so stop acting like this was so unexpected. These people would be happy to give their blood, their life, for the cause, because they believe in something outside themselves."

"I *do* believe in worthwhile causes outside of myself—just not doomed fanatical plots like this. I won't cooperate in this failed experiment anymore. If you want to play the martyr, then go ahead—but don't take all these other people down with you. I stand alone and always have. I'm better off that way. I'm going out there, and I'm going to accept whatever happens. You can stay here if you wish."

"Please, Ally. Please don't leave. We can fix this. You don't know what's going to happen to you."

"I must admit defeat here and hope everything works out. I'm sorry—I can't be a part of this any longer. I don't know what else to tell you. This was a mistake; it was great getting to know you, but this is goodbye, Osiris."

After a tearful hug she raised her hands above her head and slowly moved towards the door, stepping over bodies. "Please don't shoot.

I'm unarmed. Please don't shoot." She repeated as she went down the staircase, taking care to avoid parts of Reynard's body. She left blood-ied bootprints as she moved toward the mass of people and weapons pointed at her. Osiris realised that Ally was right: he had become a brute, consumed by his own selfish desires; he had ruined his life, and, in addition to alienating the most important person to him, ruined her life. This campaign had destroyed everything that was dear to him; with nothing to lose now, he succumbed to his fate. He exited the cabin with his arms raised in surrender. Ally was overwhelmed and thrown to the ground. Someone placed a knee on the nape of her neck, pressing her cheek firmly against the tarmac. Ally was thrown into the back of a S.T.A.T.I.C. van for carrying high-risk fugitives. Osiris was put into a separate vehicle and transported to the Federal Complex, which housed the National Investigative Bureau's head office and field offices for other law enforcement agencies. The vehicle and the convoy surrounding it went underneath the building, stopping at a series of security checkpoints. After going through the checkpoints, Ally was removed from the vehicle into a sprawling underground complex of concrete and barricades. A chain was placed tightly around her waist, connecting to the shackles on her ankles and wrists, severely limiting her movement. Awaiting her in the extensive underground complex were agents of the National Investigative Bureau.

CHAPTER TEN

The siege continued for forty-two hours. More of the Militia members left the plane to engage with the forces, but they were cut down in a barrage of gunfire. There were talks back and forth between the Militia and negotiators. The pilots had been killed by stray bullets piercing the cockpit. Militia members were demanding replacement pilots and safe passage out of the country or to the Lawless Zone, but their demands were denied. After more had perished and realising the writing was on the wall, the remaining people in the plane surrendered. From the nineteen passengers on-board, Ally, Osiris, and seven others had persisted through the standoff—four men and three women, labelled the "Clarion Nine" by certain commentators.

After witnessing the violent confrontation surrounding the incident at Haltana Airport, Portia was unnerved. The area around the airport was swarming with police and agents. Using her best judgement, she departed as covertly as possible, but she felt certain that she wasn't going to make it out undetected. But, so far, to her surprise, she was passing through a series of security checkpoints unchallenged. At the last checkpoint, police officers further questioned her. She claimed that she was one of the detectives investigating the incident and produced her badge with her new identity. The officer became suspicious and wanted to search her vehicle. She couldn't let him discover the cache of illegal items, so she had to be more persuasive by threatening him with a demotion or disciplinary consequences, as her new, fake persona was at a much higher pay scale and rank than him. She was allowed to pass through.

Equipped with everything she needed, without delay, she left Clarion—and, with it, her entire life. Everything had been shifted and disrupted. She fled so abruptly that she had no time to get her affairs in order. No time to farewell anything. She was leaving behind her apartment, her romantic interests, her career, and her identity. With her forged documents, she became a new person altogether, unable to remain who she was. Using the advanced highway network, she made her way out of the city and was caught in the early-morning traffic snarl as the roads became engulfed with activity.

Once she was out of the city, she covered much more distance quickly, eventually travelling on isolated back roads, through less-occupied areas of the country, further from the populated centres and into isolated regions, where the rule of law scarcely applied. Her destination was Delphi Township, a massive encampment on the edge of the Lawless Zone that began as a refugee camp but had developed into a thriving town. The police and other services didn't travel into the community due to an agreement that had been struck between the government and Delphi Township's inhabitants. Any justice that needed to be enforced was done by the townspeople. There was crime, but it was dealt with much more severely. Within the Township was a ceasefire rule that most of the people obeyed. The bodies of those who didn't were displayed publicly in certain areas. Outside of Delphi Township's limits, in the Lawless Zone, there was much conflict and dispute. It was the place where grievances were resolved—most often swiftly and brutally. Before sunset, sirens would sound outside the Township, signalling anyone unprepared for fighting to return to safety. At night, the Lawless Zone became even fiercer.

Sounds of gunfire and explosions carried through the vast swathes of desert outside the Township. Portia had been going down the same deserted road for hours and was beginning to succumb to fatigue. She had avoided all checkpoints and stayed vigilant for bandits who might ambush her to steal her vehicle. She arrived at Delphi Township as the searing daytime temperature was starting to fall. The colour was draining from the sky as it gave way to an inky desert night.

The streets were full of activity. Most of the lighting was provided by oil lanterns. Everywhere, people gathered in groups, gambling, cooking food, playing instruments, and getting intoxicated. There were makeshift market stalls set up that sold a variety of legal and illegal items. She felt safe there but still had her machine gun slung over her shoulder in plain sight. She parked her vehicle and walked along the dirt roads laid out in a large grid pattern. On either side were trenches choked with rubbish and a dense cluster of houses made of any material available. There was very little developed infrastructure—what she saw was mainly tents and makeshift shanties. Any actual buildings there were in disrepair.

She came to the main street and sought refuge in an anonymous lodge above a tavern, a gathering place for some of the powerful and ruthless characters in the Township. Any new person would draw attention; she felt everyone focusing on her as she entered, and the conversation grew quieter. There were refugees of all nationalities and others who did not want to participate in the wider society or who had been forced to leave it. They had their weapons resting against the tables and walls. She could hear snatches of whispers while she walked past, undeterred, approaching the tavern staff and securing a place to stay. It was a decaying room faded from the unrelenting desert sun; tattered curtains were drawn across a dusty window.

She needed to carefully plan her next move. Extremely nervous, she placed weapons all around the room, thinking that someone could break in at any minute. Her life had been irrevocably shattered—along with her reputation. She had become a wanted fugitive within her own agency. Her previous decisions had made her their enemy, one they would relentlessly hunt down. She was a rogue agent now, referred to as a "Takedown"—someone who had betrayed their duty and had to be eliminated.

She quickly became well established in the Township. She renewed acquaintances with many people she had known from her past—people from all areas, other "Takedown" agents, former criminals she had helped, individuals she had not seen for many years. They made money from mining operations and quickly got her to participate; with her extensive knowledge and documents, they secured the rights to many areas of land. She was also able to help them gain clearance and access to all types of mining machinery. They quickly made a huge profit, although Portia started to feel guilty for doing so much damage to the land and the environment.

She befriended many people and was assured safety. She even met with some of the Township's Council; they had heard the stories of her flight from the law and the fate of her associates. They were very concerned about their own future, as the government were trying to get rid of them and secure many of the mining rights they owned. They asked for her help in securing their future and keeping the government away, promising her many things if she could do what they requested. Portia discovered some legal loopholes concerning the formation of the Township and exploited them. She helped to gain the townspeople protected status as refugees and asylum seekers, who, therefore, couldn't be removed. Through an environmental lawyer, the Council contacted the governmental Department of Land Management with the information, demanding that the Township wouldn't be demolished, removed, or altered in any way. They refused to surrender any mining rights or land, citing legal precedent established in a similar situation with another refugee camp. Portia and the Council members thought they had secured a victory over the government's heavy-handed authority, but it would prove to be short-lived.

The Federal Complex was a monolith of concrete and metal, reflecting the seriousness of what took place within its walls. Agents marched Ally through a highly secured route for detainees. Crushed and defeated, she experienced a spectrum of emotions—crippling thoughts of regret and uncertainty, her dismal reality abruptly dawning on her. She felt like she was suffocating, unable to slow her heart rate. She could scarcely focus on the enormity of her situation. Her mind kept replaying the incident at the airport as she was taken through the gruelling processing phase. They recited to her the usual script, informing her of the charges against her as well as her supposed "rights." Humiliation overcame her as she had her photograph taken, the photographer cold and detached as he directed her. She placed her hand onto a designated electronic pad, and her palm print and fingerprints were entered onto a national computer database.

They placed her into an interview room that brooded with a subdued feel—the air stifling and its lighting ominously dim. The concrete walls were a dull grey, contributing to the gloom. They shackled her hands to the table and left her for hours to sit in her stunned silence. A slew of agents interrogated her, using psychological tactics like repeatedly asking her the same questions for hours. Stressed, she was unsure what exactly they wanted from her.

Eventually, an agent entered carrying a folder. Ally recognised him instantly as the same anonymous agent who had been watching her in the Hyperion Nightclub. Ally's eyes narrowed.

"Remember me?" the agent asked. He was a heavyset middle-aged man; his rounded face bore the marks of a stressful career. His hair-line was receding, and his cheeks were red and streaked with small veins. He took a seat and briefly peered at his watch. "I'm Agent Frank Blaze of the National Investigation Bureau, but we've seen each other before. The Bureau is currently investigating your affiliates, including Memphis Jackson, aka 'Osiris.' We were closing in on him that night to arrest him and question him about his role in the conspiracy to overthrow the government when you and Detective D'Amico appeared and ruined all of our previous work. Since then, we've been trying to rediscover Memphis Jackson's location and identify you. Thankfully, we intercepted some of his communications with the Militia.

"From the information we have here, it states that your name is Ally Rose . . . twenty-nine years old . . . emigrated from the Seychelles. There isn't a lot here about you. It says you started your own investment firm and filed it with the Federal Business Registry. You and your company have been investigated for fraud, but apparently, the investigation was ceased, and no charges were filed. It seems Detective D'Amico also had something to do with that. It says you started another company, Alliance Render, known as A.R. Financial, which handled money for some very lucrative companies. Not much further is known about your clientele or the specific conduct of those set-ups. It's currently handling select private investors and making a significant quarterly turnover—$20 million in the last quarter alone, this data suggests.

"The details on you are very vague. No listed contact details. No known address in Clarion on file. Ostensibly, you're a wealthy financier. I think that's bullshit. You're not a legitimate businesswoman. You're a Facilitator, like Memphis Jackson, which is why you met with him that night at the Hyperion Nightclub—to talk about the conspiracy to overthrow the government or some other criminal activity relating to it."

"I exercise my first right from Section Forty-Four of the U.R.S.C. Constitution, which disallows me from answering any questions that deliberately force me to implicate or incriminate myself in any supposed activity, crimes, or accusations," Ally replied in a detached tone, demonstrating her extensive knowledge of the U.R.S.C. Constitution.

"Let it be noted that the suspect has applied Constitutional Law in response to my questioning and is being evasive during the interview. Would the suspect like to provide a statement about the accusations levelled against them?" His dark eyes focused into a piercing gaze, like he was looking straight through her.

"I exercise my first right from Section Forty-Four of the U.R.S.C. Constitution, which disallows me from answering any questions that deliberately force me to implicate or incriminate myself in any crimes or accusations," she repeated.

The agent chuckled as he wiped some sweat from his brow. "Is that how you intend to answer every question? I don't recommend you do that. You're being charged with treason; the United Republic of the Southern Continent Constitution states the only permissible punishment for such actions is execution. You're going to be executed for your treason unless. . . ." He trailed off, leaning back in the chair.

"Unless what?" she snarled.

"I'm not going to allow you a conventional interview. It appears as though you're going to evade answering the questions anyway. What I've got here"—he opened the folder and pulled out stapled sheets of paper—"is your confession, detailing how you willingly breached the Constitution and, in forming an alliance with the Militia, actively dissented against the U.R.S.C. government and wantonly pursued acts against the country's interests. Unless you sign this confession stating that you're a traitor, you're going to be executed. If you sign this and testify against Militia members, you'll be told what to say. In exchange, the U.R.S.C. government will grant you immunity from execution, and you'll be sentenced to lifelong imprisonment. At least that's the story that will be depicted in the media and official reports. It may be subject to change before the verdict is read; likewise, it depends on what you do."

"I refuse to sign that. Aren't I entitled to a fair trial and due process? Aren't I innocent until proven guilty in a court of law?"

"Not here, you're not," he thundered. "You'll get a trial. You see, this trial—it's just a façade for the cameras, for the media, and for the populace who need an effigy to burn and a common enemy to hate. You'll get your *trial*—don't worry about that."

She stared blankly at the confession he threw across the table to her.

"I'm not signing this piece of garbage," she said after a prolonged silence. He broke into a quiet, wry laugh.

"The other defendants were much easier to convince; they quickly turned on you and were very eager to offer information. They agreed to these terms a whole lot quicker, because they knew that what we were offering was a better outcome and could enable them a much happier result. Now, what makes you think that you're stronger than them or that you're an exception to all of this?"

"I'm wise to that technique—saying that the others have cooperated with you, confessed, and then blamed me. Do you really think that I would suddenly surrender and shred my integrity to become a puppet to be used in your witch hunt? You're doing this so I'll turn against them. Did you think I wouldn't be able to see through your tactics? This process is a shameful affront to my intelligence."

"We're going to make an example out of you, to deter others from pursuing something so foolish and so subversive. We can't have the foundations of power being compromised like this, with resourceful maniacs lurking around, challenging the hierarchy. Some of the other defendants have put forth some very damning information. They've also been much more receptive to these conditions that are being offered. They may not be exactly to your liking, but they're what's being offered in the aftermath of the highly contentious matters in which you've found yourself. They are possibly more than what you deserve. If you reciprocate with our terms, then we can have a tenable agreement."

"I'll tell the court and the world during the trial what happened here. I'll tell them in detail about your corruption, that you're a hypocrite and a criminal. I'm the wolf in sheep's clothing, and you're a nationalistic sheep being led astray, convinced I'm one of you, while I fleece you, and prey on your devotion and blind faith to use for my advantage. We're not that different: you're trying to pull the wool over my eyes and blind me. I'm not some vacuous young scapegoat for you and the system to victimise. You conveniently forgot to mention during our interview Section Two Article Five, the U.R.S.C. Doctrine on Political and Civil Rights, which states I'm entitled to an impartial trial with a proper legal defence. I'm also innocent until proven guilty. I'll expose you for the fraudulent parasite you are."

Agent Blaze's tone changed instantly as he stood up. "Fucking try, you little bitch! You think you can fuck with us? The system is going to come down on you like the weight of the world. We've got all the power; we built the apparatus, the system, the one that'll be your demise. Try to resist—it'll make your life a living hell," he growled. "Get her out of here!" he yelled to the agents watching from behind the mirror. "You will sign that confession," he said as she was removed from the room.

"Your dishonesty will be your downfall, you jackal!" she shouted in response. She was taken back underground to the Federal Complex's cell block that housed female offenders, traversing an eerie, foreboding corridor, with two agents and two female guards ushering her. Naked light bulbs suspended from the ceiling flickered and droned.

The mechanical door slowly ground open, and they shoved Ally in. She stuck her hands through a slot in the door, so that they could remove her handcuffs. The cell was in complete darkness. In the isolation, Ally had an overwhelming torrent of thoughts racing through her head, diverging into bizarre tangents, and then circling around, unable to maintain a coherent train of thought. In that dark moment of loneliness and confusion, she had an epiphany. A strong sense of clarity and realisation came over her, and she thought, *If they want to play dirty and use these underhanded, deceptive tactics, then so will I. I have a few pieces of valuable information and tactics of my own that I can use before I let this happen to me.*

CHAPTER ELEVEN

Osiris met with a fate similar to Ally's. He had been interrogated and coerced into signing a false confession, which he stridently refused to do. Frank Blaze had talked to him, trying to convine him that Ally had betrayed them. Osiris had not fallen for the tactic. Agent Blaze hoped he would react negatively to that and cooperate. Osiris clung to a brief hope that he would be saved from this ordeal by the Militia, but he didn't expect any miracles.

Ally was rudely awoken by someone beating on her cell door with a baton, making a loud metallic boom. She clambered back into a corner, expecting something violent to happen. "So, have you reconsidered our little offer we discussed?" Agent Blaze said as he peered through the slot in the door, the incoming light extremely painful for Ally.

"Maybe I have. Can we talk about it somewhere else? Somewhere more pleasant?" she said, shielding her eyes.

"That can be arranged." He gestured to the guards standing by him. Ally followed the procedure for being transported from the cell. She was handcuffed again, and then crouched in a corner as they entered. They also fitted cuffs to her ankles and a chain around her waist before leading her out. She was taken to an identical-looking interview room. After she was secured, everyone but Agent Blaze exited. "You say you want to talk about this offer, off the record of course."

"I'll do it. I'll sign the confession. I'll testify against the co-accused. I'll say whatever you need me to say, but I want to negotiate some of the terms of this offer, this *contract*—whatever name makes you feel better."

"There's no negotiating the terms."

"I want to be deported immediately after the trial. I'll stay here and act out your little farce, but, when the resolution is reached, I want to be ferried out of the country as quickly as possible. You can cover it up or push a different narrative."

"Absolutely not."

"What's the problem?" she asked.

"You have still committed a crime here. You still need to be punished for your actions and to take responsibility for them. You can't just decide to remove yourself from consequences for what you've done or incited."

"How can you preach taking responsibility and punishment when you're corrupting and perverting justice in this manner? You view me as such a criminal, such a dangerous person, a threat to the country—when you're doing the same thing. I haven't committed a crime. I wasn't involved in this, at least not in the way that will be depicted in the trial. For me to agree to this show trial, you want to me to confess to crimes I didn't commit and then be punished for them. I'll agree to participate in this fabricated trial and to propagate these lies, but I want to be deported. I'm a victim of this, regardless of the outcome. If you want me to do your bidding, well, there's not a whole lot of incentive for me," she argued.

"You're in no position for bargaining. Even if you *weren't involved*, as you claim, you should have reported the information on the Militia and the coup. Failing to do so is a crime."

"I'm not aware of this. Perhaps I failed in a moral capacity, but this is no crime."

"It's a new amendment added to the Constitution, governing acts of treason and disobedience—and in a case as serious as yours, the law is retroactive."

"I didn't even hear about this; it wasn't publicised. There's always a newly minted sham law that strips away our freedoms. Just to keep the little bit of freedom we have, you make us follow an expanding set of rules. There's always some new legislation or amendment all in the name of 'progress' or 'security' or the excuse *du jour*."

"You can't claim naiveté as a reason for your innocence. That's a tenuous defence, at best. You wouldn't be able to prove that in court, given how it appears."

"I didn't meet Memphis Jackson in that nightclub on purpose. It was serendipity that we met each other there. You and I were both present, so you know that happened. There's a sinister conspiracy going on here, one that's far reaching and that needs to be exposed. I'm convinced you're involved, along with many others. I know certain individuals who have information on it. So, I suggest—if you want to keep the whole thing hidden and under wraps—that you be a bit more lenient in the terms of this *confession* deal."

"You'd say anything in this trap to get yourself out of it. I don't believe you."

"You don't have to. The information does not consider your opinion; it exists whether you want to acknowledge its existence or not, like oxygen or gravity."

Agent Blaze tried to appear unswayed by what she had said, but she could notice in his body language that he was surprised.

"If you and others are manipulating all of this, then, surely, you can manipulate the terms of the sentencing and punishment. If you'll negotiate with me on this, you'll get your conviction, you'll get your increased control, the country will get to dispatch its enemies, and I'll get to leave this dystopia behind and will not be here to pose a threat any longer."

"Here's where I don't believe you: there's some angle here you're trying to play that goes beyond a good outcome solely for you. You have something else in mind, some other agenda. I'd agree to the conditions you're asking for if I didn't think you had something to hide, or some game you're playing," he said.

"We're all playing a game for different ends. You're saying you want to help me but refuse to, because I'm a liar with something to hide. So, I'm very confused."

"This is something you *must* do—or you'll get nothing. There are other ways of arriving at the resolution we want."

"What? What are you suggesting? Torture? What kind of place has this become? Do you even stop to consider what you're promoting—or the wider implications it has for this country you claim to protect? Are you even aware of the inconsistency of claiming to defend this country's interests and yet undermine them with oppression? Or do you just blindly follow orders? I wasn't born here, and neither were you, so why put such an emphasis on dictating it and turning it into a nightmare?" she said in disbelief.

"No, I may not have been born here, but I did fight and shed blood in the wars to establish it. I didn't fight for this country only for young idealists and zealots like you to implement any crazy dogma they want. We have a difference in opinion about how a country should be run. We're equally opposed to each other's ideas, but, as a nation, we need to come to some civilised agreement. Yes, there are elements of this country I distinctly don't like and that I'd change. But you don't see me exacting that change by blowing up buildings, and killing politicians and innocent people. I find it amusing: your type's so fearless when you're hidden away, planning your terrorism. When you're finally discovered and have to face the consequences, you all crumble. You betray each other to get freedoms and rights from the legal system and country you claim to hate. Your friend Memphis Jackson turned quicker than you did. He agreed to sign the confession and implicate the remaining members, including you, in exchange for his life."

"Show me that confession, then. Now who's telling lies? Surely you can prove it by showing me the confession," she reasoned.

"I wouldn't jeopardise the case by allowing you to view such sensitive information."

"It's because it doesn't exist. I'm not that easily deceived. You're going to have to use better tactics than that. I know this is false, so don't waste my time. This doesn't seem to be going anywhere, so I will change my approach. What if I could get you more?"

"More? What do you mean? More of *what*?" he asked warily.

"What if I could get you not just more Militia members but others, other criminals and syndicates, connections, activities—everything. I've got information about Facilitators, extortion, political assassinations, false investment companies, money laundering, shady financial dealings, corrupt officials—basically an enormous amount of high-quality information that would give someone like you a raging erection."

"I have to verify anything you tell me. I can't make a deal with you solely because you've given me some supposed *intelligence*. It could be totally fabricated."

"If you want to help this country, then you have to realise that the corruption runs very deep. Other agencies, bureaus, government bodies, private organisations and companies, even some of your colleagues may be involved. Are you sure you want to hear it?"

"Now I'm listening," he said as his demeanour changed drastically.

"Once this mock trial has concluded, instead of imprisoning me, I will give you this information in exchange for you organising my deportation in secret."

"You think I can do that without attracting any attention? No, I need the information now," he argued.

"No, no—that is unacceptable. How can I trust you if I give away this information? You could simply betray me, and then I have nothing to rely on. No. Only after this travesty has finished will I give you what you want. Otherwise, I have no leverage, no motivation, if there's no positive result for me."

"As soon as the trial is over, you'll tell me everything you know. I need the entirety of it. Once it's been validated, your request will be fulfilled. Instead of being imprisoned, you will be deported from the country. I have some contacts that could potentially arrange this."

His demeanour had completely changed. In his mind, he was already scheming about how to harvest her information for his benefit. If he could expose the crime and corruption in the country, he could accelerate his character and career.

"I want a pardon and deportation for Memphis Jackson, too," she ordered.

"That's going to be a higher level of difficulty to arrange, depending on the reliability and value of your information. If it leads somewhere significant, then it is something we could consider."

"This is all for your own self-aggrandisement. I can sense that you're already planning what to do with this information. You want to harness it to expose others, so that you can grab more power to protect yourself and your acquaintances. We've fallen on opposite sides of the law, but I really think we are alike. We share very similar goals for this country, but our methods and our approaches are very different. You seem to care about the state of this place, and you seem to want to improve it, but your approach is misguided. Why would you want to do it in such an unjust way?" she asked, trying to humanise this negotiation with Agent Blaze. Even after all the dehumanisation she had endured, she wasn't very skilled at it.

"This is the method that works, unfortunately—not ideologies or movements but power and eminence. If you don't have that, you can't effect real change here. Nothing goes on without these things, and we need to ensure that we're the *most* powerful and eminent, or chaos and anarchy prevail. Then people like you start trying to change the dynamic."

"Now that I have something you want, is there anything you can do now to help in my situation? Surely, if you're the lead agent on this case, there's something you can do to improve my position."

"Not at this present time, I'm afraid. The circumstances of your detainment will remain the same for the foreseeable future. I can't start to do anything until I know I can trust what you've said," he responded.

After a long discussion, they concluded their interview, and Ally was still in the same, unenviable position, with no leverage. Ally was in a predicament now. She didn't want to disclose this information about others, and she wondered if it was stubbornness or her morals that was preventing her from providing what she knew. She felt selfish condemning others for their crimes but exonerating herself for her own crimes. Something about the idea felt wrong to her. She contemplated the ethicality of it. These people and organisations had committed terrible crimes, but did that warrant exposing them to save herself? Even if they were savage crimes, should they get away with them while she suffered?

Ally had carefully chosen the series of lies she told Agent Blaze. She was warranted for not trusting him, as he had done the same thing. She had no actual intention of confessing to any crime, and, certainly, she would not testify *against* anyone, even if they were guilty. She didn't condemn others. It was something she was strongly against morally under any circumstances. In the criminal world she hailed from, it was the ultimate disrespect and was taboo. If they wanted to use deception and underhanded methods while pretending to be righteous, then she was going to as well. She felt like she was lowering herself to their degree of pettiness, as if she were no better than them, but she had been *forced* into doing it. She wasn't going to let this happen without some form of sabotage. In the isolation of her cell, all she had was time to consider these issues as they rippled through the darkness that had become her world.

Ally and Osiris had been imprisoned in the Federal Complex for eight weeks, which by itself was a breach of the Constitutional protection for how long the authorities could detain a prisoner without charging them with an offence or bringing them to trial. To them, it felt much longer, with little information being relayed to them. All they were aware of was that an arraignment hearing was looming. They had not met with any legal counsel; they had not seen any of the Prosecution's evidence or had any time to prepare an argument for their case. Ally had enough money to afford the best legal team in the country, but her legitimate accounts had been frozen, and she couldn't access her illegal accounts.

With no warning, she was awoken one morning and informed that her arraignment hearing was commencing that day. She had been in darkness for so long that she had developed mild photophobia, a sensitivity to light that caused considerable pain in her eyes. She was forced to keep them tightly closed while she was being removed from the cell, essentially at the mercy of the people guiding her. On one of the subterranean levels, she was placed into an armoured vehicle for prisoner transport. She tried to adjust her eyes to the light by peering out of the tiny slot in the side of the vehicle. It was very painful, but she was desperate to get even the smallest exposure to the outside world after being in total sensory isolation. The destination was Clarion's Hall of Justice, which had seen some of the most high-profile cases in the young nation's history, including the war-crimes trials that followed its independence.

The streets surrounding The Hall of Justice, usually filled with tourists, had been blocked off and were all heavily guarded. Ally's head was in a furore. So many thoughts were clogged in her mind, like a chokepoint. The convoy went around the back of the building to a secured area for arrival and departure, away from the swarm of media gathered around the building. She was still trying to adjust her eyes as she was escorted into the building. She snatched only brief views of a chequered marble floor and gilded picture frames, a perfect allegory for the money wasted on pageantry while others starve. She was led into a secure interview room with a much-more-sedated feel to it than the rooms in the Federal Complex, light glinting off the stainless-steel wall panels and table. She had no documents prepared, no argument developed. She was completely unequipped to begin her trial. This compounded the mass of worry and stress she was experiencing.

While Ally was going through her ordeal, Osiris was in the same building, awaiting his hearing. He was in the same position as her. Substandard lawyers were representing the surviving defendants, so that their defence couldn't stand against the Prosecution's unlimited resources and power. The lawyers and other representatives were from the U.R.S.C. "Legal Assistance" programme, an underfunded government initiative that provided lawyers and counsel to those who had no other representation. The U.R.S.C. had a unique legal system, mixing elements from the adversarial and inquisitorial systems into one, incorporating the best parts from both systems. There were still two or more parties who were engaged in a dispute to reveal the truth, though the U.R.S.C. was wary of such a competition-oriented system, where the motivation of winning could outweigh the search for truth and justice. To counter this, they gave the judge a larger role than "impartial observer" in the case, as there was no jury.

CHAPTER TWELVE

Walking up the corridor, feverishly rushing through the briefing, was Wolfgang Stanislav, a struggling lawyer in an aggressive town. He had no experience in such advanced proceedings and had never appeared in such a high-profile case. He had just graduated from Bastion University with a degree in Law. To cut his teeth in Clarion's merciless legal world, he had been thrown into the U.R.S.C. Legal Assistance programme—despite the fact that Osiris had sufficient funds to hire the best legal team in the country.

Stanislav entered the room wearing an obsessively neat tuxedo; a sleek and precise haircut framed his thin, youthfully angular face. He was actually younger than Osiris, who recognised this as soon as he laid eyes on the man. "I'm doomed," he whispered to himself. The way he spoke and his mannerisms all seemed to give the impression that he was inexperienced and unprepared—which, of course, was the opposite of what Osiris needed. He needed representation that could stand even a remote chance against the state and come away with a lenient outcome, especially in the face of such a controlled legal setting.

"Hello, Mr. Jackson. My name is Wolfgang Stanislav. I'm from the U.R.S.C. Legal Assistance programme, and I've been assigned to your case. I have to admit I haven't been informed about this case. We have such a backlog that we're struggling to cope with the demand and attend to them all adequately. I've been reading through your briefing, and I have come across some issues that need clarification. I haven't been given any intel from the Prosecution. What they have given me puts you at the scene of the crime—which we will have to acknowledge—but the details about the evidence and how they gathered it seem suspicious. It's tenuous, and there's very little about how this investigation was conducted and how this evidence was compiled. It's all in a very grey area of legality. I've noticed multiple discrepancies—which I'm trying to address—but, Mr. Jackson, I need you to tell me what you know about this case."

"Nothing in this case is just black-and-white. They can scarcely even prove I was meeting with those people or communicating with them. There are a few links, but the only thing they definitively have me for is my arrest at the airport. Even the correspondence they have leading up to that event breaches the law. So, for them to be conducting illegal surveillance of me while trying to convict me on charges they don't even have proper evidence for is unacceptable. My rights haven't been read or explained to me at any time. I haven't even been given time to prepare. I haven't been able to get any documents together, any evidence, or any witnesses. I'm not entirely sure about what evidence is being presented against me."

"Thankfully, today is mainly an arraignment hearing, where we enter our plea and outline our case and defence. I haven't been informed about any of your communication with the Prosecution or the National Investigative Bureau. You say they've coerced you into signing a confession and manufactured evidence. I'm not aware of what they've said to you, therefore, I'm merely trying to gain insight. How have you been told to plead, or how are you going to plead?"

"Not guilty—not guilty on the grounds of duress and gross incompetence. Not guilty on the grounds of exculpatory circumstances. This trial is massively unconstitutional and highly illegal. This is a blatant show trial, where they're manipulating the components of the case and the verdict. I refuse to be steamrolled by the system. If I have committed a crime, I don't mind going through a proper trial, but I won't tolerate a false, manufactured trial. Does that sound like the hallmark of a just system? Not to mention all the other Constitutional rules they've breached with this travesty of a trial."

"I'm very aware of this. I want to help you, Mr. Jackson, I really do, but I've been thrust into this case much like you. I've got little to no sway with the legal elite of this city. It's very competitive. We'll be going up against the Department of Prosecution, who have some of the best barristers in the country. They have an extensive knowledge of the system and a disturbing amount of sway in the legal community. There are some motions I can file, but, considering what you've told me, I'm still thinking about the best strategy we can pursue. I'll stand up for you in that courtroom, but I've never gone up against such a powerful team. I still won't let this happen to you. I didn't get into this profession to allow clients I'm representing or anyone else to fall prey to improper treatment. That being considered, if they present you with a plea bargain or with certain deals or instructions, I advise that you accept then, and maybe we can settle this out of the courtroom."

His statements angered Osiris, who wanted to pursue the services of the best legal professionals in the country. Now, he'd been saddled with a novice who had a limited grasp of the real inner workings of the U.R.S.C. legal system and even less influence. Osiris decided to keep him uninformed of certain secrets, unsure of who may be listening.

Osiris said, "No, I wanted it settled in the courtroom, settled in a proper, fair, legal environment, although, if this is what I must do to avoid being unduly punished, then it must be considered. I'm innocent until proven guilty, which means the burden of proof rests on the Prosecution. With their talk about legality, fair systems, and morals, they still want to conduct their business in private. They have to prove beyond a shadow of a doubt that I'm guilty. It's not the other way around."

"I know, but it's going to be difficult getting anyone to believe you or to enter into any type of communication about it. Anything the Prosecution does decide on will be dictated by them, and it may be hard—even impossible—to change any of their terms. The Prosecution are going to be inclined to take a harsh stance on this type of crime—against the country. They don't want to appear lenient on this type of matter in the media. You're going to be made to be seen as an enemy of the U.R.S.C., and the media will distort your image. They're going to be inclined to believe what the Prosecution say about you, so an out-of-court settlement behind closed doors might be advisable."

"This isn't a trial by media. That is yet another example of how this is all a construct, of how this has all been planned out."

"I advise that you do not make a scene in the courtroom or show resistance."

"Make a scene? Make a scene! I'll *make* a fucking *scene*! I'm fighting for my life here. I don't think you understand the enormity of this because it's not you in this situation, not you facing these hopeless prospects or facing the state like this. This system plays a game with people's lives and their freedoms."

"You're correct—it's not me who is experiencing this ordeal, and I can't sympathise with what you're going through. I apologise, Mr. Jackson. That's not what I meant. What I meant to say was that you have to go about this very carefully. It would be wise to comply with their demands and be receptive towards them and what they want you to do. You don't want to ruin your chances of a plea bargain or reduced sentence by being defiant and unhelpful. You may have to be willing to compromise."

"They're doing this to *me*, and you want *me* to submit to their so-called *compassion* or settle out of court? They want to pretend like this never happened. If we let all these violations become widely known, will it help my case?"

"If we can disseminate some evidence to the Civil Liberties Organisation or the Corruption Commission verifying your claims, then it will call the Prosecution and their case into question. If they do this, then, hopefully, when outsiders go over the facts and evidence, it will reveal where they breached the Constitution." Stanislav paused and rifled through his briefcase for another document. "I'm not going to get into the legal jargon with you, but we can file this motion that requires the Prosecution to fully disclose how they obtained your confession and the evidence."

Osiris felt a small beam of optimism pierce through the looming despair. It may have been a long shot, but Osiris began to think that they actually had a chance of turning the case against him into an exposé of the corruption of the N.I.B., the U.R.S.C. government, the Major Crimes Division, and the Department of Prosecution. They hinged their defence and offence on the idea.

"After you were arrested, what happened during your interrogation?"

"My interrogation wasn't conducted properly. They tried to force me to sign a false confession that expressed my guilt and accused the others of being complicit. A confession that I never uttered violates my Constitutional rights. I won't allow them to punish me for violating the Constitution when they're doing the exact same thing. I want it to be known how Agent Frank Blaze of the N.I.B. tried to coerce me into signing a false confession and ordered me to testify against the other defendants—to not only *confess* to crimes I haven't committed but also to *be punished* for them," Osiris explained.

"If we can prove this and provide evidence to the right people in the outside world, it may attract enough attention and support for a mistrial or retrial. I know you may not want to go through this ordeal all over again, but if it's with the chance of proper justice and equitable treatment, I believe it will strongly influence the entire case being overturned."

"What other evidence has been disclosed to you from the Department of Prosecution?" Osiris asked.

Wolfgang rummaged through his briefcase again.

"Not very much at all. In fact, I've got it here," Wolfgang slid the document across the table to him. There were too many pages for him to read in the amount of time Osiris had. He looked through the index to go directly to the most relevant details. The first few pages consisted of evidence about the intercepted messages about the plan for the coup; the statements were very detailed—with a painstaking amount of data. He skipped forward; the pages that followed were statements from the arresting officers at Haltana Airport, such as Victoria Ulrich and Agent Frank Blaze, stating how Osiris had been caught explicitly associating with known Militia figures and assisting their plans to overthrow the government and levy war against the U.R.S.C. It documented their recollections of the standoff at the airport, portraying Osiris to be uncooperative and defiant. "This is tenuous, at best," Osiris said.

"They are claiming it as the truth," Wolfgang said.

"What is truth? You said you want the *true version* of the incident but *whose truth*? The so-called 'truths' we've been taught are created. It's all ultimately subjective . . . just modified to serve different agendas. Some of this happened, but other parts are embellished with their brand of what is real. Whose truth is correct or valid is, ultimately, a matter of perspective. They don't want to hear our truth. They have made their own, and that's their rendition of the truth, the supposed facts," Osiris said, emptily. Wolfgang didn't know how to respond; clearing his throat, he changed the subject back to their defence strategy.

Upon finishing his consultation, he left Osiris to formulate his defence, while he went to another interview room to meet with Ally. She had formed the same impression of Wolfgang as Osiris had. She thought he exuded the presence of someone out of their depth—an inexperienced beginner who wasn't versed in such high-calibre legal battles. They had a similar conversation where he talked about exposing some of the details of their illegal treatment to outsiders and gathering support for a fairer retrial. He also hinted at the possibility of the Prosecution cutting a deal. She was excited about this, but the extremes of emotions she had gone through limited her from being overly enthusiastic. He also showed her some of the small pieces of evidence he had been given. She read through some of it and was shocked by the blatancy of the inaccuracies and lies within.

She drafted an affidavit declaring her version of the truth and of the facts, and signed it. In the room, they formulated their defence. As Wolfgang was explaining something to her, she glanced upward through the narrow viewing window in the door to see Security Officials outside. They entered, signalling that the trial was ready to begin. Ally shuffled from the room into the spacious corridor, Wolfgang walking behind her and the officials. The lighting on the corridor's ceiling produced a bright sheen on the highly polished chequered floor. Lawyers and barristers congregated on the staircases that branched from the hallway. Their indistinct conversation echoed from the high marble walls and ceiling. The throbbing in Ally's chest reached a crescendo as they approached Court Room Number Four of the Hall of Justice's Eastern Wing. It was a chamber that could accommodate dozens of people.

Inside Courtroom Number Four, only certain members of law-enforcement and the media were allowed. Two Security Officials opened the heavy wooden doors, and Ally entered, surrounded by people. The first sight that everyone got of the defendant was of a confused young woman who could barely open her eyes, which made her appear vulnerable and mistreated. She was painted out to be some terrorist monster, but all the people saw was an individual who did not personify that whatsoever. She felt so many eyes scrutinising her. She walked past the aisles of onlookers; her chains rattled jarringly. Ally and Wolfgang were seated at a table with only a microphone on it. Opposite her, the Prosecution counsel talked and passed documents amongst themselves. The Prosecution consisted of high-profile barristers Scarlett Resnik, Roger Chenoweth, Aisling O'Riordan, Nadezhda Vyshinsky, and Abdallah Bin Saleh.

The court clerk, a young woman, entered from a door behind the bench. She approached her desk next to the Judge's and stood at a lectern. "All rise. The court is now in session; presiding is the honourable Judge Sophia Bettencourt."

Judge Bettencourt entered from the same door and took a seat. "Please be seated," she declared. "Welcome, people of the court. I am bringing this session of the Established High Court to order. The Court will now be hearing details concerning case number nine-zero-one-two-five: *The people of the U.R.S.C. versus Ally Rose*. Would the clerk please read the indictments aloud for the court."

"Yes, your honour. Concerning Case number nine-zero-one-two-five: *The People of the U.R.S.C. versus Ally Rose*, the defendant, Ally Rose, is accused of one count of High Treason against the U.R.S.C. and its government, committing crimes outlawed by the Constitution. The defendant, Ally Rose, is also indicted on one count of purposely withholding information of a threat to the U.R.S.C. or its government."

"Regarding the case of the U.R.S.C. versus Ally Rose, On the first count, an indictment of High Treason, how does the defendant Ally Rose plead?" the Judge asked.

She leaned in toward the microphone. "Not guilty, your honour, on the grounds of legal exculpation," Ally answered. There was an expected shift in the atmosphere of the room, the level of chatter steadily rising within the crowd.

"Silence in the court," Judge Bettencourt said. "Before I proceed any further, I must ask the members of the gallery to please refrain from reacting to the pleas being entered by the defendant. On the indictment of purposely withholding information of a threat to the U.R.S.C. or its government, how does the defendant, Ally Rose, plead?"

"Not guilty, your honour, also on the basis of legal illegitimacy regarding Constitutional breaches, unlawful imprisonment, and illegal evidence." There was no audible rise of conversation in the courtroom.

"Let it be noted that the defendant has pleaded not guilty to both charges, case number nine-zero-one-two-five, the U.R.S.C. versus Ally Rose, will now proceed into the preliminary phase by conducting another hearing. The court will now discuss the matter of detaining the defendant and the relevant proceedings for continuing to trial."

Roger Chenoweth, counsel for the Prosecution, said, "Your honour, due to the severity of the supposed crimes, the high-profile nature of the case and the defendant, the Prosecution also considers the vast wealth of the defendant and her link to other known wealthy figures and organisations throughout the country. We believe the defendant could easily access an adequate sum of money in order to leave the country and is, therefore, highly likely to evade justice. The Prosecution would also like to state the fact that the defendant is an immigrant with links to other countries, particularly France and the Seychelles. Your honour, we would ask that any type of bail or conditional release be denied, as the defendant poses a significant risk of fleeing."

Wolfgang Stanislav countered, "Your honour, the defence argues that the defendant should be released on a bail order. The defendant is a registered U.R.S.C. citizen and has expressed to me no desire to leave the country. The defendant's accounts are currently frozen, so she would be unable to afford or orchestrate any type of transportation from the country. The defendant is a professional and responsible business owner, who should be treated with respect, dignity, and the presumption of innocence. If a conditional release were granted, the Defence believes it would give the defendant more opportunity to advance their case, as they have expressed to me. They believe they have had an insufficient amount of time and resources to prepare for these proceedings, your honour. It is, in fact, her right to adequately prepare for any proceedings that may arise."

"Would you agree, Mr. Stanislav, that, if released, the highly public profile of the defendant would render her a significant risk for attempting to leave the country to escape justice?" Judge Bettencourt asked.

"Your honour, like I stated, the defendant has no intention of leaving the country and is unable to, due to the restrictions placed on her accounts. As per the bail order, the defendant would be prohibited from approaching any of her known contacts in order to fund her escape. She would also be under strict conditions which would deter her from such a transaction or even any correspondence regarding it."

"With the arguments that have been presented to me concerning the case nine-zero-one-two-five, *The People of the U.R.S.C. versus Ally Rose*, I deem that there are insufficient grounds to warrant a bail-order release of the prisoner into society to await trial. The seriousness of the allegations against the defendant, as well as the defendant's immigration status and financial position indicate to me that the risk she poses of escaping the country is too prominent to ignore. They are to remain in custody until the next stage of proceedings. As legal counsel has been appointed to the defendant, I am setting a date for the preliminary hearing of this trial one week from today at 9 a.m. on the twenty-first of March, two thousand and twenty-two. This session of the Established High Court of the U.R.S.C. Hall of Justice has been called to order.

The defendant may now be escorted back to custodial remand to await the hearing. The Court will now hear the next pending case."

The courtroom erupted with chatter. Everyone focused on Ally like an exhibit. Due to the high-profile nature of the case and who she was, instead of being transported to one of the city jails to await trial, she was taken back to the Federal Complex to be detained. Travelling on an alternate route of staircases and corridors before they exited the Hall of Justice, Ally tilted her head back to see a media helicopter hovering above the building as she was placed into another transport vehicle.

Osiris's hearing went even worse. He was indicted with a series of charges, his role in the coup much more evident than Ally's. The Prosecution had amassed a large body of evidence, through all the stages of his involvement in the coup, and could definitively prove his guilt. They had every intention of presenting this. The Prosecution also presented arguments similar to those against Ally, as to why he should not be released on bail; due to his vast wealth and connections, he was too much of a risk to be released. The mere discussion of it was fodder for the media and the masses. Memphis Jackson was a stateless individual; his citizenship was revoked due to the crimes he had committed throughout his life. Behind the scenes and with a lot more evidence, the conditions of his confession were even more stringent. The growing commotion was leading to more Militia members being discovered and brought to trial. These arrests spurred even more attention on the entire ordeal, fuelling the fire of the public's interest.

CHAPTER THIRTEEN

Portia had been following the case extensively, as it had garnered considerable attention from media outlets across the nation. There was much talk of it around the Township. The people there were worried about their future and the future of where they lived. Portia had been hearing updates on the case through the Township's independent radio station. She sat in her hotel room at the end of the day and listened to the broadcast. She was outraged by what had happened to Ally and Osiris, so disgusted, that she felt obligated to disclose the dossiers and information she had. She felt it was her duty to her friend. She couldn't sit idly by while these atrocities went unchecked. She didn't care about her own safety or the consequences anymore. The case had caused anger throughout the country, resulting in widespread protests and furious debate. Various personalities from all spheres came out in condemnation of the trial and the authoritarian government. Despite campaigns to distract and divide the population, which worked to a certain extent, a larger section of the people, regardless of their circumstances or views, were uniting in their dislike of the regime. The "ripped from today's headlines" slogan adopted by the movement was: "We can't breathe."

As dusk descended over the plains, Portia got into her vehicle and, under the veil of desert night, travelled along an isolated highway from Delphi Township to Paloma Ferry, a sweltering tropical city on the far north coast. Along the highway, it was completely dark, offering an unpolluted view of the night sky. It would take her more than one night of driving to reach the city in the far north. She had been using drugs to stay awake. She continued driving through to dawn; as the heat rose, waiting at a rest stop for nightfall gave her the best chance of entering the city.

As she got closer, she encountered new challenges. Protests there had caused so much disruption and damage that burnt cars littered the long, empty highways along the approach to the city. She had to weave sharply around them. The feeling of unrest was palpable. It was eerily still and silent, with none of the usual indicators of civilisation. Dark figures gathered in groups on the side of the road, disturbingly watching her. Further into the city, the military and police had installed barriers throughout. She could travel only so far before their barricades blocked the road. They rushed around in vehicles, battling protestors; buildings were on fire, and widescale looting was in progress. Some of the streets were eerily quiet, while others were surging with commotion. Many of the roads had been blocked by debris, and autonomous zones had been set up by protestors.

It was impossible to find any accommodations in the city, as all the businesses were closed, and only the essential services were operating. She arranged to stay with an old friend, an exile who'd exposed secrets and was now living in a secure commune of people with similar beliefs in the empty plains outside Paloma Ferry. Their security system alerted them to her presence as she neared the commune. Her friend stood out in front of his heaving, dusty cabin, waiting to greet her as she arrived.

A melancholy moment arose when they first laid eyes on each other; they pleasantly reconnected and reminisced. Portia was relieved to have secure shelter with a reliable friend; a warm welcome was just what she needed after losing everything. She travelled between there and the city, disseminating information to the largest underground resistance organisation in the country, who specialised in leaking classified and sensitive documents in print and digital form. To ensure it would be broadcast, she gave another copy to a trusted journalist and former agent she knew, who was working for the largest—and one of the last—independent media companies.

The information was damning in its scale and all-encompassing in its disclosure, identifying people from almost every agency in the country. It listed the companies that were providing donations and slush funds to political parties, and lobbying for laws beneficial to them. The political parties gave tax breaks to corrupt organisations and helped them store money in illegal accounts. Vast criminal empires were being afforded protection and immunity from their crimes; protected land areas were being sold for resources. The criminals funded conflicts around the world to control the drug supply; intelligence agencies destabilised other countries to install puppet regimes furthering their interests. The police deliberately incarcerated the poor and impoverished minorities; there was massive exploitation of prison labour; the military-industrial complex was being funded with enormous black budgets, while living conditions in the country were neglected. There was pervasive control of media by a few elite magnates to further the government's stranglehold on the general population. The shocking list of crimes and injustices went on and on. The revelations shocked the country.

Great numbers of people began to voice the outrage that Portia felt. Suddenly, the accused, including Ally and Osiris, became the faces of a revolution. Their images were adopted as the symbols for persecution and victims of oppressive regimes. So wide was the impact that they become icons throughout the world. The people of the world had a sudden but authentic interest in the case. They were imprisoned rebels becoming anti-heroes who embodied disobedience and the rebellious spirit. Their faces were graffitied on items throughout the country and the world, including the Israel-Palestine segregation wall. This prompted Mihalis Konstantinos, a famous civil-rights barrister and activist, to take action. He was a highly regarded and accomplished figure in the legal domain, representing many high-profile clients; his name was synonymous with protecting the bastions of legal freedom.

The firm that he operated had tried to start correspondence with the N.I.B. regarding a meeting with Ally. But, at every turn, the N.I.B. kept refusing for reasons that were ultimately illegal. Agent Blaze and others were reluctant to give such an influential character as Konstantinos access to the case. His law firm cited a list of rights which allowed them the opportunity to conduct an interview with the defendants. When the N.I.B. refused this request, the law firm contacted the media with details of how this completely legal request had been denied, further highlighting the discord and lack of due process for the case.

Despite the efforts of the mainstream media to distort the reality of the rejected request, an immediate backlash arose among the public, who feared their own prosecution—with good reason. Countless protestors, rebels, and groups had been labelled illegal across the country. These cases garnered some attention, but the nation's primary focus was on the Militia defendants, particularly Ally and Osiris, as their story became a polarising factor, romanticised by some and disavowed by others. After confidential negotiations, barrister Mihalis Konstantinos managed to secure an interview with Ally. There was much contention over whether the interview would be monitored by agents.

Konstantinos and his legal team travelled to the Federal Complex and requested a meeting with Ally. She was trying to sleep, which had become even more difficult as a storm raged in her mind. She tried meditating to gain greater clarity on her choices. She was unaware of any of the arrangements being made with Konstantinos concerning her case. When they arrived, it was decided that only he could speak with Ally. She could hear the muffled sounds of movement and muted voices outside her cell. An agent opened the small slot in the door. Light flooded in. "You have a visitor," they said as Ally shielded her eyes with her forearms. The agents and guards then left, allowing them some privacy for their conversation, even though they were still being watched and recorded through cameras.

"Hello, Miss Rose."

"Who—who is that? I can't see you." she said in a dreary state, her voice raspy.

"Miss Rose, my name is Mihalis Konstantinos. I'm the main barrister for the legal firm I operate, Konstantinos and Partners. I've seen the publicity generated around your case recently. The improper way in which you're being treated and how your trial is being conducted have caused me to come here to talk to you. I want to offer you my services and representation. I understand that, as part of the conditions of your remand, your accounts have been frozen, so I want to offer this service and representation to you completely free of charge. Are you experiencing any pain from being kept in this dark environment?"

"Yes—it's excruciating."

"That's in direct breach of the Constitution. Are you being allowed out for daily exercise?"

"No. I'm in this cell every hour of the day and night. I have no perception of the outside world. I know it's night now because the lights are on in the corridors, but I have no concept of the actual time or date."

"That is another breach of human rights. Ally, you are being treated illegally and in a grossly unconstitutional manner. I'm here because I want to represent you in your case. I've talked to some of my partners in the firm, and we've assembled a team of some of the most experienced legal professionals in the country—with a very extensive knowledge of the law—who are also willing to help." Konstantinos had suffered in refugee camps overseas before migrating to the U.R.S.C. He had turned his life around to become a law professional with a focus on human rights, deciding to fight for others against the same inequalities and injustices to which he had been subjected.

"I can't believe this," Ally said as she moved towards the slot in the door. "You're my saviour, but I don't know whether to trust you."

"When I saw that you had been arrested and were being subjected to this type of treatment, I was enraged. This country has become a circus, and people like you are suffering because of it. I refuse to let the state walk all over you," Konstantinos said, with a defiant, professional manner.

"You've come to my rescue in my darkest hour. I don't know what to say. This is such a shock. I'm honoured that you'd do this for me, however, I don't want to mistakenly place my faith into that strategy. You've come here with this proposition, and I'm unsure if you have some type of hidden agenda."

"If there are as many violations as I have observed, in conjunction with your testimony, this is one of the strongest cases of illegal incarceration I have encountered in my entire career. With all due respect, Miss Rose, we do not have to offer you our services. Even if you have committed these crimes of which you are being accused—the answer to which I don't want to know—you are still entitled to due process."

"Yes, but the government have almost-unlimited powers. This is a cancerous growth deep within the body of this country."

"I am aware of this. Recently, the extent and full scope of it was released by a whistle-blower from the Major Crimes Division. . . .

"Portia," Ally whispered.

"Pardon?"

"Nothing—please continue."

"This whistle-blower was from the Major Crimes Division and had a comprehensive collection of the most secretive information ever revealed in this country. It has had an unexpected, massive impact. You would be unaware, but, outside these walls, the country's worst people are being made to face their crimes, and everyone's campaigning for you and cheering you on. Mass disobedience and rebellion have been inspired by the actions that have taken place here. Your case has been the catalyst for a major reckoning."

"Listen to me: If you're here merely to further your career or personality, then leave me alone. The lives of people cannot be played with, as if freedom were only a game. If that's all you're here for, then I'd prefer if you did not help me. The very concept of celebrity lawyers is anathema to me."

"I can assure you that's not what I'm here for. I'm not here to win favour with my career by helping you. This is why I got into law. You're right—much too often, it turns into a game. But I want to try to address the injustices that have been committed against you. The reason, Miss Rose, is that our legal firm has been harassed for defending certain individuals. The government have interfered with our firm pursuing the proper course of action and achieving a just outcome. I've had threats, made enemies, and been ridiculed as consequences of searching for the truth. It shows how dysfunctional our society is and how far this civilisation has strayed from its foundations. Consequently, my firm is currently drafting a writ of *Habeas Corpus* to be heard in the Federal Court of Appeals as we speak."

Ally soared with hope upon hearing this. "This makes me much more confident in my case, but I don't want to expect too much and be disappointed. I was an unwilling participant in this whole event. I'm not like how they're portraying me—I'm not some fanatical terrorist. I was only trying to live my life and find a place in this insane world. Even though I *may* be guilty of some crimes, as you remarked, I still deserve my due legal process and an unbiased trial."

"I agree, Miss Rose. I'm not concerned with what you may or may not have done. If what you're telling me is true regarding your involvement in this, then I believe that you should be treated normally by our justice system—but not in the farcical manner that we're witnessing. Be assured, Miss Rose, that we are working extremely hard on your case, because being prepared is half the battle. We will advocate for your release or, at the very least, a re-evaluation of the circumstances involving your imprisonment and trial."

"What happens now?" Ally inquired.

"This is probably one of our last legal resorts. Whether they decide to actually hear it in court is another matter altogether. They're either going to reject the declaration immediately or rush it through so that it's defeated and out of the way. It won't be surprising if it isn't successful and they create some false evidence that justifies incarcerating you. I think we are just bystanders in this trial; the judicial process—the entire legal system—has become absolutely tyrannical. This system will do whatever they're told to do by those in power. We're paralysed while they conduct this procedure. This is pandering to the fear in people, who will always surrender their rights in the name of safety. Showcasing individuals like you as a common enemy, another threat to be afraid of, is a strategy. If they have that clearly defined enemy, that image, they can pass any law they want. I apologise, Miss Rose, but this is a common occurrence."

"No. I'm starting to think that, perhaps I should reconcile myself with the fact that I *am* one of those criminals who should be prosecuted. I've done a lot of atrocious things in my past—none of which I'm going to disclose—for which I faced no apparent consequences at the time.

The Pendulum has swung through and sent me on a different course; this period of my life may be when I atone for all that. I think that this may be my reckoning, the time in my life when I accept some punishment; I can't avoid it all my life. I didn't commit the crimes that I'm being tried for currently, but I have committed others. If this is what I must do to make up for those, then I should wait to see how this situation develops."

"If you want to atone for the wrong things you've done, then that's respectable of you, but you should have the chance to do it in a safe atmosphere that's part of an adequate system. People need to see and know how our system is transforming into something that strips people of inalienable rights. A warning needs to be sent that our democratic systems are degrading into something unrecognisable. We can't be silent while it morphs into a weapon used to promote evil and negativity. If it continues in this fashion, then anyone could be next. The government has broken a litany of laws here; they shouldn't be allowed to keep you in these conditions. The numerous breaches of the Constitution amount to a major human-rights case."

"A lot of lives have been ruined in my wake. I don't want to resurface any more than I have and expose myself to more danger. I don't want to live my life in fear of retribution for what I've done. I understand that you want to warn others of this rape of justice and freedom, but I think I may have to step away from this and let it run its course. Though we must negotiate the conditions of this trial and confession, I refuse to testify against the other defendants. I also don't want to confess to crimes I haven't committed. I struggle enough with what I've already done," Ally remarked.

CHAPTER FOURTEEN

This unexpected appeal twist generated even more hype and attention in an already sensational case. It was a developing story followed closely by the entire nation, whose citizens continued widescale demonstrations and protests. The application was summarily denied in a very public manner. The Prosecution claimed to have new documents proving how they were justified in imprisoning and bringing Ally to trial. The Prosecution did not disclose the full nature of the documents; they were saving those disclosures for the trial. Judge Bettencourt, in accordance with what she had been instructed, decided to deny the writ on the grounds that the country had sufficient reason to detain her.

Konstantinos stayed with Ally for hours, answering all of her questions and talking to her like she was a normal citizen, with all the rights commonly afforded to people on trial. Ally felt honoured that he would take the time to stay with her. It was the comfort and company she craved.

Ally was not surprised by the ruling; she had accepted that this was more of a play than a trial and that she was merely part of the audience watching it. She may as well have been seated in the public gallery. The preliminary hearing would continue as scheduled. Konstantinos informed Ally he would be appealing the outcome, but she was no longer concerned. She accepted this situation as her destiny, and she was going to do the only thing she could: in a sense, resign, live with the result, and endure.

From time to time, Konstantinos would come by her cell and inform her of the progress of the appeals and the case. He also made sure to apprise her of the fact that there was a growing public movement to overhaul the country's laws. He was her only link to the outside world. She had been completely removed from society, like some pariah or outcast, and her intensely private struggle was being shared with a nation. Soon, the date for the preliminary trial was upon them. Ally felt calmer about the transportation process; it was her only fleeting exposure to the outside world, and it made her more appreciative of small pleasures.

She sought counsel with the formidable legal team Konstantinos had compiled. They informed her they were seeking to file for a mistrial due to Constitutional breaches and using illegally obtained evidence to evince a false confession. Documents had surfaced from Portia's dossier outlining the N.I.B.'s and the Major Crimes Division's illegally obtained evidence on members of the Militia at the start of the investigation. The government continued using it up until Ally's and Osiris's arrests. Ally was stunned to learn that some of the channels they had been monitoring them on violated the country's rules regarding surveillance. All of it had been made public, yet nothing had been done to end the trial. The government had been covering it up and claiming that it was a lie disseminated by the Militia to cause dissension and distrust in the government and nation. With a fierce legal team to support her, Ally regained some of her will to fight and went in more confident than she had previously.

A different clerk came out and announced Judge Bettencourt, who started the proceedings with the clerk reading the current details of the case aloud to the court. Judge Bettencourt called upon the Prosecution. In their opening argument, they outlined how they intended to prove she was guilty. With the evidence from the nightclub and the airport, in conjunction with other tenuous evidence unrelated to Ally, they prosecuted their case. They exhibited pages from reports by the Major Crimes Division and the N.I.B., which were riddled with inaccuracies and lies. They summarised the report of the incident at Haltana Airport, showing photographs of the aircraft and stating how Ally had committed crimes by willingly travelling with the co-accused with intent to help in the coup. This was their main focus in their argument, as it was the strongest way to link her to the coup.

When it was the Defence's turn for the opening argument, Konstantinos attacked the Prosecution's evidence, calling into question its legality and relevance, to which there were many objections from the Prosecution. Konstantinos stated not only that Ally was innocent but also that the evidence against her was illegitimately obtained. He went into detail about how Ally was the victim of an illegal investigation, one that was part of a wider network of governmental conspiracy. He cited the release of Portia's dossier and other legal precedent regarding unethical investigations in the country's history.

The Prosecution called Agent Blaze to the stand. He outlined how Ally and Osiris had been seen together at the Hyperion Nightclub and how they were also both involved in the siege at Haltana Airport. His review of her was scathing; he attacked her character and suggested that she was a dangerous lunatic who deserved her punishment.

When it was the Defence's turn to question him, Ally whispered to Konstantinos several damning questions to ask Agent Blaze concerning corruption and the illegal nature of the Hyperion Nightclub surveillance operation. These revelations shocked people in the courtroom. Agent Blaze was evasive in the face of the questioning, and Konstantinos was repeatedly stonewalled by Judge Bettencourt. Konstantinos attacked Blaze's credibility and raised questions about how he had compiled the evidence, hinting at the illegality of the Prosecution's tactics. Agent Blaze avoided answering the questions factually or completely.

The Prosecution asked for a brief recess, which Judge Bettencourt granted. During the recess, they met with Ally and Konstantinos in an interview room. Ally was led in to see the Prosecution all sitting on one side of a large table, with Agent Blaze standing behind them. Ally and Konstantinos took their seats on the other side of the table, and Roger Chenoweth began talking.

"In the wake of current developments, Miss Rose, we have been conferring. Some issues have arisen unexpectedly; as a result, we have had to . . . *re-examine* our position. We have evaluated the terms and conditions of our plea bargain, Miss Rose. It would be pertinent to reconsider your options. If you do not comply with our recommendations, then we have no choice but to find you guilty of the offences of which you have been accused and pursue your execution. This is now no longer negotiable, Miss Rose. You have an opportunity to begin cooperating with us to achieve our objectives. If you do not, we will take the necessary steps to condemn you to death.

"If you do, however, begin to follow our instructions, the outcome will be more beneficial to you. It has come to our attention that you are the bearer of some highly sensitive and important information that is important for us to see."

Ally sat in silence, considering a vast array of options. She stared hatefully at Agent Blaze, who avoided eye contact. He had betrayed Ally by disclosing the deal they had created. Ever since the meeting had begun, she'd felt this was their main agenda. Ally leaned back, and Konstantinos whispered something into her ear, recommending what she should do next. "Perhaps I do—perhaps I do have some knowledge that may be valuable to you, and yet, I'm interested in how you know this."

Scarlett Resnik answered, "We were informed by an undisclosed source that you may possess certain intelligence that could help us immensely, which is why we are offering you a more advantageous plea bargain."

Ally looked up to Agent Blaze again, who darted his eyes away. His expression morphed into one of stoic discomfort at his deception being exposed.

"Where is my incentive? You're not giving me many options here. I don't see the purpose to any of this for me. Why should I comply with you when you're going to execute me regardless of what I do? I didn't know executing somebody could be so bureaucratic and prolonged."

"You misunderstand our proposition, Miss Rose. We are asking for your compliance in the proceedings that we are conducting. We need you to follow the direction which this trial is taking, as opposed to resisting and making the process more difficult. The country would like to offer you a favourable outcome in exchange for some reciprocation on your part, Miss Rose. We need you to be an actor within this performance. You have a part to play in advancing our agenda, and the country is willing to overlook some of the offences you have committed. But, to do this, you must submit to our directives. This trial is an important step for introducing sweeping changes to the country's laws and Constitution to combat the growing range and number of problems. These are necessary changes, Miss Rose, which will be put into place with or without your cooperation.

"Therefore, Miss Rose, you can be a willing participant in these events, or you can remain resistant. But you must understand that what you choose to do will directly influence the punishment you receive. We have no choice but to force you to answer our questions by negotiating with you. A decision to assist us with the intelligence you have could make an enormous impact on your future. From what we have been told, you have a lot of damaging evidence relating to many individuals and organisations—evidence which we could harness for several beneficial outcomes. If the quality and extent of the information you claim to have is true, we can use it to combat the entrenched crime and corruption in this country.

"Giving us this evidence could mean the difference between you facing imprisonment at a facility and being executed. Your imprisonment will then be subject to review, with a possible chance of your release once an extradition agreement can be reached. Once you have engaged in these proceedings, you will be granted a safe passage from the U.R.S.C. But be aware that you will be denied re-entry for the remainder of your life," Resnik continued.

Ally again conferred with Konstantinos. She leaned over and whispered, "What should I do? Should I ask for deportation like we've discussed?"

"I'd be careful, Miss Rose. You don't want to reveal everything prematurely or ask for too much. I'd advise that you ask what more they're willing to offer."

"I want to be deported immediately after the trial, and I want a deportation order for Memphis Jackson," Ally said and then looked at Konstantinos. Without speaking, his demeanour communicated that she had made a mistake by not following his advice.

"Unacceptable. The offences you have committed cannot go unpunished, Miss Rose. You must face consequences and a custodial sentence for your decisions and your behaviour," Bin Saleh said.

"We cannot guarantee that this will be exactly how everything will unfold, but we will consider this request, and we will inform you of our answer," O'Riordan added.

"If we did enter into some type of deal, then how long would it be before we would be eligible for deportation?" Ally asked.

"We're unable to comment or say at this stage in the proceedings. We would at least have to consider a significant term of imprisonment—perhaps twenty-five years—before we could even move forward with those arrangements. The process for your departure from this nation could take many years. If you cannot guarantee an extradition plea with another country, then you will remain imprisoned here. Re-entry back into society would be completely out of the question. Due to the level of attention this case has been attracting from around the world, many nations would be unwilling to accept you as an asylum seeker," O'Riordan replied.

"There would be an equal number who gladly would," Ally retorted. "I understand what's going on here now. You've been discovered for your deceit, and now you want to keep the status quo, because you've become threatened. You should've executed me when you had the chance. Now, you need me to assist in this little game you have created, because it has gotten out of your hands, and you're desperate to regain control. You've seen the secrets uncovered; you've seen the stories being leaked and the writing on the wall. You tried to keep it confidential and covert, and now it's spreading like a virus throughout your nation, infecting people and turning them against you. You need me to help advance this fantasy, because without me and my participation, you can no longer finish what's been started here.

"It seems our fates and the fate of the country and its future have become intertwined. That's amusing. If you want to keep your power and monopoly, I suggest you start being more open to my demands, because we're all in this now, far too embroiled to turn back now. Unless you want me to tell everyone what's taken place here and before, unless that's something you want me to do—which, I thoroughly advise, would be against your interests—because if the word *revolution* starts being thrown around, when they storm this place, it'll be your heads they are after, not mine," Ally said.

"We need to see proof of this before we go any further," Konstantinos whispered.

"I digress. I've been informed that if we are to proceed with this, then we need to see some proof. You had that false confession drafted up pretty quickly. Now I want to see a contract or something in writing, some indicator that this is legitimate."

Ally was doing a lot of bluffing, trying to make them insecure.

"If I cooperate with what is being proposed, all I want is for you to guarantee the safety of Memphis Jackson. If you can alter the conditions to allow for his deportation to occur simultaneously with mine and to the same destination, I'll serve this time in your facility. I don't care about that. I only want safe passage for Memphis Jackson and me to leave the country, and I want no harm to befall him.

"I won't testify against the other defendants. I'll admit to the offences I have actually committed. I won't admit to these false accusations. I don't see why that would change anything if I'm already condemned. I want to be eligible for deportation as soon as possible. If you can do this, I'll submit. I'll yield to your conditions. Memphis Jackson and I will leave this country, and we will not return. This would be a desirable outcome for everybody."

They conferred quietly among themselves. "We would need some time to draft up and produce any contract or agreement," Chenoweth conceded.

Konstantinos said, "See to it that you do. I will be assessing the contract's clauses and conditions before my client signs anything. If it is not to my liking, or if I think it is manipulative in any way, my client will not be signing it. Unless you have anything else to say, I believe that will suffice for this rendezvous."

"We have nothing further to currently propose," Vyshinsky replied with a heavy accent.

"Then if you'll excuse us, my client and I will be leaving now," Konstantinos stated.

Ally thought she had made a major error in telling them she had information and agreeing to plea deals. She thought it may be her downfall. What she didn't know is that it had actually massively helped her case. Agent Blaze had been forced to share that Ally had mentioned she had sensitive secrets and information. Blaze was unwittingly forced to bring that aspect of the case into the public record; what he wanted was to extract it from her in secrecy and use it for his own gain. In the wake of their disintegrating case and increasing threats to their positions, they had to change the plea deal. Now that they had, it meant that Ally would have much more influence over the decision and her future. True to their nature, there were elements of the negotiations that were a carefully woven lie, coercing Ally into a false sense of security. Their thinking was that she would reveal more secrets if she felt more comfortable. That the Prosecution was open to negotiations and agreeing to certain conditions was a lie; they were planning to deceive her until the end, although Ally was preparing for this.

CHAPTER FIFTEEN

Following the meeting, Ally had another consultation with her team. They were all aware that, due to the controlled structure of the trial, their efforts were becoming more pointless and whatever they tried was going to be ignored. They had to change their approach; their main focus now was on changing public opinion strongly and hoping for an encouraging conclusion from that. The press coverage was skewed in favour of the Prosecution and the government—especially by the reporters who had been contracted to cover the trial—but the people's trust in these sources had been eroded. Unfiltered events from the trial were being widely leaked.

Ally was led back to the courtroom, and the hearing continued. "Courtroom Number Four will now be called back into session to resume hearing case number nine-zero-one-two-five, *The People of the U.R.S.C. versus Ally Rose*, before the court was dismissed for a brief recess. The Prosecution was cross-examining the defendant. Would the Prosecution like to continue with their questioning of the defendant?"

"Your honour, we withdraw our request to cross-examine the defendant at this stage of the hearings. We believe it would be prudent to refrain from cross-examining the witness until such time as the actual hearings for *The People of the U.R.S.C. versus Ally Rose* go to trial. The Prosecution is quite satisfied with the quality and volume of evidence we have presented; it demonstrates that there's enough probable cause to elicit a guilty verdict and a conviction," Resnik said. This was simple subterfuge; the Prosecution needed more time to adequately control any damage resulting from the hearing and to draft up an agreement with Ally in exchange for more cooperation on her part.

"If the Prosecution have no more questions for the defendant and have nothing further at this time, will the Defence be presenting any evidence or calling any witnesses to testify? Or would the Defence like to begin with their closing argument?"

"Your honour, the Defence will not be presenting any evidence or calling any witnesses at this point. The Defence believes that the Prosecution is responsible for this, and the evidence they have brought forth again has to be scrutinised. They have produced evidence of questionable origin against my client. They have not established a probable cause to find my client guilty."

"Does the Prosecution have any rebuttal arguments to make?"

"No, your honour. The Prosecution is satisfied with the case and standard of evidence we have presented and has nothing further to add at this point," said Resnik.

Ally knew it would proceed to trial but still felt a pulsing nervousness within her.

"Very well, then. This pre-trial hearing has concluded. Based on the evidence that the court has seen, I find that there is sufficient evidence to warrant a probable cause of guilt from the defendant, and there is a clear link emerging between the defendant's actions and the accusations being put forward against her. Accordingly, the U.R.S.C.

will be seeking to advance to the trial phase, in which the defendant's guilt or innocence will be decided upon. I am setting the date for the first hearing of this trial for two weeks from today, to commence at 11 a.m. on the fourth of April, two thousand and twenty-two, so that both sides may prepare. Case number nine-zero-one-two-five, *The People of the U.R.S.C. versus Ally Rose*, is now dismissed. The court will now be hearing the next case."

The next case was Osiris's pre-trial hearing, and his situation seemed more desperate. They had amassed an extensive body of evidence, including recordings of Osiris talking to known Militia members, incriminating photographs, and reports identifying his whereabouts and his encounters with members regarding the coup. They called to the stand one of the analysts in the case, who demonstrated that Osiris had been identified as a person of interest, as he kept appearing on their surveillance and recordings. Like the co-accused, there was a definite pattern emerging showing the probability of his guilt.

Still, when Osiris's lawyer cross-examined the analyst about the specifics of their investigation—and even the legality of it—the analyst became argumentative and evasive. Osiris's lawyer also reminded the Prosecution and the Court that associating with these people, in and of itself, was not illegal. In most of the instances they were referring to, the Prosecution had not established that any actual information about the coup had been exchanged. Osiris had simply been seen in the presence of these people. Thus, his lawyer managed to inject some doubt into the Prosecution's case and challenged the admissibility of some of the evidence. As in Ally's case, most of the "evidence" and allegations brought against him were false.

The Prosecution was not worried by this. They called an N.I.B. Reconnaissance Operative, known only as "Operative X," to the stand, who reaffirmed the analyst's deposition.

The female operative said that Osiris had been noticed during one of the N.I.B.'s covert-surveillance operations on people in the nation who were considered potential dissidents and problems to law and order in the country. Osiris's name began appearing multiple times during their ultimately illegal surveillance. She said that Osiris was a deranged fanatic who was actively seeking to destroy the country by being party to a violent attack and inciting anarchy. When it was the Defence lawyer's turn to question her, she couldn't recall how the evidence had been collected—only that it had been collected during the inquisition. Even though she appeared to know more than she was saying, the case that had been built against Osiris was looking increasingly difficult to sway. It was still widely believed that the case against him wasn't fully legitimate, but his involvement in the entire ordeal was more evident than Ally's.

Osiris, like Ally, had also been in negotiations with the Prosecution after the hearing to discuss the possibility of a plea deal or compromise they could reach. Like Ally, he had some sensitive information concerning the illicit and criminal realm of the United Republic, but he was reluctant to share it for many reasons. He did not want to give away the information prematurely and have nothing to bargain with. He had to carefully reassess his objection to informing on other people. He realised the predicament he was in and that revealing the information was a way to get himself out of it. At this point, he was willing to resort to anything.

In the evening of the day of these hearings, there was an explosion of media coverage and countrywide protests. The unrest and damage were mounting, physically and emotionally, all around the country. Various places were vandalised or burned, and protestors marched en masse through the streets to fight with police. Growing movements supporting the government began to emerge and clashed with the anti-government forces. The morning after, before the sun had even risen, a joint operation was carried out by the N.I.B. and the A.C.E., the Agency of Centralised Espionage. The home of Japanese journalist Hazuki Yamamoto—*and* the office of the media company she worked for—were raided. She was a known dissident against the government and vocal critic of current president Saige Rico. She had been discovered sharing sensitive information about the trial and revealing details about the Prosecution's fabricated evidence. She was accused of being a foreign spy, arrested, and detained, to await trial for espionage.

This caused an immediate uproar across the company and added even more frustration. Media outlets were claiming that this was a violation of rights for disclosure, reporting, and freedom of access to details. This was a boost for Ally, Osiris, and the other Militia members. More questions were being asked about the future of the nation. If journalists were now not only under scrutiny but being arrested and imprisoned, who would be the next target? Citizens were growing increasingly worried and uncertain. Living conditions had been deteriorating, and crime was out of control in the U.R.S.C. A growing wave of other social and legal problems was sweeping the nation. The bright utopia that it had been portrayed as was devolving into a dystopian disaster.

Ally had been forced back into the darkened solitude of her cell. For her, sleep was not an option. She had been mentally preparing, thinking of answers, questions, and strategies to help her. In the total darkness, there were no distractions; she could focus solely on what was approaching. She noticed that being deprived of light had heightened her other senses. Today, there was a massive protest and riot occurring outside the Federal Complex; Ally could hear a few of the muffled noises. Outside, military personnel and police shot dead many protestors and injured others, which caused parts of the city to descend into a frenzy. Almost every place that the leaked documents showed had been caught up in the crime and corruption were burnt down or attacked. Throughout the U.R.S.C., people occupied the front lawns of the Houses of Government and financial districts in all of the major cities. The turmoil and unrest in the country were making international news; the whole world was carefully watching the events playing out.

Ally's only source of information about the world beyond the prison walls was Konstantinos, who was hoping this growing turmoil would be the catalyst to get her case over the line. She was doubtful; she was wondering if any real change had been effected. If so, would it be beneficial over the long term, and how would it impact her? Konstantinos also explained to her that the Prosecution were still making excuses and delaying the plea-deal contract. They had moved quickly to bring forward the first hearing, in order to end the trial quickly and to clamp down on the tension and anger across the country. Their bid was successful, and they were going to trial ahead of schedule.

With the trial approaching, there was an ominous sense of suspense in the country. People were awaiting the result and were actively invested in the case. Most could see that the accused were going to be victimised and chastised by the system. For many people, this was a turning point. People began to realise that Ally and others were being unjustly treated and targeted to serve as an example for others not to interrupt the dynamics of power, prestige, and establishment. It was a clear case of authority intimidating and trampling over people with its might. When people saw them condemned like this, it was the end of their trust and belief in the country, its operations, and the people responsible for everything.

Ally's legal team forced discussions with the Prosecution and members of the government. The negotiations began to lean in their favour, as people in the legal system and the government who were invested in the country's control were concerned about the amount of backlash. This issue had forced a reckoning they could no longer contain. Despite their efforts to suppress the outrage, it was a chokepoint that seemed to be building, heading towards a disastrous climax and descent into chaos. An opinion was beginning to surface that maybe they should alter the outcome of the trial to a more favourable one, or declare a retrial altogether and start again.

This was a precarious position. These negotiations would chart the course of the country's future. There was also a concern over *more* damaging information being leaked. To protect their secrets and the extent of the corruption, the government's strategy shifted towards *appearing to fix* this problem while continuing to undermine it through covert tactics. It was decided to continue the trial; certain elements were going to change, and that could result in a different outcome. The deception would take a new form.

The day of the trial had arrived; the country was at a boiling point. The trial had reached a critical junction—it would either end favourably or cause even more outrage. During the transportation phase to the Hall of Justice, Ally's convoy was attacked by armed protestors along the journey, causing serious delay. Hordes of police clashed with them. Ally could open her eyes only briefly but saw flashes of the main streets filled with carnage. Fireworks flew in random directions and exploded in aggressive colour, and thick plumes of tear gas obscured large areas. On the front steps of the Hall of Justice, the protestors faced off with the police, with the press on the flanks. The scene had the feel of a Renaissance painting depicting a horde of people grinding in a melee. Before the trial was set to commence, Ally had an important meeting with her team. The main issue of the conversation was the status of the contract.

Ally said, "I'm highly concerned about the fact that they have brought this hearing forward. I'm also worried that there is still no confirmation on the terms of the plea-deal contract we arbitrated. I don't want to go out there without being informed of what's going on. I feel utterly lost. Helpless. What should I do?"

Konstantinos replied, "I'm growing more apprehensive about that as well. I think we need to meet with the Prosecution and discuss that. They're going to call you to the stand, so we need to see evidence of this deal before you disclose anything. I'd be very cautious about what you say on the stand. They have forced you into a delicate balancing act; you must straddle the line between giving them what they want and entrapment. If you apply Constitutional Law Forty-Four and refuse to answer their questions, they may revoke the conditions of the deal, and you may face execution."

"Is that the reason they have brought this forward? To use this plea deal to extract what they need from me, while rushing it through the court to reach their desired conclusion?" she asked.

Another barrister replied, "I have no doubt that this is one of their tactics—withholding details and deliberately being vague as ways to control the developments. It adds more stress and makes our case more difficult. If we don't know what to disclose or what's in our best interests, then they can extract whatever they want from us. We are, essentially, blind, and we may be sabotaging ourselves. They want us to make a mistake."

Ally said, "I'm also fearful that this is another one of their machinations. If they have falsely led me to believe there would be a contract or a plea deal, I would give them what they desire, thinking that I'm helping myself. Do you think they're going to call me up to the stand today, or you think they're going to delay doing that until another day? I mean, it *must* be today. Should we be concerned if they don't?"

Konstantinos explained, "I have strong reason to believe they are going to call you to testify today. I'd be surprised if they don't. Everything they do will have a strategic reason behind it, some element they want to work to their advantage."

"When I am called up to take the stand, what answers should I give to their questions? I need to know so that I'm not walking into some trap. I'm falling apart here, and I need your help."

Konstantinos said, "I'm going to tell you exactly what to say when you take the stand and what answers to give to certain questions. We can't be prepared for *every* potential question. They might try to delay this contract—or it may not even exist. Their strategy might be to try to get you to reveal something or implicate yourself." Then Konstantinos instructed her what to say and went over it with her rigorously. The atmosphere in the courtroom was one of agitation and tension. This was the most critical moment of the trial so far, and the country's attention was focused on this courtroom. Everywhere, people stood by, waiting for developments to stream through via radio, television, or digital news sites. All conversation immediately ceased when Ally was escorted in. Judge Bettencourt welcomed the court and started the first hearing. The Prosecution's opening statement said they intended to prove Ally's guilt by questioning a host of witnesses, including her. Of all the evidence they'd gathered, they believed the witnesses had the most compelling evidence.

Konstantinos stood to deliver his opening argument. He realised that the effort was most likely in vain, but he was hoping details from the case would be shared amongst the people campaigning for justice and transparency within the government agencies. In his speech, he intended to show the extent of how ludicrous the case against Ally was. He would undermine the credibility of the Prosecution's evidence and turn the spotlight on the *real* problem: The unchecked governmental power that could easily lead to a dark period for democracy.

The Prosecution first called to the stand an analyst from the N.I.B. who'd intercepted communications about the flight and the correspondence between Militia figures. It was all only tenuously tied to Ally; she had never met most of the people they were discussing. Ultimately, they would use the analyst's testimony to show how Ally ended up meeting with Militia members in the siege at the airport. He revealed communications starting from when the coup was first discovered by agents, to them deciding who would be investigated, what they needed to find out, and how.

Konstantinos cross-examined the analyst, questioning him intensely about the details of the investigation. For the first time, they seemed to make some progress and clearly had the advantage. Konstantinos got the analyst to confess that Ally was not identified at all in the investigation until only hours before the arrest at the airport. The analyst tried to argue against his earlier statements. Konstantinos persuaded the Court to read the transcripts aloud, and it showed that Ally was identified as a "person of interest" only *after* she'd been seen at the Hyperion Nightclub. When they had confirmed her identity, Konstantinos proved it was only hours before she was arrested.

Sharpening the focus of his questioning, Konstantinos forced the analyst to admit the agency was unsure of what Ally's exact role was in the plan for the coup. He went even further and got the analyst to admit that they couldn't even connect her to some of the Militia personnel identified in the investigation. Konstantinos had managed to destroy the analyst's credibility; the Prosecution was furious. This could damage their case and further tatter their image.

CHAPTER SIXTEEN

The mood in the public gallery—and in the nation-at-large—had changed.

Media reports turned more sympathetic to Ally. The government's threatening of the media had not been received well among liberals, and the factual evidence that had been uncovered in Portia's dossier had turned many organisations against the government. In retaliation, the government had shifted away from supporting them, and, as a result, many of the offending organisations were subject to funding cuts and sanctions.

The government's hold was weakening, and the situation was growing more dire. The Prosecution called Agent Blaze back to the stand to repair some of the damage done by Konstantinos.

Blaze further corroborated how Ally came to be caught up in the coup investigation and gave specifics of her arrest. His demeanour was completely different from his earlier testimony; he was calmer in his answers, more concise, and less scathing on Ally's character. He recounted in more detail how she figured into the investigation and was identified as a person of interest. He went through the timeline of her being sighted with Osiris, the subsequent search for them, and the point at which they had identified Ally. He detailed how the investigation continued and how the accused resurfaced when communications between members was intercepted, which led to them being arrested at the airport.

When it was the Defence's turn to question Agent Blaze, his answers were inconsistent; he had given detailed answers when it helped the Prosecution's case but was evasive with questions posed by the Defence. Konstantinos read from a document leaked by a journalist that showed they had intercepted intelligence about the coup plans in an illegal operation but, due to the seriousness of the threat, continued regardless. Agent Blaze denied this and questioned the authenticity of the document. He went on to say that, if the document was real, it was classified intelligence that should not have been released, as it jeopardised the nation's security. Konstantinos, of course, used this to further attack his legitimacy.

The Prosecution needed to regain control, so they used the best tactic at their disposal: They called Ally to the stand to testify. It was the most anticipated event of the trial thus far, since her last testimony had been discontinued. "Be very careful with your answers, Miss Rose. Remember what we discussed."

"Of course, I remember," Ally replied as she was escorted up to the stand. She opened her eyes enough to see out into the public gallery. All attention was focused on her. They chose Aisling O'Riordan to do the questioning. "Miss Rose, could you start, please, with telling us where you were born?"

"I was born in France."

"When did you immigrate to the U.R.S.C.?"

"I was a teenager; I was sixteen years old at the time."

"And why did you immigrate here to the U.R.S.C.?"

"I was told it was the place to go to seek opportunity."

"Have you found opportunity here in the U.R.S.C.?"

"No . . . not necessarily," Ally replied with a cold, detached tone.

"Is it true that you have a background in finance and that your current occupation is as a financier?"

"Yes, that's correct."

"What company do you work for?"

"It's my own company that I established: A.R. Financial."

"What is your role in this company?"

"I'm the C.E.O., and I handle large investments and manage money for a number of my clientele from business organisations."

"When did you establish this company, and where was it located?"

"I established the company approximately two years ago, when I moved from Boheme. I have documents that could tell you these details exactly, but the government has denied me access to any of it in order to prepare for this. I have barely been able to engage with any type of representation. Everything in this trial has been manipulated against me." She glanced over to Konstantinos. He was waving his hand in front of his neck in a cutting motion, gesturing for her to stop.

"Miss Rose, is it true you were once investigated by the Major Crimes Division for fraud and embezzlement of your clients' funds?"

"Correct. That is true, but the investigation was dropped, and no criminal charges were ever filed."

"When did this investigation begin, and where did it initially take place?"

"It began approximately three years ago, in Boheme, before I relocated to Clarion."

"Miss Rose, it's understood that, shortly after the inquiry into your previous, insolvent company in Boheme, you left the city for

Clarion, which you made your home and resumed running a company. Was your decision to relocate to Clarion influenced by this investigation?"

"No. I'd had a desire to relocate for some time. The damage to my reputation was not major, but I was impacted to a degree where I thought that relocation was an effective choice."

"Where was this new location for A.R. Financial?"

"The company was run from an office in a business suite of the Aeolus World Tower, in the city's Financial District. But it's no longer there, as we are currently moving locations and have not yet found another." Ally had to be extremely careful about what she was saying. Her company had no legitimate address. She had made it up to use as a shell company for money laundering and hiding proceeds of crime.

"Why was the case continued when you relocated to Clarion?"

"I can't recall. I'm unsure as to why the case was continued, as nothing was found in the searches of either my home or of my office. Both of these searches, I might add, were illegal. I was not told about any developments—and I don't know why. Like I explained, the case was eventually dropped without any legal repercussions for me, my employees, or my clientele, which is why I was never disallowed from trading or operating companies."

"Then, from what is outlined in some of the reports about A. R. Financial, identities were created for ghost employees who never existed, incorrect and misleading tax data was filed, shareholders were intimidated into silence, there was subsidising and profiting from organised crime, and the company handled and hid funds for a number of known criminal entities such as the Mafia. How do you respond to these claims, and why was nothing ever done about this?"

"I have no knowledge of these claims. They are outlandishly false; none of this took place in my company. Those were all initial allegations that the Major Crimes Division unfairly made against my company.

The reason nothing was ever done about these matters is that there was no basis for anything to be done. It is a legitimate company."

"How do you explain, then, how these deposits of millions of dollars, including one deposit of $9 million, were put through your personal accounts and into offshore holding accounts only weeks before your arrest?"

"They were from bonuses I accumulated as the C.E.O.; some came through donations from certain clients."

"It says here you paid very little tax on your exorbitant earnings; did you transfer those funds into offshore accounts to escape paying taxes on these bonuses?"

"Of course not. I transferred them to offshore accounts for security and financial stability."

"Which clients gave you these deposits, and how much did they give?"

"I can't recall right now, but these were legal under the U.R.S.C. tax laws. Voluntary donations from companies did not have to be kept on record at the time. I know the law has changed since then, but at the time, there were no records kept."

"In reports filed by the Major Crimes Division, it states that 'Through initial inquiries, there is evidence to suggest A.R. Financial is running a Ponzi scheme or similarly engineered type of pyramid scheme, targeting investors through fraudulent financial activity to gain a dishonest monetary advantage.' If your company is legitimate, why would they deduce this?"

Konstantinos stood up before Ally could answer. "The Defence is objecting, your honour, to this repeated line of questioning. The defendant is not on trial for these matters; these questions are irrelevant and serve only to depict the defendant poorly. The Defence would ask that the Prosecution change the focus of their examination at this time, your honour."

Judge Bettencourt admonished the Prosecution to ask relevant questions pertaining to the case.

"Is it true that one of the detectives from the Major Crimes Division who investigated you was one Detective Portia D'Amico?" O'Riordan continued.

"I cannot recall who, exactly, was involved, as it was a long time ago." This answer frustrated the Prosecution; they needed Ally to admit to her connection to Portia.

"You're saying you cannot recall if Portia D'Amico was ever a part of the investigation launched into A.R. Financial for fraud and misappropriation of funds?"

"That is correct. I cannot recall if she was ever part of the investigation."

"Why can't you recall? That seems to be your answer to a lot of these questions—you can't recall. Do you have selective memory of what transpired?"

"It was a long time ago, and I was never aware of all of the identities of the detectives on the case."

"Do you know if she had anything to do with your case being thrown out?"

"I don't believe so. If this is true—which I'm unsure of—I have no knowledge of her being responsible for getting my case thrown out."

"What is your connection to Detective Portia D'Amico?"

"I know her only from when she was investigating me. She interviewed me on a number of occasions, and that was the only contact I had with her."

"Miss Rose, why, then, were you seen with Detective Portia D'Amico at the Hyperion Nightclub?"

"I didn't expect that I would see Detective D'Amico at the nightclub. We encountered each other randomly. I was there for social reasons completely unrelated to Detective D'Amico," she lied, trying to diminish her responsibility.

"Why were you also sighted in the company of another defendant, one Memphis Jackson, at the Hyperion Nightclub?"

"I also encountered him there by chance. We would both frequent the venue, and, on this occasion, we were both present at the venue simultaneously. We were not there for any reason concerning illegal matters."

"What is your relationship with Memphis Jackson?"

"Memphis Jackson and I are friends."

"Has your relationship with Memphis Jackson ever been more than platonic?"

"I don't see how this is relevant. I don't want to publicly reveal such private matters. This is not a forum for some sordid gossip rag. This is an outrage."

"Objection to the question, your honour, on the grounds that it is irrelevant," Konstantinos said, standing up.

"The Prosecution will withdraw the question," O'Riordan said indifferently.

"Do you think your previous history with Memphis Jackson was the reason you were identified as a person of interest in a police search to locate you after you were seen fleeing from the Hyperion Nightclub?"

"How would I know that? All I know is we were concerned for our safety, as we were being followed by certain people, and we didn't know why. At the time, we didn't even know they were law enforcement officials. We thought that our lives were at risk, so we removed ourselves from the venue."

"Was your previous involvement with Memphis Jackson the reason you decided to get into this coup plan to eject the current government, commit treason, and levy war against the U.R.S.C.?"

"Initially, I didn't want to be a part of this coup. It's not the smartest way to bring about change. I got involved because of a connection to Memphis Jackson. I tried to persuade him not to get caught up in this coup. I was hoping I could protect him somehow. I thought that, if I was there, I could help and look after him. That is what you do for the people you care about. I'm not some insane terrorist. I'm not someone waging war against this country. I was apprehensive about his safety, and I made the mistake of taking part in this crusade by the Militia. I was not even a member of the Militia before these incidents, nor did I have anything to do with them or any of their ventures."

"What knowledge did you have about the coup before you made the choice to commit to it?"

"I had no knowledge of them—what their ideologies were or anything about what they were doing. I didn't know the exact nature of what I was getting into. I didn't realise the extent or the scale of the undertaking."

"Yet you were aware that what you were doing was illegal. Did you decide to continue with these actions knowing they were unlawful?"

"I knew there would be risks involved. I wasn't told important details about the coup; I wasn't even sure what my role would be, or if I would even be needed. No, at the time, I was there because I had a vested interest in Mr. Jackson's survival. I was not aware, that this was so serious or I wouldn't have done the same thing in retrospect. I would have distanced Memphis Jackson and myself from the entire notion."

"What did you find out about the coup after you made the decision to remain involved, and is Memphis Jackson the individual who connected you with the other defendants who were arrested following the operation at Haltana Airport?"

"I'm not sure. I was not present for any contact he had with them. I was also not informed of any plans he had made with them. I had not met any of those people before what happened on that runway," she lied again, trying to make herself and Osiris look better.

"How is that possible, if you were with him in the time before you travelled to the airport?"

"Like I said, any communication with them wasn't made in my presence. I was not physically there when any plots were made. I had no idea what was happening at the time. I was not in the position to be asking questions, nor was I concerned with asking any. I just knew we were getting onto a flight at the airport. I wasn't even sure of the destination. We were being pursued illegally, and we feared for our lives."

"Miss Rose, are you or have you ever worked as a Facilitator?" There was a gasp in the public gallery.

"Of course not. I'm appalled at your question. No, I am not or have never been a Facilitator. I am an educated businesswoman and university graduate with acumen in the finance and investing industry."

"Did you think at all about how many innocent civilians would perish in the crossfire of this attack, or is collateral damage and mass casualties something that you do not care about?"

"The Defence objects to this question, your honour, as it's inflammatory and speculative."

"The Defence is denied. The Court will allow this question; the defendant will answer the Prosecution's question." Ally dropped her guard.

"If by 'innocent people,' you mean sycophantic drones like you, fawning, without a spine—then, no. I didn't spare a thought about or care about how many would die. I didn't care if all of them died. Is that what you want me to say? Is that what you want to hear?"

"The Prosecution has no further questions at this time, your honour."

This questioning had cast Ally in an unfavourably negative way and would become the sole focus for some of her critics. Konstantinos tried to restore her image through his examination and questioning, but he couldn't repair the damage she'd done. Ally was taken from the stand. She felt that she had damaged her image in her deposition. As she was escorted back to the Defence's table, she overloaded her mind with questions. *Did I perform properly? Were the answers I gave correctly worded? There were some that I wasn't prepared for.*

She said to Konstantinos, "I was trying to follow your advice about how to respond."

"That outburst about 'innocent people' was completely uncalled for and an astounding example of stupidity. You played right into their hands by responding from an emotional place. There were some questions you responded to moderately well, but there were others that cast you in an unfavourable light. You rebutted most of their questioning, but you made a mistake in trying to *make a statement* about the injustices you've been experiencing. That outburst will not be forgotten in the sentencing phase."

"What does this mean for me?" she whispered.

"That was good testimony. They had you on a few questions, but you stood fast without disseminating too much. Unfortunately it doesn't bode very well in the context that these protests are impacting the trial—and they don't want that. Your little tirade won't perform any miracles for us, either."

Judge Bettencourt interrupted their conversation and announced an end to the initial hearing. Now that it had gotten underway and had been verified as a definitive case, there was no stopping the momentum. The Prosecution was persevering under the direction of their superiors. Judge Bettencourt declared that another hearing would take place the next day and every day after until the case was concluded and a verdict had been reached. She also declared that, due to the protestors disrupting the transportation, compromising the building, and threatening the safety of the trial, Ally would now be detained in the Hall of Justice Remand Centre. It was a jail housed inside the sprawling complex, where inmates were awaiting sentencing to determine what type of facility they would be transferred to. Courtroom Four had a reputation for draconian sentencing. It was referred to as "Four—Free No More."

Ally looked at Konstantinos. This development had taken her by surprise, and she didn't know how to react. This change meant that she no longer had access to the agents or any of the people with whom she could negotiate a deal. Bartering an arrangement would now be much more difficult and convoluted.

After the closing statements, while they were still conversing about the ruling, Ally was escorted away from the courtroom by officials. She didn't know when her next chance would be for consulting with her barrister. She had to rethink her options.

Still stunned by the ruling, she was put through the Hall's processing systems. It was like an interconnected macrocosm inside the Hall that relied on every one of its components. She was photographed, given a new number, and issued clothing but no other necessities. Ally felt humiliated being subjected to this process another time. The huge public awareness of the case and her situation had led to a full-scale revolt within detention facilities all across the country.

Now, Ally was being transported through the Hall in secret. She would not be placed in the general population of the Remand Centre. Her image had become too recognisable, and there were already bounties being offered for her death. A heightened sense of unease lingered with many others in the facility who were facing the same treatment as Ally, Osiris, and the other Militia personnel; they would be looking at equally dismal fates. Rioting had already erupted, and some areas of the massive facility were on lockdown. Ally was taken through a complex network of tunnels and corridors, through many security doors, and was placed straight into a cell in the solitary-confinement section. This treatment had originally been banned by the U.R.S.C. but had recently been reinstated as a way to lower the overwhelming crime rate.

Ally reeled as she acclimated to her new environment. She was no longer in complete darkness, although it was still too painful to open her eyes. She remained in a world of uncertainty. She would call out to the guards, asking them to schedule a meeting with Agent Blaze. She was desperate to talk to him. There were a lot of issues she needed to clarify, and she came to the realisation that she had to be more receptive of him and hope that he would reciprocate. She was desperately pleading her case, but her cries were lost in the cacophony of noise within the facility. Her pleas were now no different from the cries of many others who were subject to the same unjust treatment by the tyrannical system.

Time and time again, she would make attempts to gain the slightest amount of attention. When she did, she told the guards that she needed to talk with Agent Frank Blaze from the N.I.B., but she was denied or ignored, leaving her in a static, empty void where she was left wondering what these changes meant for her. Ally was wondering why this was happening to her, but she felt it was part of a wider destiny and that it had happened for a reason, though she struggled to find that reason. She questioned herself deeply about why it had all happened. She wondered if it was punishment for all the things she had never been caught for. She'd always known that she would have to suffer some consequences for it eventually. She was aware enough not to think she could escape any ramifications entirely, and she was beginning to challenge many of her personal beliefs.

It was no wonder that Ally had come to see her personal philosophy in terms of a pendulum-like effect.

CHAPTER SEVENTEEN

The next day, the protests outside continued, the sky was completely overcast, and the greying clouds added a miserable overtone, seeming to mirror the gloom and foreshadow the unfolding events. Ally was consulting with her legal team again when she asked for a meeting with Agent Blaze. Her Defence team were a little hesitant at first. Ally had to be vague about some details. After some persuasion, she managed to convince them. When they agreed, Ally requested that the meeting be between only her and him, and they had further objections. Ally insisted they attempt to establish some rapport and get him to agree to an interview. Konstantinos went to orchestrate some form of engagement.

When Agent Frank Blaze came into the room, her legal team left with startled looks on their faces. Ally was still wary that they were being recorded or listened to. Blaze said curtly, "We need to be quick; I'm not supposed to be talking to you right now. If anyone sees me, this whole thing is blown."

"I had to. I needed to talk to you in private, but I'm not sure how far that privacy extends. I want to continue this interview, but only if what's said and debated remains confidential; I think it can benefit both of us. You betrayed the trust of the first deal we made. I was hesitant to reveal anything to you and trust you enough to devise a deal. I'm probably making another mistake by even setting up another meeting, but I know the value of what I have—and I think you do, too. Did you do it deliberately? Why did you let that opportunity slip?"

"I didn't want to do that—to say what transpired. Some of the other agents in the bureau and people from the Department of Prosecution found out about our liaison. They forced me to reveal what happened during that interview. They were threatening to take me off the case and to implicate me as well. They knew the possible value from an insider. They wanted it also as they thought it could elevate them into a better position. I wanted to hear what you could offer."

"What if we could still pursue something? What if we could make something happen in secret? You could still utilise what I know for your agenda. I'm starting to think we are not so different; I don't want to be doing this, but if you can give me some behind-the-scenes assistance, is that something you would do? If this trial deteriorates any further, maybe I would be more inclined to share with you the knowledge I possess. I believe that it can help the both of us, elevate us into a better position, where we need to be; it can change both of our fortunes. You can no longer claim this is about justice and punishment when this is about status and position and money. None of it matters to me anymore. I'm fighting for the things and people I treasure," she said.

"After everything that you've said, all of a sudden you need me."

"I don't need you. You're my rescue from this sinking ship. You're my ticket out of here. I'm trying to make as many deals as I can to ensure I get out of this place. I need what you can facilitate. I need your power and networks. Can you make it happen, or are you just trying to elicit something out of me with false promises?"

"If we do this, it has to be with total confidentiality. I've become more open to the idea. This is going to be exceptionally risky and hard to conduct, but if you can give me some information about the people in the Department of Prosecution and their collaborators, then I would be very interested. It also may not happen for some time; it isn't going to be an easy feat to keep this from being discovered," he responded.

"How exactly are you going to fulfil your promise and set up this whole exit plan?"

"I'm still working on some of the components of it all. There are some things I don't know about this tribunal and the decisions being made. Most of what we're planning will have to take place after the verdict, after you're sentenced. Getting you transferred and securing the transport for your departure will have to wait until the attention and hype from this case has faded. That's not likely, as it's getting so much focus and is putting the country into such a state of pandemonium. You still may be imprisoned for a while, but if any word at all gets out about this, then I'm not going to be ruined, and you're getting the blame for everything."

"I already am."

"I can't stay any longer, or else I'll be disciplined for talking to you. We need to meet again." When Ally's legal team came back into the room, Konstantinos asked her what had taken place. She responded by saying: "We were just discussing the case." Eventually, he grew frustrated by this.

"You need to be totally transparent with me, Miss Rose. You need to tell me everything, so hiding information from me will not help your case."

She leaned in close to him and talked softly but with rage in her voice. "Listen to me, you glorified gambler. I'll decide what I tell you or keep from you. I didn't ask for your representation. You approached me. At this time, I can't release to you what happened during that meeting, because, like you, I'm also trying to help myself and my case. Divulging that to you now would have a detrimental impact, which I, for one, don't want. Does an ambulance-chasing viper like you understand that?"

He looked at her with an expressionless face. "I think this is all having a negative effect on your reasoning and rationale."

"Tell me you understand before I strangle you with your necktie."

"I understand, Miss Rose. I'm trying to help; if you don't want my services, I can withdraw from the case."

"It's a show trial; the outcome has already been decided, and you're not having this grand influence on it like you think you are. This is not some popularity exercise to feed your hubris or megalomania. What is there for you to do? At this point all you can do is secure a better outcome. I'm going to do this my way. This is not about you. Now do what you came here to do and save my neck without telling me how to live in what may be my last days."

With some tension amongst them, they were called in to commence the second hearing. They went through the standard procedure to start the hearing. The Prosecution started by calling some of the agents from the N.I.B. who'd worked on the surveillance team that had tracked Ally, Portia, and Osiris's movements. They gave evidence that showed the doubt around Portia D'Amico and the multiple scandals she had been embroiled in.

Ally deflected this by asserting that she couldn't answer for Detective D'Amico's actions and how it had nothing to do with the events central to this illegitimate, comical trial. The agents pieced together some of their movements around the time of their arrest. The N.I.B image technician on the stand said, "In exhibit twenty-two, here, the defendant, Ally Rose, can be seen with Memphis Jackson and Detective Portia

D'Amico from footage on a surveillance camera located in the foyer of the Olympia Building, only hours before they were arrested together on a private jet bound for the Lawless Zone that was carrying other known enemies of this country. We believe they were at that location to procure false identity documents to aid in their escape."

They called to the stand Victoria Ulrich and other S.T.A.T.I.C. personnel who'd been present during the arrest. They detailed how they were able to approach the plane with the element of surprise and detain the defendant. They gave little detail about any other pieces of the incident.

On Konstantinos's cross-examination, they were extremely hostile towards him and were refusing to go into any detail, citing that it was a risk to their ongoing engagements, public safety, and national security. Ally was annoyed that the Prosecution could get away with being evasive while blackmailing her into complying with their orders and the way they wanted the case to work. Overall, it had been an extremely unpleasant day for them. The people in control of the case against her carefully chose which small portions of information they would selectively feed to their reporters, who would spread it to the public. Their case was quite weak and was lacking in major areas; under normal judicial circumstances, Ally would be found not guilty and would face no penalty on the grounds of inadmissible evidence.

But now the system was being held hostage by criminals. Enduring days of false testimony against her, when a hearing was in session, the stress of everything had gripped Ally, and a tempest of emotion and rage swelled until she could no longer contain it. While Detective Trent Wardrop was giving testimony rife with falshoods, she interrupted. "You're a liar and a disgrace," she uttered, summoning her strength. "This is a disgrace," she shouted. "A joke, an outrage, a poorly acted, absurd comedy. This is a total miscarriage of rights, of justice, of sense and decency. You've taken everything away from me without any proof, and now you want to take my life, despite the fact that I have committed no real crimes. These proceedings are heresy that's merely hearsay. You've deprived and disadvantaged me in every conceivable way. To think I will simply accept it is an insult to me."

"Miss Rose, be quiet," Konstantinos said through his teeth.

"No, I will not be quiet. I have been quiet and gone along with this charade. The time to be silent is over; I was silent through all of the blatant subversions of the law. I was silent as I was presented with false confessions by Agent Blaze. I was silent as I was listening to this perjurer sitting on the stand."

"Miss Rose, please control yourself," Judge Bettencourt decreed.

"Or *what*?" Ally shouted.

"Or you will be held in contempt of court," Judge Bettencourt said calmly as the Security Officials surrounded her to take her away. One of them went to grab her arm, and she pulled it away.

"You want me to stay silent because you're afraid I might speak the truth—so I don't leak any truth that's seen as harmful or classified. This country has come to prosecute and punish those who seek the truth. You don't want me to reveal the facts I know about these corrupt people caught up in this. I have knowledge about things that would shock you and destroy everything. So, go ahead—wait until the truth comes out and exposes you all. I'm not the only criminal here. You can't do this to me while your crimes continue unanswered. You just want to keep me silent so I don't interrupt the dynamics of this deceitful little game that you're playing. When your lies are exposed, you'll face the aftermath."

"Miss Rose, you've given me no choice; I am finding you in contempt of court. I ask that the officials please remove the defendant. This hearing has been cancelled due to the defendant's disruptive behaviour and disrespect towards the court."

"*Disrespect?* There's nothing here *to* respect. All of you are criminals like me—but, at least I know what I am. This is not an institution to be respected. I don't masquerade around pretending to be righteous with an undeserved, inflated sense of importance and prestige. You're criminals with self-imposed titles and no moral integrity." She made other personal attacks toward the judge, which angered her further. "I know how you took a bribe from the state to convict certain political dissidents. . . ."

"Enough! Enough, Miss Rose! I will not have you scandalise this courtroom with slander; these outbursts have no place in this court-room. This is a civilised court of law—not some public house for you to indignantly voice your gripes."

"It's not slander. It's the truth, and you'll see it before it blinds you. How dare you reduce my struggle to merely voicing gripes? Open your eyes, people! They're lying to you," she shouted as she was taken away from the courtroom.

In the following days of cross-examinations, the Prosecution's plan was to continue haranguing her with questions until she revealed more damning, unfavourable testimony or evaded the question with Constitutional Law Forty-Four. This appeal to the most authoritative law of the land was an increasingly resourceful weapon for both Ally and the Prosecution's witnesses, who could effectively use it as a mask, to absolve themselves of any possibility of incrimination. Though Ally was smart and continued to play the cat-and-mouse game, she lied about every aspect of her life but didn't contradict herself. After rehearsing it hundreds of times, she told the same lies and stories over and over again, so that she didn't undermine her credibility, which ultimately worked in her favour. She said nothing that confirmed the assumptions of the Prosecution or made her seem guilty of anything. Rather, she gave the impression that she was a normal person in an undesirable position for making bad decisions.

CHAPTER EIGHTEEN

While Portia continued her life in Delphi Township, she gradually became more receptive to the lifestyle. She had been used to living in a thriving city, a metropolis, where anything was available. In the Township, certain resources could become scarce; it was so isolated that it relied on deliveries from contracted companies. With all the turmoil in the country, the supplies had to be rationed; water became the most prised commodity, above anything else. Around half of the Township's water was extracted from underground reserves.

Portia was still staying in the room above the tavern. In the early morning, the heat was already searing. She was contacted by a representative sent by the Council. The young man knocked on her door, saying that they urgently needed to speak with her and asked her to attend a meeting. She was not expecting this, which alarmed her. She pointed a shotgun at the door, unsure if it was a trap. She thought that if someone wanted her dead, they wouldn't have knocked first. Taking no chances, it was a stressful moment as she asked him questions that only people in the Council would know. Once she had confirmed he'd been sent by the Council, and confident it wasn't an ambush, she slowly made her way towards the door and opened it.

The man told her that the Council had requested her immediate attendance. He said he hadn't been given all the details, but he told her something about the government taking the Township to court, trying to close it, and take over their land claims and everything else they owned. Portia had trouble processing the revelation. She thought they had been promised immunity and no harassment from the government—but this was morphing into a rampant overreach.

Taken aback by this development, she was seized with fury. When she emerged from the tavern, she was immediately accosted by the many vendors who congregated in the Main Street. They offered all sorts of commodities. An elderly man nudged a live crayfish with rubber bands around its pincers toward her. A woman pushed a broken wooden cart towards her filled with a cache of weapons; another woman aggressively shoved a briefcase brimming with drugs towards her. A pre-pubescent girl offered jewellery from a glass case, and several people were offering exotic animals and human slaves. She ignored them and continued walking. There was a public bus service in the Township, but the vehicles were neglected wrecks, and it could be challenging to make it through the snarl in the streets, attempting to manoeuvre around a seething mass of stalls and people.

The Council had some core members, people who had escaped horrible conditions to come to the U.R.S.C., only to experience more hardships. Some of the members had helped gain autonomy for the Township in landmark, precedent-setting legal cases. They had fought to gain recognition and rights from the government after travelling to the country illegally. They had also been through a lengthy struggle to secure somewhere to reside, but were vanquished to remain in the desert, which had both worked to their advantage *and* been a curse.

The Council was a shifting organism. Warlords and other influential merchants and suppliers in the Township could secure a place. They had ensured their position through careful alliances or bloodshed and ruthlessness. Even though it was a diverse mixture of people, some with nefarious intentions and others with more-innocent approaches to the decision-making, they all shared an attachment to the location and tried to balance their differences. Their various interests came together for a wider purpose after adversity had affected everyone.

She arrived at the Council building; it was a disused centre, built to process the illegal immigrants arriving in the U.R.S.C. It was a bland, beige-coloured building with razor-wire fences and barred windows, the harsh climate deteriorating it very quickly. There seemed to be much unrest and nervousness around the place. The people seemed to be in a confused limbo, some of them looking at Portia with extremely dismayed expressions. Their faces were fatigued and their eyes wide. She went into the chamber, which had desks and long wooden seats haphazardly placed around the room and graffiti covering the walls. She could perceive the atmosphere of unease and worry in the members' voices. Their chatter ceased when Portia entered, their attention focused upon her.

An elderly African woman addressed her. "Welcome, Portia, to this meeting of the Township's Council. As you have already been told, we're summoning you on such short notice because we have a pressing concern, something that has just come to our attention. It appears the U.R.S.C. government are taking the Township to the High Court with an affidavit stating the land belongs to them and that they're reclaiming it and any mining leases or other land contracts that exist here. They're planning to dissolve the Township and send the inhabitants away to different camps—yet to be established—around the country. We're worried this will not happen and that many will be imprisoned or deported to another country. This has alarmed us greatly as it was completely unforeseen. They have no programmes in place to keep families together; they want to evict every single person from the Township and take it back so they can control all the contracts and other money-making elements we've set up here.

"We don't know what to do about this. We thought we had been given immunity or protection with the agreements we had drafted with the government, but, with no warning, they have completely disavowed that agreement. We need your help, Portia, which is why we consulted you. We are aware that you have a very pervasive and far-reaching influence, which is why we brought you here. We asked you to this meeting to help the Township, to help it continue to grow, to help its people live unafraid of unchecked authority removing them from their homes. The members are unsure what to do in the face of these developments. We know that we will have to compete and face the might of the government. They have already been trying to sabotage this place and essentially starve us into submission. The Township has offered you protection, Portia. Do you think that you could do the same in our time of need? If you don't help us, then there will be no future here, and there will be no place for you to stay."

Portia now understood why the place was in such an unusual condition. This development unsettled her, yet she wasn't surprised by anything anymore. "I promise that I'll help you in your fight, not only for welcoming me so graciously into your chambers and Township, but accepting me as one of your own. The kindness and friendship that have been extended to me is overwhelming. It's not an easy life out here, but it's one we chose to live, free from oppressive law and the burdens of society. I won't allow this to happen to you or anyone else. I was a law enforcement official for ten years, but this is not the proper application of law. This is thuggery, an example of the government coming down with the entire scope of its power on those who are weak and disadvantaged. Where's this hearing taking place and when?"

"It's being held in High Court, in the nation's capital; they gave us only two weeks to prepare," another member replied.

"This is not going to be an easy battle. We have to send some representatives to the nation's capital to appear on behalf of the Township—the most distinguished and eldest members of the community. We need to show the public that the people they're ejecting are the vulnerable and the disadvantaged. Some of the Aboriginals who had ancestors who occupied this land—before it was even Australia—have claims, and the government have recognised those. We also must amass a powerful legal team to stand a chance against them. I'm afraid to say this, but the outcome has most likely been determined—just like the coup trials which we are all currently watching, as that, too, will have a bearing on our fate."

"We can't pay for this," an audience member remarked.

"I have some money I can offer to help to fund the legal battle, but I don't think it will be enough to cover *all* the costs. We must use some of the Township's money, and we have to persuade some of the wealthier, more prestigious residents to put some money towards the effort. We have to tell them the seriousness of the threat to the Township, otherwise, they may not be persuaded to help."

"We don't have enough for a fight like this. We are running out of money, and we need it to buy water and food—there won't be enough to pay for this *and* what we need for survival," a member said.

"The Township has been running low on money, most of our operations around here have already been taken over by rebels or the government, and, due to the protests around the country, it has become harder to get the things we need to survive as a settlement," a second member added.

"We need to view this as what we need to live; if we do not do this, we will no longer have to worry about that, as there will be no Township to bring any supplies to. It's true our money and other assets are running out. How are we going to pay for this, Portia?" the African woman asked.

"I've got a lot of money I can funnel into this; we will have to auction off some of the Township's reserves of minerals and gemstones. Some stock has to be taken from the officially recognised dealers that the Council are invested in. Other dealers who aren't from the Council will also have to offer some of their hoard so that this can continue," she replied.

"Are you sure this will work? We used to do lots of business. We used to sell many things to people and places all around the country. Now, with the trials and craziness it has caused, it has ruined everything. This has all been stopped because of protests."

Another member asked her a question before she could reply. "Will this be enough? The members of the Council have some wealth between them, but, these independent merchants will not sell their collection."

"We must convince the independent brokers working here to sell some of their reserves and then send that to the large auction houses and jewellers in the cities. It's the only way to pay for this whole charade. Otherwise, we won't get the right legal representation, and we'll be trampled. People should not be trying to hang on to these minerals out of greed; it could be all swept away, regardless. I know some people in the legal field with whom I can re-establish contact and who will be able to help us out with representation, and they have a great amount of knowledge about the way that these transactions are handled, not to mention a great deal of power. Without my influence and what I unearthed, Ally Rose would have been relegated to dealing with the Legal Assistance Programme.

"It would be the same for the Township—we would be appointed a lawyer who doesn't stand a chance against the overwhelming power of the Department of Prosecution, bolstered by the government and their unfettered resources. That's what they do—they swarm over any potential foe like a tidal wave of superiority, leaving everyone unable to match them in their wake. I won't let this happen." Portia paused momentarily to think. "We must take back some of the things we've lost and make a bold statement that we're not going to go down easy. We'll have to sabotage some of the government's mining plants and other infrastructure. We must try to negotiate with the rebels, get them on our side, and fight against a common enemy."

The meeting continued for much longer. Portia took a seat and listened while they discussed other matters affecting the Township and its surroundings. Though it was dominated by the shock of learning they were possibly going to be evicted, the conversation kept coming back to the same dominating topic. Portia partially listened but was gazing out the window, watching a cloud drift above the far reaches of the rugged landscape beyond, while she thought about her plan. She came back to reality when the meeting concluded. She knew with whom she needed to consult. She exited the room into a long hallway, striped by cool areas of shadow and glary shafts of sunlight that streaked through the doorways; all available space was cluttered with boxes of ammunition and weapons. She looked left and right, seeing people gathered all along the hallway in groups, talking about the meeting and voicing their concerns. She found and engaged in further talks with the people who were experienced in combat or criminal activity. Leadership of the Council was like a revolving door—and there was never a shortage of people who were in perpetual competition to gain a place in it.

Portia found herself in an uncomfortable position, as these people were unpredictable and volatile. However, she succeeded in getting some of them alone to talk to about scheduling raids and attacks on the government, who, without warning, had seized much of their land and income streams illegally. They would start by sabotaging their contractors' mining operations, intent on regaining control of their lucrative mines and land leases. She knew they wouldn't be shy about violence; it would be necessary to inflict it against the overbearing authority of the government or anything else threatening their way of life. Portia motivated them to meet her at night in the tavern below her room.

At the meeting, they were seated at a large wooden table, drinking and doing drugs. The space was illuminated only by the light of many candles, as they endured rolling blackouts—some areas of the Township were now without electricity. Their attention was fixed on Portia as she told them what needed to be done, like some outlaw preacher in the desert night planning to stop the apparatus of evil. The light flickering around her highlighted her facial features from different angles as she looked at the people gathered around the table.

Portia said, "This is what we need to do: We need to get the rebels from outside the town to help us fight the government and let them know that, if they don't act, then the federal forces would come after them next. We must reach a truce with the rebels; if they refuse, we destroy them," Portia said drunkenly. "We have to send out a few people to try to repair our relations with the rebels. There are government sites located close by that we can sabotage and disrupt. The Township also needs to reclaim the various land and other sites that were in our control. It's the only way to fund this entire operation."

"You don't know these rebels. They're not going to give up their gains, and most of them will not form an alliance with us. That's why they chose to be rebels—outcasts even—from this place. They will look at us the same way they look at the government and the Mining Department. They will think we're coming to take away what they believe is theirs."

"Like I said, anyone who doesn't align with us or surrender what they have taken will have to be eradicated. It's critical! Otherwise this Township is destined to fall, and we'll have no place to hide—which won't matter because we'll all be dead."

As their perceived leader, Portia was in a fortunate position, where she could help plan the dangerous missions but didn't have to risk her life carrying them out. Over the course of the next few days and nights, teams were sent out on many different missions. There were large-scale battles all across the desert. They attacked road convoys with explosives, destroyed factories and refineries, disabled machinery, derailed freight trains and wrecked rail infrastructure, raided mining sites, and took workers hostage as leverage in their demands to the government to let the Township remain and to give back what they had stolen from its people. The terrified hostages were shown on broadcasts across the U.R.S.C. When they refused the so-called "terrorists" demands, they executed the hostages. There were many casualties, but it did start to produce the desired effect.

Not every mission was accomplished, but the government were significantly disrupted. The Township formed an alliance with some of the rebels and regained some vital mining sites from the Mining and Mineral Department. The government counterattacked by sending a huge military presence into the desert, which was an acceleration of their plans to close the Township and force out the members. The disconnect was so obvious and apparent to everyone. They had taken away the Township's means of survival by force, yet were viciously fighting back when those same citizens simply tried to reclaim what was theirs. Most of these people just wanted to live their lives, without having to tangle with such powerful overseers, who were seemingly impossible to reason with.

Portia began taking criticism from the people she was working with for not visiting any of the mining sites or being present during the missions. To address the issue of her absence and prove she was engaged, she took them up on their offer to travel to one of the gold mines. She wanted to show she wasn't taking advantage of the people doing the hard work. In her hotel room, she loaded weapons to prepare, and they departed just before sunrise in a convoy. It was late in the morning when they arrived, and she was horrified by what she witnessed.

These unfortunate people working in snaking, unsafe crevices that would often become their tombs. There had been many shaft cave-ins and collapses, resulting in many deaths here. The gaunt people hauled themselves out of the claustrophobic spaces—fissures of greed, like weeping sores on the earth. She witnessed the warlords searching out and beating the miners ferociously. She watched one woman have her clothing torn off and beaten to death for hiding a piece of gold. The living quarters for the miners were unsanitary; it was an overcrowded shantytown. Angry-eyed people were squatting in hovels, their faces bearing the fatigue and punishment of the work. All of it was overwhelming to process; when she swivelled her head, she saw tragedy everywhere, from all quarters. Her impulsivity reached a crescendo when she confronted the warlords running the mine and berated them for their cruelty.

She left in disgust, ashamed and disappointed with herself. She had taken advantage of people yet again. Even when she had good intentions, she reverted to hurting people. She started to think, *Is that my nature?* This sparked in her a deep desire to help the exploited, yet she found herself repeatedly straying from that vision. It forced an ultimatum: she would no longer help with their legal troubles unless they improved the mine conditions. They begrudgingly listened to her, and the conditions there gradually improved. Traumatised by what she saw, she decided to no longer be part of the mining.

CHAPTER NINETEEN

Deeper into the trial, days passed, and the rigmarole was repeated. On the twenty-fourth day of the hearing, the proceedings were interrupted. Security Officials came and approached Judge Bettencourt. They talked to her, and she looked concerned. Protestors outside had broken into the Hall and were clashing with officials. "As a result of the unrest around the country, upon which this case has undoubtedly had an influence, and due to the breaches of security and the ongoing uncertain conditions relating to the civil unrest, I am immediately delaying this trial until further notice when it is deemed safe to continue," Judge Bettencourt announced. There was a sense of confusion around the courtroom and the public gallery. While Ally was still unsure of what was unfolding, she was quickly surrounded and escorted back to her cell by a mass of officials before anything could happen to her—and before she had a chance to escape.

Some of the protestors were armed, and gunfire was exchanged. The sounds of gunshots and shouting reverberated throughout the Hall. It was evacuated and immediately placed into lockdown; Ally was told none of this, as she was in her cell. She was told only that protestors were attacking the building. Ally could occasionally hear unsettling noises, a discordant blend of screams and gunfire as the Hall around her descended into anarchy. Outside, many civilians and law enforcement personnel were injured or killed. There were many attempts by protestors to set the Hall of Justice on fire.

The hearing and entire trial had quickly been suspended; it took hours to get the Hall of Justice under control. This was an unprecedented event in the Hall's history. They had many prisoners who needed to be evacuated. Some had already broken out and were participating in the widespread destruction. The authorities had resorted to shooting anyone on sight, and bodies littered the Hall. Outside, masses of people swarmed around in a hive mind. The situation was rapidly deteriorating; law enforcement eventually regained control of the building and forced the protestors back outside. This caused everyone's cases to be delayed. Nothing like this had ever taken place in the U.R.S.C. The country was no stranger to unusual experiences, but this level of chaos was unprecedented. Everything was shifting faster than could be comprehended.

As the night approached, the fury and number of protestors surged, but law enforcement personnel regained control of the perimeter outside the Hall with merciless force. Many non-violent, peaceful protestors were killed or savagely injured in the hysteria. Every department or branch available had been dispatched to locations across the country, from the U.R.S.C. military and special forces to S.T.A.T.I.C. agents. But, by this time, the governmental resources that kept police and military supplied were starting to become scarce. In some cities and towns, the protestors had completely taken over parts and were repelling counterattacks. The U.R.S.C. had been birthed out of a fierce, protestive spirit, and the public were not going to go quietly. It was seen as an inalienable right to protest, to embody the revolutionary spirit, and redress absolute power or unfair conditions. Now that they had gained so much, to have it all taken away seemed unthinkable. Law enforcement had to drive the people away from the Hall, forcing them back to the surrounding streets. Some gained access to nearby buildings and attacked from all angles, it resulted in massive casualties for both law enforcement and civilians alike.

The breakdown and suspension of the trial process, it was evident, would last much longer than expected. The people in the Prosecution Department and the government were hard-pressed to reckon with the damage, to intervene, and bring a resolution to the trial that wouldn't result in annihilation of the country. Ally had been rendered into solitude and submission. She listened to the periodic jolts of the unrest erupting around the Hall, unsure of when the next noise would sound. She was still told nothing of what was unfolding. It was obvious that the entire place was in an uncontrolled state of upheaval and confusion. All entrances or exits were completely restricted. She couldn't talk to her legal team about what was going on or about when the trial would resume.

While this was happening, with almost no coverage from the media, the trial of Hazuki Yamamoto was beginning, as well as of the high numbers of other people who had suddenly been accused and brought before a court. While the citizens were distracted, the legal showdown for the control and rights to Delphi Township started in Palisade. A delegation of the most-important citizens of the republic had made the pilgrimage to be present for the beginning of what was to decide their future. Already, it was appearing unfavourable for the residents. A raft of laws had been hastily changed to replace the old agreements, ratifying and legitimising the government's greedy intentions to take over.

The Defence, which comprised some very prominent barristers and human-rights activists from around the country, rebutted by showing portions of the Constitution which allowed for them to remain on their land. They followed this by using evidence, notes, and the subsequent treaty from the original trial, which showed legal precedent that the privately owned land and mining leases couldn't just be taken without warning or due process. It was a highly regarded ruling, a defining moment in the nation's young history. When they gave the land to people who had fled from turmoil to start again in the U.R.S.C., the historic ruling also had made possible the formation of other Townships and Communes around the nation. These enclaves were the primary *loci* of vehement protest. The whole world was watching closely—these struggles could change the whole dynamic of the U.R.S.C. and affect great numbers of its residents.

What followed was an agonising time for Ally, Osiris, and the others, as they were told nothing about where they were going to be transferred to. Ally had daily visits and briefings from her counsel, but these meetings were disappointingly ineffective, with their lack of any hard intelligence on her imprisonment or on what was going to happen. The protests outside had not stopped. There were more incidents of protestors breaking the containment lines around the perimeter, gaining entry, and sieging themselves on the roof, displaying anti-government, anti-establishment banners, burning effigies, and destroying the place. Those people were being murdered in droves. There were growing calls to defund the resources for the police and give the funds to other groups in hopes of addressing the out-of-control crime statistics in the U.R.S.C., as well as other disturbing violence, drug-addiction, and mental health statistics.

The idea was conceived with the intention to take some of the pressure off the underfunded and overstretched law enforcement agencies and free up their resources so they didn't have to combat every problem in society, some of which they had no expertise in and weren't equipped to handle. This caused a deep divide within the population; the idea wasn't properly explained, so it was dismissed as dangerous or infeasible. Ally wasn't concerned about which facility she would be transferred to; she was more upset about the prospect of a looming execution at the hands of the U.R.S.C. Her legal team were trying to get retrials and appeals or whatever they could to save their client from being put to death. They would tell her about the efforts, but they were weak and ineffective. The prisoners suffered many beatings from the staff along with murders, riots, and fights. Currently, Ally's facility was still in lockdown due to the numerous breaches and insurrections within it when it was stormed by protestors.

Born from the struggle was a growing Resistance called the "Naught-For." They were having success interfering with the government by using a guerrilla-style campaign, which was becoming indistinguishable from the shattered Militia. The Naught-For Resistance movement was an increasing concern for those in control. In a concerted effort, the many government agencies, bureaus, and departments all undertook surveillance and spying operations to identify the hierarchy within this Resistance. They encountered a problem when it was discovered that this Resistance didn't have a conventional structure, like the Militia. They identified a few Resistance insurgents who had been sabotaging and attacking, but they soon realised that this adversary was different. It was more of an ideal, a movement, forming in the minds of the people and drawn out into practice through oppression. It was an ideal that had the power to dismantle the unchallenged authority and leadership they had suffered under.

This was carefully monitored as the movement was increasing in its far-reaching support. It got people together from different backgrounds who may not otherwise interact to share a common goal. There were different ideas being discussed amongst the collective community, from radical solutions like the coup to other, non-violent visions. The government wanted to end the unity and tried to shatter it through racial, economic, and political divides. It began a campaign of false-flag incidents in different parts of the nation, attacking religious sites, famous landmarks, protest groups, and communities, aiming to incite racial violence to divert attention away from its more sinister acts. To a degree, this strategy worked in creating large-scale hatred and distrust, leading to harrowing bloodshed.

Security had been tightened after the breach of the Hall of Justice; Ally was allowed only sporadic meetings with her team in one of the jail's depressing interview rooms. She tried to convince Konstantinos to set up a secret deal with some of the powerful people he knew. He was initially opposed to the idea, but Ally had swayed his opinion to the point where he was more considerate of the proposal. "You need to help me, Mihalis. You need to put together a deal to get me out of this, released from prison, and deported back to France, Australia, anywhere. I want you to talk to some of the people you know in powerful positions. I need you, Mihalis. Now that I've been transferred here, my connections have been severed. You have to be the mouthpiece and start plea bargaining."

"I want to, Miss Rose, but I don't want to jeopardise my very career. They've tried to arrest me many times for the work that I've done—raiding my office and putting surveillance out on my employees and myself. I'm not entirely sure who I can consult at this point or if I can do anything without being spied upon. The government has many eyes and ears around now, trying to dismantle this Naught-For Resistance and stop those organising protests and dissent around the nation."

"I'm going to be *executed*, and you're concerned about your *career*. That's why you should do it in secret, even if I have to serve some time in prison while you do everything from the outside. Talk to someone, and influence the report, or get it changed—apply some pressure if you need to. Who would we need to speak with in order to put together a contract or plea deal behind the scenes?"

"That would be someone in the Executive Office of the U.R.S.C. Judiciary and Law; it's who the Department of Prosecution and the Judge ultimately work for and are appointed by. They're a branch of government, with many smaller, internal divisions that control all of the prison facilities and everything concerning the law, the courts, sentencing, and justice within the legal system. Most of the people there are appointed by political ministers, who give the high-paying jobs to their friends and allies. A committee will write a report determining where you are sent, which should be handed down after you're sentenced."

"I know some things about illegal activity within the Executive Office and the political identities linked to it. Can you get me into a meeting or talks with any of the people higher up in the Executive Office? Maybe then I would be in a better position to do some bartering and use my information as leverage against them."

"I don't know about that idea. It has the chance of getting you an even worse result. Amongst other things, those people won't like you endangering their positions and power."

"They have already been endangered through their horrible conduct. They can make this whole debacle better if they change how they're conducting this and actually listen to what the people are saying to them. If anything, I'm stopping all this from descending further into disaster. I can make things much worse for them."

"You're far too impulsive, Miss Rose. You must be more strategic; you have the right mind for this type of thing, but you reveal your cards too soon. We can do this. I have seen that you're not how they have portrayed you in the media—not at all. You're very intelligent, and it's a shame that you're here when you have such potential. They seek to denigrate you and paint you as a deplorable person not worthy of anyone's admiration or sympathy."

"No, I'm much worse. I'm a monster, Mihalis. I don't believe this was all destined to happen like this; I don't believe that we don't have the wherewithal to take charge. While I'm still breathing, this is what I'll vow to do. They've played dirty—and, now, so will we. The time has run out for regular tactics, for playing by the rules. This is the fire, and we must fight it with fire. The people in the Executive Office are worse criminals than I am, and we're going to have to blackmail them to get what we need. We must make them know they could be exposed and themselves put on trial if they don't open up to the prospect of creating a better deal for me. Then we have some leverage—we have something that could turn the tables. You need to get me into a meeting with someone in the Executive Office."

"Miss Rose, that's going to be very difficult to achieve. I know someone who is working there at the moment. I can contact them and see what I can do, but I'm not making any promises. This isn't going to be easy, or it may not happen at all. I will make an attempt, and I'll let you know what happens, whether they accept or reject our offer."

For the next two days, Ally waited nervously for news about whether Mihalis had come through and had accomplished getting them into a meeting with someone important in the Executive Office. She knew it was a secretive place; not much was known about it by the public. She went through stages of hopeful optimism, to pessimistic disappointment, and, finally, to futility. She was still isolated from the other prisoners but was allowed short periods for exercise. Apart from that, she was confined to her cell. It was a massive contrast to the lifestyle she had been leading. She didn't miss the vanity elements or the luxury penthouses as much as she missed the smaller, simpler pleasures she had been now deprived of.

CHAPTER TWENTY

It was the early morning of the second day after Mihalis' and Ally's meeting. Mihalis had fallen asleep at the desk in his home office. He received a phone call. He was startled awake, lifting his face off the stack of papers sprawled on his desk. Still weary from the minute amount of sleep he got, he answered without checking who it was. "Hello. Mihalis Konstantinos speaking," he said drowsily.

It was his assistant, a young female paralegal, who was frantic. "Mr. Konstantinos, Sir—you need to come down to the office right now. There are agents here from the N.I.B. and the A.C.E. They're going through our databanks and mainframe, requesting access to documents I told them we don't have—but they're insistent on searching the place. They're gaining access to all of our personal, private material and files. I need you to come here immediately— *Excuse me! You can't go in there! You can't access that without permission from Mr. Konstantinos.*" He could hear her talking to someone and a commotion taking place in the background. *"Excuse me! I informed you that you had to wait until Mr. Konstantinos arrives before you're allowed to look through that folder!"* She was distracted and panicking.

"Listen to me, Claudia. Calm down, and tell them not to do anything else until I arrive. Tell them not to touch any more documents or search through anything else until I arrive, or I will have them charged with offences relating to the privacy act."

"Yes, sir."

"Have they said why they are there? They have already conducted searches of the office and found nothing of any value to their case—or whatever their objective is."

"No, they haven't said anything. I've been trying to request to see a warrant, but they are refusing to show it to me."

"Who are the main agents in charge? Has anyone presented themselves to you and stated that they're in charge of the operation?" Konstantinos inquired.

"Yes, it was an Agent Frank Blaze from the N.I.B. and Agent Yue Zhang from the A.C.E."

"I'm going to call their agency offices and find out why this is happening again and what clearance they have been given. Try to stall them until I get there. I apologise for this, Claudia." On his rushed trip to the firm's office building, he was on the phone, being bounced between departments by the agency offices. When he arrived, he immediately confronted Agent Blaze, who had made his way into his office and was rifling through the papers in his desk. "Agent Blaze: I *thought* I could smell something that was rotting. What the fuck are you doing here, tearing through my office *again*? You've already ransacked the place once, looking for apparitions or whatever it was you believed was here."

"We have a warrant to be here," Blaze growled back.

"Yes, but why are you here again? If you didn't find anything before, then why return and cause this inconvenience? To what do I owe your presence in my office again?"

"We're looking for any evidence or information that you may be withholding from us. We're here to conduct another search in case you have anything about this trial that we don't."

"You failed to find any before because there is nothing here that we are keeping from you. The same can't be said about your agency."

"Listen, Mihalis—you slimy fuck." Blaze lowered his voice. "It's come to my attention that you've been making deals with your associates from your past who are in the Executive Office, making plea deals regarding the future and fate of a client of yours. These deals may be detrimental to that client and their present dilemma, because they already have arrangements in place with other individuals."

"Perhaps. I'm not at liberty to discuss such things. I can't confirm or deny that they actually occurred," Konstantinos explained.

Agent Blaze banged his fist on the table. "You'd better fucking tell me what she said and who you've been talking to."

"She hasn't told me anything. That poor young woman knows nothing. She is under surveillance and is isolated in confinement for almost every moment of the day. How could she possibly tell me anything?"

"I know that she's been telling you about some of the figures she has information on. Now you're utilising it to work behind the scenes and destroy everything I've done. *That stops now!* I need that information to wield the power and the change that it represents. I am going to be the one responsible for releasing that intelligence and reap the rewards that it offers. Then I'll be in a much better position to negotiate my way up the ladder—right to the top, where I'm in charge," Blaze said.

"I'm sorry, but I don't know what you are talking about."

"How honest do you think she is being with you? She's an untrustworthy little whore who uses her little innocent façade to persuade others and get out of trouble. There's been some whispers that you've grown very attached to this case, enough to break the law and pursue secret, illegal meetings in order to influence the High Court's decision. There's a lot going on that you don't know about."

"Don't come here with your unfounded conspiracy theories and paranoid fantasies, trying to coax something out of me. What are you hoping to achieve with this pathetic little ruse?" Konstantinos asked.

"Did you know her real name is Alexandrine? Alexandrine Chevalier? She's a Facilitator, and her *company* is fake and acting as a cover for her illegal money laundering from the proceeds of Facilitating and financial fraud. She's been deceiving you, me, and the whole country. Everything she has said is a lie. She is selective with what she wants to divulge because she wants to get out of this by any means necessary. She's a criminal—but not in what we thought she was doing and indicted her for," Blaze explained.

"You're lying. This is all to gain more control and manipulate your way to the top."

"No, it's all in this report. Ask her yourself. I know everything now, and, if you want to stop me from making it all public, then you'd better tell her to confess what she knows. I can make sure she gets executed. If she still wants to make a deal, she's going to have to do it with me—or nobody at all."

Konstantinos said, "How can I be sure of this? You could be bluffing. That's just one of the cheap tricks you employ. I've never heard of any of that. How do I know it's true?"

Blaze retorted, "It is. Now that we've come to a stalemate, she can't make a deal without me. Don't you understand? With all these new laws, I've been given all the power, and after these Militia court cases are over, I'll be in line to become head of the N.I.B. Then, I can do as I please. You've lost. There's nothing left for you to do but align with us and what we want."

"There was never any chance to win," Konstantinos said, emptily.

Blaze kept coming at Konstantinos. "It's well known that you originally worked with your connection in the Department—*and* that you fell out with him when he was a barrister. But now that he's in the Executive Office, you're seeking him out for a secret plea deal. That was quite ambitious of you, and it was also quite stupid."

"What did you do?" Konstantinos asked.

"I didn't do anything, but, without him or his recommendations, there'll be nobody to give their input to change that report. It won't be altered to favour Ally Rose. Seeking out an arrangement like that is a criminal offence," Blaze threatened.

Konstantinos stood his ground. "We've been forced to find alternatives in our fight against the people who have infiltrated this system! They're the criminals! I didn't enjoy the notion, but I'm running out of options and time."

"You *admit* to it then!" Blaze said. "Well, now, if you want to make a deal, you have to come to me. You have to surrender what you know to me, or your associate won't be making any more deals . . . ever," he taunted.

"We had become estranged from each other. I gradually came to loathe him and his ideals. He is the complete opposite of the type of person I once knew, but that doesn't mean you can just *assassinate* him. Just because we didn't see eye to eye doesn't mean you can just murder him or whatever you're planning to do to him. I'll take an eye for an eye, and blood for blood, if that's what you want to do," Konstantinos said, vehemently.

"I wouldn't be making threats against an agent if I were you," Blaze said, indignantly. "You don't have any more options. Now that everything's collapsed, you have to go through me. If you still want to save Alexandrine Chevalier's life, you'd better start complying."

"Congratulations!" Konstantinos said, sarcastically. "You've managed to manipulate this to your advantage and your gain, no matter who you had to run over or destroy to get it. I sincerely hope it's everything you've ever wanted. Enjoy it while you can, because, soon, all that will be taken away from you. You came here to tell me what you needed. Now, go! Get your saber-rattling, power-hungry arse out of my fucking office."

Agent Blaze stood in the doorway and turned around. "I'll be seeing you again soon."

After Blaze was gone, Konstantinos left to try to secure a meeting with Ally. He couldn't get close to the entrance of the Hall of Justice because the protestors had set up camps and tent settlements in the streets around the Hall, in an "Occupying" type of protest. There had been clashes earlier in the morning and the night before, but he still had a hard time gaining access to the Hall despite the relatively peaceful state of things. But the mood seemed to hum with the ominous energy of something sinister about to occur. The government had placed spies and secret police amongst the protestors to identify Resistance members. After weaving through the tents and groups of people, it was still a struggle for Konstantinos to get through the barricades and fencing erected by law enforcement.

He was in a state of mixed emotions as he finally made his way inside. He believed he had a good rapport and relationship with Ally. He was unsure of why she would lie to him, and he was enraged over what Agent Blaze had been doing. Ally was brought into the room. She had a jaded aura about her; her normally prominent, rosy cheeks were deflated and pale. Cracks were etched into her lips, and her hair lacked its usual lustre and volume. Usually immaculately coiffed with a vibrant bounce, it was frayed and unkempt. Her blue eyes were lifeless, a void of stone. "There is much to discuss, including some disturbing updates I have been made aware of."

"At the moment, I don't care, Mihalis. I don't care about this any longer."

"I have been told many things about you lately, many disturbing things. I'm very upset that you kept crucial details from me. I was trying to help you, and you didn't even tell me your real identity? Why did you do that? I wouldn't have done anything with it if you had just told me," Konstantinos said, frustrated.

A look of surprise suddenly appeared on Ally's face. "How do you know this?" she said in a sinister voice.

"Agent Blaze knows everything, and he said he was going to release it."

"It's irrelevant. I'm not on trial for what happened in my past. I kept it hidden only to ensure my survival, so that it couldn't be used against me. I apologise for not sharing this with you, but I fear I'm becoming more like Agent Blaze, willing to say or do anything to escape from this, no matter the cost or sacrifice. What were you doing with him?" Ally argued.

"You will be on trial if he releases it. I was trying to make a deal with my contact from the Executive Office, a Director on the Board of Prisons and Sentencing, but Blaze found out about it. He raided my firm, pretending to be looking for withheld evidence; he informed me that he knew about my secret meeting and plans to blackmail the Director into silence or try to get him removed from the Executive Office. He wouldn't tell me how he'd discovered my intentions. My contact assured me there was nobody who knew about the meeting."

"Who is this person?"

"I didn't really tell you because the connection is someone I used to know. He was one of the first people I met when I migrated to the United Republic. He became like a mentor; in time, we gradually started a firm together. We had a lot of differences on the way we wanted to obtain justice and became increasingly opposed to each other's ideas. I wanted to focus on human-rights issues, but he was anti-human rights, and his opposition seemed to grow every day. He became less focused on the truth and morality and more about money and position.

"Eventually, we became almost completely estranged, and that's when I left to start my own firm. Then my son was framed for selling classified secrets and put on trial for treason. Similar to your own case, my son was facing execution, and I tried to get the Director to help because he had changed careers to join the Executive Office. I begged him to confer with his powerful friends or use his position to get my son a lesser sentence, but he didn't do anything about it, and my son was put to death five years ago. He was about your age when he was murdered," he explained.

"I remember hearing something about that. See? We all have parts of ourselves that we withhold. All of us are biased—and, ultimately, flawed—representations of whatever truth is. I knew it! I knew you weren't telling me everything. You can't condemn me for keeping certain aspects of my life a secret. It was for strategic intents and purposes; I was certain there was some other reason you were doing this," she replied.

"The reason I've been doing everything for you—taking these risks and working so fastidiously—is that I wanted to make sure that didn't happen to you. See to it that you weren't doomed to the same fate as my son—it's too late for him. If you haven't noticed, I can walk away from here right now if I wanted to. But I saw something in you, something in your case about the treatment you were receiving. I was hopeful that we could reach some better outcome for you that doesn't involve execution. Agent Blaze wants to prevent the Director from implementing changes to your sentencing report. He got his hands on a file somewhere that had evidence about your real identity, your profession, and the status of your company. He's manipulating everything so that we make a deal with him only; he's trying to get rid of the competition. Admittedly, I didn't want this fallout and danger introduced into my life, but I was doing this for you. I was not going to walk away from this, but, after the way Agent Blaze has come after me, I'm in this now for some of my own reasons," he said sternly.

"I know this must be true. It may not be the best truth or one you would rather forget, Mihalis, but I know this is your gritty, raw truth, stripped bare. What do you suggest we do?"

"After they have done this, it means anything will be possible going forward. I have taken some risks, but, now, I don't care about this anymore, either—or about the consequences. I'm willing to take any risk or do whatever is required. I'm no longer going to worry about doing things properly, transparently, or fairly. I tried to do this in the correct manner. I tried to be exemplary in what I was doing, not out of pride but to demonstrate how a case such as this should be conducted. Yet they have repeatedly shown such a disrespect and disregard for this situation and for justice. Now I'm going to do the same."

"Let's do this. Let's destroy them together. I know we've had our disagreements, but are you with me?" Ally asked.

"Fuck it—I'm in. I have to warn you, though: This is not going to happen overnight," Konstantinos responded.

"It will be all the sweeter when we triumph and crush them! Thank you for telling me all of this. I'm sorry that I said I didn't care earlier. I've gone so numb, so exhausted; I don't keep a record of all the times I've fallen—only the times that I rose up to keep fighting," Ally said with resolute courage.

Konstantinos knew that, if he could get a meeting with a high-enough-ranked politician, he could make a world of difference for Ally. He saw in her the same qualities his murdered son had; he felt a growing attachment to her and wanted to fight for her.

"Miss Rose, your situation leaves me helpless. I need a bartering tool to help repair this whole quandary or something I can do to ensure that people will be compelled into talking about and settling this matter. I can't wait for knowledge to appear out of the ether . . . I guess that's ridiculous."

Their eyes met, confirming their understanding, as he slid a piece of paper toward her. She wrote down secure locations where some of the damaging files were, what he needed to do, and how he could access them without her present.

CHAPTER TWENTY-ONE

After that meeting, he went from there straight down into the underworld, immersing himself, contacting people he had normally spent his career representing. Konstantinos immediately retrieved the files. Armed with Ally's reputation-destroying facts and evidence, he was even developing a contingency plan in his head to break Ally out of prison, though it was unlikely.

The country's most important political sphere was the nation's capital, Palisade, where the nation's laws and bills were passed. It was where the Federal Parliament sat and where the nation's most esteemed politicians worked. Armed with some of Ally's incendiary files, he embarked for the capital the next day. It was 600 kilometres south, a relatively short distance to travel. But it had been made nearly impossible with the protesting: Flights were disrupted or cancelled, and parts of the highway network had been blocked. Passing the checkpoints into cities was notoriously difficult in the daylight and now banned at night. Konstantinos secured some transport there and a forged checkpoint-clearance certificate after he consulted a Facilitator.

The capital, of course, had *the* most security around it of anywhere in the Republic, stopping any insurrectionists from getting in. There were stringent security checkpoints along every entry and exit into Palisades. Disruption was growing in the city, which housed five million people, out of a total population of eighty million. There were blockades and a huge military presence. An enormous amount of money had been spent on fortifying the city.

There were protests by privileged, idealistic students from the prestigious universities in the capital. Konstantinos—even after seeing that they were being unfairly attacked—thought they didn't embody the spirit of what this fight was about. They were pampered and largely sheltered from this crisis; many of their parents and family members were the people perpetrating these crimes. He listened to their listless chants and subdued, disparate protest—the perfect allegory for the sanctions and excess restraint exerted on the city. Messages in graffiti were sprayed on most surfaces, and almost all the buildings had been boarded up, showing that, although the capital *appeared* normal, anarchy was bubbling under the surface. Palisade was in a carefully curated lockdown and curfew.

While Ally and others were suffering in the harsh conditions of the prison system, Konstantinos was meeting with influential people in fine-dining restaurants and high-end lounges. He was no stranger to the criminal underworld and the art of persuasion. It was a miserable, rainswept evening in the city, which cooled some of the tensions. The downpour seemed to shrink the activity on the streets, and the wet ground reflected the glittering city lights. He was meeting with a Director on the Board of Prisons and Sentencing within the Executive Office. The restaurant the man would be dining at was a frequently used meeting place for some of the most powerful figures in the country, overseeing some of the most important meetings and decisions that had shaped it. The restaurant felt warm and inviting, providing shelter from the rain.

Konstantinos was taken through the candlelit establishment to the table, past well-dressed diners, looking around at them suspiciously. But, to the people there, he was like a background character, and they paid him no attention. The Director was seated in a booth, secluded from the other patrons. They were enclosed and sheltered by the surrounding high walls and thick wooden panels, hiding them and protecting the nature of their conversation. He was already eating when Konstantinos took the seat opposite him. The other activity in the restaurant faded into the ambience as they focused on their business.

The Director said, "It's been a while. You must think that this is a very important case for you to be scheduling a meeting. I thought you might prefer an illicit meeting like this and settling our case out of court. It's how all the most crucial business is done in this country," he said in a taunting manner.

"How can you sit casually at this restaurant like nothing's wrong—when the world is burning down out there?" Konstantinos enquired.

The elderly Director responded, "It very well may be, but if you were willing to step out into that jungle to discuss this, it shows me that it must be of some importance to you. The show must go on—even if the place is falling apart. A man works up a powerful hunger trying to hold the world together and keep it turning. It will *keep* turning, despite the unpleasantness that we're experiencing and the inconvenience that has accompanied it. Your client is causing quite a commotion within the country, quite a stir. We can't have this upsetting the balance of power that we keep over this fragile nation—it already appears to be sliding towards disaster. We're stuck in a predicament—we can't appear to be lenient on her, yet, giving her a less-harsh sentence would ease some of the hostilities the whole ordeal has caused. I've become very adept at guessing the reasons and motives behind the people who come to me. I'm guessing that's why you're here."

Konstantinos pled, "I know that the outcome of cases and instances like this aren't decided in courtrooms. It's decided in fine restaurants like this and in the stifling boardrooms of the privileged class, not on the streets where it happens but sheltered away from public view, from prying eyes. I need to know that she won't be put to death—that she at least has the chance to live."

"Don't despair . . . I made sure that nobody followed me here. Did anyone follow you here?"

"No—I made sure of it," Konstantinos assured him.

"Because if anyone finds out about this, we'll all be court-martialled. Many of my colleagues and friends with a vested interest in this affair have become concerned. This meeting was scheduled because something needs to be done about this," the Director said.

"It may be in the best interest of the Department to change the power dynamic and control from slipping and degrading any further—there could be an insurrection, but I'm not confirming or denying."

"What do you mean?" the Director snapped.

Konstantinos replied, "This isn't just a normal case. I've never seen a case with so much meaning for the country and its future. This is the biggest challenge facing the nation since it was founded. If it's not met with the proper response, it could break this country; either it survives this—or it's over. There may be some intel floating around in the ether, damaging intel that would be better left undiscovered. There may be certain people around with harmful knowledge at their disposal who are waiting on the outcome of the trial before deciding what to do with it. This ugly mess could degrade even more; the outcome for my client impacts not only her but a whole score of others. What my client decides is what will happen to the others, and a lighter sentence for her may calm the people who are beating down your doors and sharpening their guillotines. I've come here to request that you give my client a lighter sentence. If you could fabricate it to the mainstream media and say that she was given a tough sentence, your department can still maintain the image of being harsh on offenders and making an example out of her to deter and discourage other people."

The Director said, "There's a lot of people who want your client and the rest of those Militia people dead. They've been a thorn in the side of this country, and the disobedience they've inspired has caused untold damage to the economy. If this is what's required to get this madness to end, then it's something I will recommend to the other Directors on the Board. All measures will have to be taken to ensure that this isn't discovered, or our careers are over. We need your client to keep this confidential; they should be told as little information as possible.

"We would have to completely cover up the details, and any path we pursue would have to result in some form of imprisonment of your client. At least until such a time when these riots and protests are over and the attention has died down. Nobody knows exactly how long that may be—the civil unrest around the U.R.S.C. appears to show little sign of stopping. There has been a lack of momentum reported in the media, but this is not true. Our reports show that the ranks of the Naught-For Resistance are, in fact, increasing in ferocity and numbers. The destruction and costs are mounting."

Konstantinos pressed the issue. "That could all go away if you change the rules—just a slight alteration. It's not just for my client's benefit. *I* need this surveillance to stop, and *you* need these protests and this scrutiny to stop. I've got people intercepting my mail, harassing my staff, and threatening my life. A better outcome for my client translates to a better outcome for us all. There have been photographs and footage leaked of the regime and military's crimes against unarmed protestors. Members of the international community are outraged and are viewing us as an increasingly rogue state, a failed state, which already has a reputation for being unlawful, for having a bad record of human-rights violations. There are already discussions about some going to court for crimes against humanity, sanctions, and other tariffs on trade and goods. We can't let it get to a tipping point. If you don't find a more humanitarian solution to this, then we all go down with the ship. I know that no one wants it to end up like the Nuremberg Trials or the show trials in Stalin's Soviet Union." Konstantinos had to sell the idea to the Director, making it sound appealing for them as well as for Ally.

"I have seen this, and the U.R.S.C. will come out of this unscathed. Many of these nations saying these things have a long history of abuse and crime—the same ones for which they are denouncing us," the Director rebutted.

Konstantinos insisted, "This is exactly what you are doing to my client. She'll be left to be punished and made an example of, yet the very people who are denouncing her are guilty of crimes themselves. This is not acceptable. If you want to keep your monopoly and your privileged position, your high-level friends and secret dealings from being released, then I suggest you take another look at the report for my client, as it is also in your best interest for self-preservation."

The Director countered, "If this first traitorous report that was released by the anonymous whistle-blower and law enforcement defector did nothing to hurt us, then we will emerge from the aftershock as we always do. We will wait out this scandal."

Konstantinos said, "That is where you may be incorrect. A great number of our citizens seem to be seeking a major awakening. Have you not seen the commotion out there? I guess you may not have, as you are most likely sheltered from it. Like you said, *the world keeps turning, and it's business as usual* for your type, safely hidden away in places like this while there are people out there are suffering, fighting, and dying. Why can't you have some mercy? Do this for my client and help end this? It isn't a matter of business or career. This is about life—human life. You couldn't even do it for my son, for my family, when we needed it the most. At least, do it this time," Konstantinos said accusatorily.

"I told you there was nothing I could do about his case," the Director replied, defensively.

Konstantinos said, passionately, "There were things you could have done for him; you just chose not to do them. There are so many other phenomena that can't be controlled that, when you have the possibility to change this and soothe this savage beast, you should take it. This episode that has shaken the pillars the country rests upon could be its undoing."

The Director said, "Understand that I'm doing it for my interests. I will see to it that the report on your client shows updated recommendations. This favorable action on your client's behalf needs your silence and cooperation to work and help calm those angry crowds."

Konstantinos said, "It will. It means they are being listened to, not undermined and fought against. It would show a huge shift in reasoning and rationale for the extremely unpopular institutions of power. If any of them want to be left standing, this is the best solution."

The Director warned him, "If any of this gets found out, I'm absolving myself and the Executive Office of any implication. You must understand that you're taking the entirety of the risk."

"I'm willing to accept those risks for my client. I've become quite invested in their future and safety. I'm fearful for them, and I don't wish to see this happen," Konstantinos replied.

"Farewell, Mihalis. I'm sorry that we cannot meet for longer and under better circumstances. You must go now, before our location is compromised."

"Farewell, old friend."

Now, Konstantinos had only eighty-four hours to make an impact behind the scenes in the capital. Eighty-four hours to get everything accomplished—it became a whirlwind, a blur of limousines, political galas, and offices. He went to the less-reputable, dubious parts of the city, where a lot of business took place behind the scenes that would have consequences for the whole country and population. He had succeeded in getting close to whom he needed. He was reserved in his approach—he knew this was a dangerous venture and that people around the capital would be conferring among themselves, and his presence had disturbed many people. He had to stay in a sleazy motel by the railway lines, frequented by drug addicts and destitute people who were invisible to those in the Capitol buildings, far removed from the glamorous hotels in the heart of the city and frequented by delegates and esteemed politicians. He noticed that he was being followed and closely watched. He would peer through the soiled curtains to see vehicles farther along the street, keeping surveillance. When he left his hotel, the vehicles would begin following his.

He had some unsettling encounters with people intimidating him. On a cloudy, moonless night, he was waiting for a meeting in a park on the outskirts of the city. The rain had stopped, and leaves stirred along the damp ground. Out of the darkness lurched two men in black suits. Konstantinos' heart dropped when he saw them, and he was unsure whether to run, his hand on a firearm he had for protection. They confronted him, accusing him of causing a lot of trouble around Palisade to attract their attention.

"You've been making a lot of noise around here and showing up in a lot of places. Powerful people are talking—people we work for. You threatened the wrong person and have been advised to stop and disappear from the capital, or you might disappear forever. If we have to meet again, next time you won't see us coming. You're being watched closely." One of them men quickly pulled open his jacket, showing

Konstantinos his holstered weapon before they receded back into the darkness like spectres and were gone.

Konstantinos was shaken by the incident but not deterred. He abruptly cancelled the meeting after he told his contact what had occurred. Konstantinos had secretly recorded and videotaped the encounter. The man rescheduled the engagement at a more crowded, safe location. What his contact told him was worth risking his life for. Konstantinos suspected that Agent Blaze had used freelance cyberterrorists and hackers to compile the truth about Ally, which the man confirmed. He knew some of the best ones worked in the technology district of the nation's capital; he knew some of them had joined the Resistance and went to seek their services the next evening.

CHAPTER TWENTY-TWO

In a cramped and run-down internet café with a gritty urban presence, Konstantinos and his guest were sitting in a booth. Across the room was a large window; a neon sign suspended at the top radiated a tranquil blue glow, and an ocean of rain droplets beaded on the window and caught the light. The woman, known only as "Access Memory," looked out at the cluster of neon signs and advertisements crowding the street. Her eyes darted around in childlike curiosity, as if they were hypnotised by their vividness. She was roughly the same age as Ally and had a youthful complexion; her slender face was wistful and difficult to decipher, even though she had worked with Konstantinos before.

"Who was it who approached you to get those files on my client?" he asked.

"It was some special agents from the cyber bureau of the A.C.E. Through files that were stolen from them, the Resistance discovered an Agent named Frank Blaze had approved the search, and they said they wanted all of the details on the people who've been on trial—Ally Rose and Memphis Jackson. There was talk around the tech district about agents recruiting the hackers, who were working with the government in developing some of their secret programs and viruses. Many of them had gone underground or joined the Resistance. I declined because I didn't want to work for the government. All they needed was a program created to hack into Ally Rose's company mainframe and steal encrypted files. I know who they recruited to do it, though."

"Can you tell me?"

"Another hacker, a freelancer, who goes by the name 'Kill Switch.'"

"Why did this 'Kill Switch' person help the government when they're trying to destroy people like them?"

"I can't answer that. It's angered and threatened the freedom of many people. The way we're portrayed, many people see us only as neutral mercenaries, essentially willing to help whichever side pays the most. The administration wanted to recruit who it could or eliminate them; it's also why many have fled or gone rogue.

This probably isn't the most ideal spot to meet. I think we've made a mistake meeting here. Are we safe?" Access Memory droned.

"It's fine. We should be safe here. This is a perfectly respectable internet hub and café for the city's tech workers. No illegal activity is taking place here," Konstantinos reasoned.

She looked unswayed. With her chin resting on her hand, she had a detached disposition, like her mind was always somewhere else.

"How do I find them?" he asked.

"To do that, you're going to need the services of a Facilitator. I can't do that," she replied.

"Are you sure? This is so we can hopefully stop the government and throw them out of power. I can make it worth your time," he bargained.

"Sorry. I'd love to help you shatter the institutions of control and dominance, but there is a standard of self-preservation I need to sustain.

Even if I wanted to, I'm not sure where they are, so I can't take you to them. Remaining incognito and difficult to locate is part of our trade."

"Why did you join the Resistance? What made you take the risk then?"

She explained, "As a hacker, as someone who works anonymously in the shadows, you can probably understand my penchant for defiance. The government have been trying to target the tech community. Before, they used to leave us to the shadows and would reach out to us when they needed a program created to hack a foreign nation or company, or to interfere with an enemy or spy on them. They've been placing more sanctions, more restrictions on tech companies, questioning them in parliamentary enquiries, and invading their privacy. We became the enemy, which is why many of us joined the Naught-For Resistance and which is why I wasn't going to help the government. I may have spied on a lot of people and created programs for the cyber bureau in charge of misinformation and interference, but I had to draw the line somewhere. I had to take a stand for something or settle for nothing. It seems like they're turning on everybody and making a lot more enemies than friends. That's why they want to get every cyberterrorist, cyberpunk, hacker, and freelancer they can on their side, because they are fine with using them against their enemies, yet they are not so fine when those same people start targeting them."

"If this 'Kill Switch' can't help me, would you be able to? I need to get some classified files from the government about this trial and discover the true extent of their deception and criminality."

"At this time, the way things are, it is too dangerous to be doing that. I joined the Resistance, but I don't plan to be found out and trialled like that Ally Rose. I just don't know if it's a good idea right now—the timing seems a little precarious."

"If you don't help me bring this oppressive regime down, then it will only get worse, and they will hunt and persecute you with even more ferocity. With your expertise, we could cripple and seize control of their systems. There isn't going to be an ideal time; there isn't going to be a moment where everything is perfect—so we need to strike *now*," he pleaded.

"Perhaps you're right," she said with a depressed tone.

"I know you're well informed. If you knew what I know and have seen some of the things I've seen, then you would be much more willing to help."

"We will be doing everything we can to aid the Resistance and sabotage the government and its spying agencies. In time, they will unravel," she vowed.

"It can't be done without you. The government can't be defeated and replaced without the assistance of people like yourself. They are too powerful and pervasive without their systems turned against them or repossessed, then the Resistance will fail, the last defenders of freedom will fall, and all these protests and movements will be all for naught."

Next, Konstantinos met with "Kill Switch," who was a much more paranoid and cautious hacker. A nervous individual with behavioural conditions, he almost cancelled the meeting halfway through due to suspicions they were being followed or listened to. He was wanted by law enforcement agencies, including the N.I.B. and the A.C.E., for previous cyber-attacks and hacking into their systems. He was now linked with the Resistance and was being pursued for the knowledge he had about their inner workings. The government got him to work for them by offering him immunity from prosecution for his past. He was opposed to the idea but had no choice. Konstantinos could see that he wanted to help but something was holding him back; he wasn't entirely sure what that may have been. Konstantinos appealed to him by saying that they would be working against the authorities, and he couldn't get what he needed to without his help.

"Kill Switch" needed further encouragement. Konstantinos could feel he was losing him; he searched his brain for something to say that would change his opinion. "Kill Switch" wanted to cancel the meeting again. Konstantinos salvaged the meeting and convinced him by saying that they would be getting back at the government for using him as a pawn and that he was crucial to the future of the Resistance movement and the nation.

Konstantinos said, "Many lives depend on your decision." Then he saw "Kill Switch" thinking intently about it, the thoughts ticking over in his mind while his eyes darted around like they had for the entire conversation. "Kill Switch" finally agreed to help. He quickly hacked into government and law enforcement servers and got anything that Konstantinos asked him for.

Now Konstantinos had files about Agent Blaze authorising the assassinations of various people and law enforcement members, including himself, his staff, journalists, and hackers in the Resistance who had disseminated secrets and the crimes of the N.I.B. that he could use to extort him. Konstantinos knew he would comply if his position were to be endangered in any way; the man wanted to climb his way to the top and didn't care whom he trampled on to get there.

Konstantinos returned to Clarion with a wealth of interesting developments he could exploit. One of the reports he'd obtained was from Agent Blaze himself. He planned to expose the Director and have him removed from his role so that Ally wouldn't get a lighter sentence.

Before Konstantinos could do anything, Agent Blaze exposed the Director and the breaches of his duty and the law to an internal commission. It was leaked through to the public and morphed into the next scandal, which the Executive Office denied. Yet, in an obvious and transparent damage-control effort, they removed the Director from the Board.

Konstantinos was devastated; without his changes to the sentencing report, there was little hope for Ally—she would be at their mercy.

He was incensed with Agent Blaze; he wanted to get back at him but couldn't afford to have people questioning his recent unlawful escapades. There were claims levelled at Konstantinos that he was the unnamed barrister from the report who'd met with the Director in the capital, which he completely denied. It was something he could be disbarred and indicted for.

While the protests outside remained a menace, their intensity ebbed and flowed. They had been going on for so long that some questioned whether they had lost some of its momentum, thinking that they were not being listened to. People felt disillusionment; there were so many casualties and so much damage mounting that they lost the initiative to continue. Many saw it as a failure. Instead of gaining the freedoms and relaxation of law they were fighting for, the protestors were facing a swathe of laws and orders introduced that were regressive—reversing the nation's growth and prosperity. Other people thought it had come at the cost of too many lives to go unavenged; it couldn't be all for nothing and abandoned. There was a general consensus that the way the fighting was done had to be adapted and reworked.

The uncertainty continued for three gruelling weeks, until the protestors had been driven back and there was some level of normality brought back into the situation—but it was at the cost of many lives. It had been an immense struggle to regain control to the point where they could resume Ally's and Osiris's trials. It had been valuable for Ally and the others, as they had precious time and windows of opportunity for more preparation. The Hall was taken off lockdown status after being given clearance to continue hearing legal matters.

Without warning, Ally was hauled from her cell, with little briefing about the tumultuous events that had made the case seize up entirely, bringing unwanted effects for everyone involved. It appeared now that no one was getting out of this completely unscathed or immune from the fallout. She was taken to the interview room to see her legal team.

Konstantinos was looking at her with a sense of wistfulness. Ally said, "You are looking so defeated; the look on your face does not bode well for me. You may as well inform me of all the glorious details because I'm a blank slate. I have absolutely no idea what has transpired or what's going on. I know from what I can hear that it's a whole ensemble of chaos out there, but I need you to tell me what else is taking place."

Konstantinos said, "Miss Rose, I'm sorry to be the one to inform you, but we have only just found out ourselves. The government is calling for an abrupt end to these trials. They claim that public safety has been compromised in light of the massive outcry the trials have spawned, arguing that the trials have been inciting violence. They're saying that fake news and reports have caused pervasive, far-reaching attacks on citizens and other members of the community. They've decided to forego the rest of the hearings, and they're deciding to move directly into the sentencing phase. I'm sorry to be the bearer of this bad development."

Ally was not disillusioned. She had thought they had something much worse to tell her. She even felt a small sense of relief, but her emotions became clouded, and nervousness set in.

"No, no—this may be good. This is beneficial for us—this could be just what we needed. There was no influencing the decision; there weren't very many legal avenues we had to win that case, so what does it matter? It's not a 'hell or high water' situation. This is what we wanted—to create enough of a commotion to bring about a mistrial or achieve something through these demonstrations and protests I'm told are happening across the nation."

Then Ally realised the implications of what she had been told. She had been so focused on her own thoughts and ideas that she was delayed in processing this new turn of events.

Konstantinos said, "Miss Rose, I'm afraid you aren't comprehending the magnitude of what this means. Everything that's previously been said, discussed, or put forth in the court is all meaningless now. All the deals and negotiations we made have been for nothing. Everything that we could have done to change the government's opinion or rework to help us has been ceased entirely. All the deals you made in secret are going to be rendered useless."

"How do you know this?" Ally replied immediately.

Konstantinos admitted, "Because it is what's going to happen. It has been made to happen that way. They wanted you to believe that you had a chance of getting a better sentence so that you would follow their direction and give them what they wanted. Everything has been misrepresented deliberately and is coming together to work against you, when it should have reinforced you—the document leaks, all of it. Your case, combined with the Township's and the arrested journalists' case, has caused such a major response from the population, they're rushing to the finish so that they can put an end to it *their* way. They want to rid themselves of the complications this has created and get it out of sight and out of mind."

"Look at all of you, pathetic—so ready to stop trying when it's all looking bad, and *I'm* the one who is optimistic. This has taught me something valuable: that I shouldn't surrender to what's apparently laid out, like some linear path to follow. I'm not afraid of what's going to happen; if I was not meant to be here, I wouldn't be here. I'd be on the other side of paradise. But here we are, so we're all going to go in there, and we're going to fight the good fight—like it's victory or death. Whatever may happen now may not be the ultimate destination, so while we still can, before they cut the head off this hydra, I'm going to give them a fight they will never forget. I'm going to give them the fight of my life. You're either with me in this, or you're not. If not, don't even worry about stepping into that courtroom."

"What happens if you are sentenced to die?"

"I'm going to fight that as well. I'll still try to barter some deals secretly—that's how this country seems to run. I must, at least, try, but if I do get executed, you have to promise me that you will carry on the fight for righteousness, to continue to campaign for the values and rights I was not afforded so that this does not befall any others." Ally felt like she was putting on a mask, one the world would see, to veil the worry and pain she was feeling; she felt she had to be brave. If she faltered, there would be nobody to help her; she had been used to being isolated but never to this extent.

CHAPTER TWENTY-THREE

The courtroom was eerily empty; none of the public and only a few selected reporters were allowed in after the breaches and riots that had broken out at the Hall of Justice. It was only the Defence, the Prosecution, Judge Bettencourt, clerks, and security officials. All of the spectacle and power had been taken away; it felt like a private meeting between them with Ally's life at stake. It was not broadcast, making it easier to cover up the outcome and deflect attention, which they had also done by scheduling many other trials that day in a mass persecution of their enemies.

After the hearing started, the Prosecution began arguing their case for which punishment she should receive. "Your honour, the Prosecution believes that, given the circumstances of the case and the highly destructive outcome that was narrowly averted, due to the seriousness of what it meant for our nation and considering the defendant's role in this, we believe the risk posed to the country by someone like the defendant is far too great to ignore or treat without the severest punishment. With the evidence we have presented through this trial, we have consistently and repeatedly demonstrated that the defendant, Ally Rose, being of sound mind and judgement, was aware that her actions were criminal, highly illegal, and in direct contrast to the values, laws, and interests of the United Republic. Our evidence has shown that the defendant was indeed aware when she decided to assist a rogue insurgency cell with their unlawful and treasonous aspirations. Therefore, the Prosecution is asking your honour that, when considering sentencing for such a disturbing and treacherous case with an equally troubling defendant, it would be appropriate for you to place upon the defendant a sentence of death."

This set the tone for the rest of the hearing as they summarised their case. Ally looked at Konstantinos with confusion. She looked over at the Prosecution like what she had just heard was surreal, a conversation in a dream. She couldn't slow her heart rate or the tight feeling in her chest; she was seemingly possessed by anxiety.

Konstantinos delivered his closing argument to the largely empty courtroom; Ally was completely dejected and heard only the conclusion: "This is something we can apply the slippery-slope fallacy to. An outcome like this is unthinkable not only for my client; its implications for the rest of us are grave. If something like this can happen to the defendant, who has been failed by a massively flawed system and let down by a lack of due process, in a trial without any fairness or legality, then who among us is next? Who is the next person who falls victim to a witch-hunt perpetrated by those in power? Those with power can deflect attention from their own crimes and then dictate to us who our next enemy is. I am asking your honour and the court to please not allow this deprivation of liberty and rights to continue, not just for Ally Rose but for everyone, for the future of this country and its future generations, who deserve to look forward to the same freedoms we enjoy now. I am pleading the court and imploring your honour to show mercy on the defendant, for both her own sake and for the sake of all our citizens. Nobody wins when authority goes unchecked by justice. Thank you, your honour. That concludes the Defence's closing argument."

At the end, the Prosecution appealed to the judge's sense of reason that execution was the only outcome to stop her from menacing the U.R.S.C. any longer. After a brief period of deliberation, Judge Bettencourt emerged back into the courtroom. There was a shared sense of anticipation in the people present in the courtroom, a mutual sense of tension.

Konstantinos leaned over to Ally. "Before we hear the verdict, I would just like to say it's been an honour to represent you, Miss Rose. I know we've had some differences, but whatever happens now, I will continue to fight for you, and I'll continue to uphold the ideals and spirit you've imparted to me."

"That's condolence talk. Don't admit defeat; don't get into that mindset of negativity. This is a setback, an obstacle that needs to be overcome. Whatever happens here, this is not the end. It's not over—it's never over. For what it is worth, I thank you for helping me."

"Can we have silence in the court. The court has reached a verdict concerning case number nine-zero-one-two-five, the *People of the U.R.S.C. versus Ally Rose*. On the indictment of purposely withholding information of a threat to the U.R.S.C., I have sufficient evidence, beyond a shadow of doubt, to find the defendant, Ally Rose, guilty. And on the other count of high treason against the U.R.S.C., I also have sufficient grounds to find the defendant, Ally Rose, guilty. The Prosecution has shown you willingly engaged with the Militia of your own accord, with full knowledge that what you were participating in was illegal and treasonous, and had serious legal ramifications. You are a dangerous individual, Miss Rose, and you have demonstrated through your behaviour that you have renounced your right to remain in our society, and that you pose an irrefutable hazard to our country and way of life. Therefore, in accordance with Section Sixty-Seven of the Constitution, I am imposing on the defendant, Ally Rose, a penalty of execution. You are sentenced to be executed by the U.R.S.C. through means of a firing squad. You will be imprisoned at one of the United Republic's facilities to await the date for your execution. The verdict has been reached, and this now concludes case number nine-zero-one-two-five. You are dismissed, as the court will now hear the next case. Would the Court's Security Officials please escort the defendant away to await transportation."

Ally dropped her head, her breath taken away. She had anticipated this and was prepared for it, but, still, the sting was difficult to endure. The enormity of it was still sinking in; the reaction it elicited was one of shock, and many others shared Ally's disbelief at the verdict. In a disarrayed state of breathless disbelief and horror, Ally was taken away from the court; she wanted to shed a tear but couldn't. She felt like she had been broken, shattered into a stunned silence. She was in such a rage, she wanted to murder everyone in the room.

Konstantinos came to see her afterwards. She repeatedly requested him to bring her a gun, which he declined. He told her they were going to settle this without violence. Ally had always used violence as the perfect way to get what she wanted. It was the tool she resorted to, but now she knew it was going to do nothing for her. "Perhaps I don't want a resolution to this; perhaps I'd rather die in a storm of bullets and fire."

"Miss Rose, we did not come this far to do something foolish like that. I need you to be alive so that I can help you. I'm going to keep this going while you're in prison. This is where the real battle begins."

The verdict was deliberately changed in the reporting and statements issued to create uncertainty and to calm the angry citizens, spreading propaganda that the outcome was much fairer. It was broadcast around that Ally, Osiris, and the others had been sentenced but were still in talks with members of the Prosecution and the Executive Office. It was reported they were given life imprisonment with the possibility for parole if they demonstrated good behaviour, and, if they were released, they would be deported and unable to return to the U.R.S.C. This was to cause widespread confusion and uncertainty about the legitimacy of the verdict.

In reality, Osiris and the other Militia members were sentenced to be executed. Hazuki Yamamoto and a string of other journalists were sentenced to execution for treason and security threats, and so were the various other individuals who were put on trial. In an attempt to clamp down on the backlash these cases had created, it was all covered up by creating ambiguity around the series of events and plunging the population into a state of unknowing. It was taking shape as one of the darkest days since the formation of the U.R.S.C. Many considered it the day it transformed forever into something foul and oppressive. It was touted as the "Loss of Freedom" and "Paradise Lost" by many. If they couldn't get it back, then it would change into something hideous and unrecognisable.

While this was raging, the Township members were entering into the final phase of their trial. It was closely scrutinised, and the result was highly anticipated. The lawyers for the government and their interests used a surprise tactic that caught everyone off guard. They cited a new law inserted secretly into the Constitution stating the government could reclaim land in an emergency or disaster situation. This was met with disgust and disappointment. Under the current circumstances, they declared a state of emergency and needed to reclaim the land to address the emergency. The citizens who were present were crushed by the decision. All their rights and judgements had been stripped away under the new law.

They immediately appealed the ruling. The new law was the perfect excuse for them to seize land wherever they wanted. Now they could take back their mining leases without being challenged and use them to fund the containment effort and pay for the rising damages bill brought on by their own shortsighted actions. The megalomaniacs in power were too blindsided by greed to consider their paradox. It created havoc instantly after being passed. They thought they had solved the problem, but they had only created another. It had awoken fierce anger in people—and not just in the Townships and Camps. They began to take land away from farmers and the agricultural sector. They took land away from other criminal groups, from private miners and citizens, causing more conflict to ignite. They had made more unwanted enemies who now joined the fight and rallied against them.

Two weeks had elapsed before the report, unedited from the Director, was handed down in all its condemning magnitude. A copy was given to Konstantinos' office after much delay and bureaucratically slow movement. It was worse than he feared. He had to break the grim news to Ally that it stated she was designated the worst type of offender who posed the biggest threat to society, the nation's security, and its future. She was to be sent to the highest classification of prison for the most serious offenders who were a greater level of danger and required more serious incarceration terms.

Many factors were considered in the case. One element was the severe overcrowding in the country's prison system. It had one of the highest rates of incarceration in the world. It also had staggering rates of recidivism. There were certain pipelines that existed within the U.R.S.C. that funnelled vulnerable people and targeted marginalised groups and ethnicities into prison. It was largely being privatised and used to exploit prisoners for profit. A growing percentage was privately owned. There weren't many other facilities that were equipped or funded for containing such a high-profile inmate. There were also massive shortages of correctional workers.

She was being sent to the Skyline Outpost Federal Prison Facility, with security classified as "Super Maximum," a place that struck fear into offenders. It was where political prisoners, dissidents, and those who offended against the U.R.S.C. or its interests were imprisoned. Being sent to Skyline meant you were never seen again. Some never saw civilisation again. It was located in an isolated area far into the desert, completely cut off from everything; there was no trace of other people around in any direction. It was so secluded that it was an extended journey, taking many hours to complete, further exacerbated by disorder caused by the incidences of violence and demonstration. With that presenting such an obstacle, parts of the journey had been stopped or interrupted.

The first part of the newly reformed transportation process involved Ally and dozens of others being transported on an aircraft specially modified to ferry the nation's prisoners between different facilities. The decommissioned military aircraft was departing from the city's Aeolus Airport. It was methodically carried out. The imposing convoy raced through the blocked-off streets, with a surrounding security presence. Protestors tried to attack the convoy, but they were unable to get close enough. The city felt stilted and oppressed, carved up by the barriers and forced apart. People lined up at the fences that blocked the streets to get a glimpse of the convoy. They threw Molotov cocktails and other projectiles. Those who crossed the barrier were shot by snipers.

At the airport, the prisoners were taken out of the vehicles and escorted like cattle through the cargo-bay area at the rear of the air-craft. Ally felt it was a degrading process, rigorously performed, with no margin for error. On either side of her were heavily armed guards, lined up. She was taken into the cabin, a crowded network of doors, cells, and glum metallic caging. She was placed into one so small that, because of her height, her shoulders were pressed against the metal cage and her knees against the door. The weather conditions were conducive to flying. It was a sunny day with only a few scattered clouds, high visibility, and little wind activity. The plane soared off the runway and away from the city, climbing high, hoping to avoid any rocket fire. Their destination was the city of Halley Beach to a Processing and Transfer Facility. It was much closer to Skyline Outpost, and, from there, she would be transported via bus the rest of the way. Ally had found out her co-accused were also being sent to Skyline Outpost. She wanted to reconnect with Osiris and discuss all the tumultuous events that had transpired. She wanted to apologise for certain behaviours; she also needed some apologies and answers from him, and certain points clarified concerning the course of events.

CHAPTER TWENTY-FOUR

Without incident, the plane touched down in the coastal city of Halley Beach, in the country's tropical north, with a population of half a million inhabitants. It was small, although, like Clarion, it was a city divided. Gripped by panic and fear, large areas were without electricity or water, which had a catastrophic impact on the people affected; fighting broke out to keep people out of the parts that were unaffected. It was locked down and carved into different sections. The fighting there had become more about vital resources. It was like a vision into the apocalypse, and, for some, a reliving of the earlier conflicts that had created the country. Bombs exploded, fires raged uncontrolled, food was left rotting, shops and businesses were looted, hospital casualties remained unattended, buildings had collapsed, bullets tore through every target. When Ally stepped out from the plane, she felt the tropical heat instantly. She saw there were towers of smoke billowing into the air from places all over the city; she could hear fleets of sirens wailing and distant gunfire.

The Processing and Transfer Facility they were going to was a complex outside of the city. It had been spared the worst of the city's breakdown, but there was heightened security from recent attacks and a surge in violence and escapes. It was the largest place of its kind in the U.R.S.C., processing tens of thousands of prisoners annually. In the previous two years, they had processed and transported two million people. The overcrowding, noise, and unpleasant odours in the place were unbearable. With the massive backlog, the prisoners weren't processed for days. The amount of movement and activity there was astounding; there were many stories and people intersecting and fleeting, leaving an imprint behind from so many interactions—in the wake of so much energy, memories, and suffering.

Ally had such a transitory feel toward everything, like she was no longer herself but a residual, a ghost. She was locked in with so many others that there was no space to move. When it was her turn to be processed, she was entered into the prisoner database. Her identity was further stripped away from her. She was assigned a number by which she would now be identified. No longer was she "Alexandrine" or even "Ally." She was "Prisoner Number 19-842112."

She was then given a designation for offenders on a scale of low to maximum, based on their risk to themselves, other prisoners, and staff. It was also calculated based on the type of security needs that the person required. She was placed at the highest designation in the scale, meaning she needed a high level of supervision and degree of caution. For less-serious offenders, this rating could change, but she was told that, for crimes like hers, there was no possibility of changing her designation. She got her first glimpse of the dilapidated bus which would complete their journey. It was battered and had a distinctly unsafe appearance. Because Skyline Outpost housed both males and females, they were conveyed there separately.

They departed before daybreak, watching civilisation fall behind and give way to the desert. The temperature in the bus was sweltering as they were travelling through when the heat and sun were the most intense. Ally had heard a lot about this facility, but it remained mysterious. Very little was known by the public—only that it was where the worst offenders were sent, due to its remoteness. Not much was known about the conditions, but they were, apparently, the harshest. They had been travelling for painstaking hours through the night, stopping only briefly to refuel.

The next day had dawned, and there was still no signage on the side of the road indicating that it was close. It would be hours more before the facility came into view, the only feature that loomed dauntingly in the distance as they came to the end of the rough dirt road. When they got closer, it was not what Ally had thought. All the speculation about it appeared to be wrong. The landscape around it was featureless, with very sparse vegetation adapted to survive. There were no signs of life or civilisation, only the meeting of earth with sky and red dirt that stretched endlessly. It evoked a feeling of dread and hopelessness in Ally, now that she had to rely on this wretched place to survive in this barren abyss.

Initially, it didn't resemble the imposing, brutal place it was portrayed as. It didn't appear to be incorporated; it seemed like a town or settlement of its own placed in the desert with many scattered, disparate buildings widely dispersed throughout the enormous space of the facility. There appeared to be fencing only around some buildings and the paths linking them together, separating different areas within the grounds. There was no fencing on the perimeter or any security features, which Ally thought was unusual.

The place was not what she expected. Prisoners were gathered near the fences to watch the new arrivals coming. The warden and other high-ranking officials in the facility made an appearance to welcome the new arrivals and induct them into the place they would spend the remainder of their lives. For some, that would be much shorter than others. When they had stepped off the bus, the warden of the facility inspected them from where he was standing. It was still early in the day, and already the air was extremely humid and still. His eyes scanned them from behind mirrored sunglasses; the prisoners stood in a line, not daring to speak. The uncomfortable silence was broken when he cleared his throat.

"Welcome to Skyline Outpost, where all your dreams come true. Formerly an abandoned cattle station that the government transformed into the happiest place on Earth, a modest fifty-square-kilometre oasis in the desert and your home for the next however many years until forever expires. I'm the warden of this facility. You've probably all heard about this place, but you have to come here to really know what it's about. Because of your actions, you have been removed from society, and, because of the nature of your offences, you have been deemed too hazardous to be incarcerated in another facility. So, you've been sent here, to total deprivation from the outside world.

"You were probably expecting a bit more security. As you can see, there aren't many fences around here. There are no towers. We don't need them, because, if you escape, where are you going to go? There's nothing around in any direction. You're obliged to stay here. It's a bit of a mutual thing. We don't have much supervision, and you can stay here and go about your business without being disturbed by huge amounts of security. Everyone thinks this place is a fortress, but it doesn't need to be. Its best defence is the inescapable terrain. You feel that heat . . . on your face . . . and skin . . . sweltering . . . almost knocking you over . . . feel that dust in your throat . . . choking you? Well, get used to it, because that's all there's going to be. If you escape, and we don't kill you, that desert will.

"You may not be aware that our rule here is that no one's allowed to hoard or collect any water, and it is not to be traded. You will be

given a per-diem ration of water, and that's it. There'll be no excep-
tions to this rule. I don't care if you're dying of dehydration. We do
things a little differently here; the government and private companies
have contracted us to perform manufacturing work for them. There
are also various other labour projects involving mining that we have
been contracted to do by the Corrections Department. For some of
the more fortunate souls amongst you, when you are not performing
these duties, you have been granted a relative amount of freedom to
move about certain areas of Skyline Outpost as you like. This is not
to be taken as an opportunity to do anything you want. Out here,
religion goes away, society goes away, decency goes away. Out here,
I'm the master of your destiny. Out here, I make the rules you hear;
you'll do well to remember that. It will make your time here much
more tolerable," he said with his strong American accent.

The way in which the prisoners lived was not what Ally had
expected. She saw that the housing there for some inmates was rather
unique and different. Instead of a conventional structure, most of
the people there were accommodated in large surplus military tents
that were shared. Many individuals were allocated to the same
tent. There were bunk beds and cots placed within; the only thing
between an inmate and the elements of the unforgiving desert was
the tent. She was issued a red jumpsuit, the prisoner uniform for
people on death row. While this was happening, the warden came
to meet her while she was in a holding area. He advised her not to
make a commotion. Her case might fade from memory, and there
was a chance she could escape execution. Ally was repulsed by the
man but heeded his advice.

But, because she was on death row, she was not being housed
outside. She was in one of the buildings with other inmates sentenced
to execution. Ally was now acclimating herself to her new reality. She
was not used to being told what to do and when to do it. She had

become very accustomed to setting her own schedule and doing as she pleased. The day would start at 4 a.m., when they were awoken by a loud siren that blared across the facility. There was no cafeteria in the death-row section. They were strictly prohibited from leaving their cell, outside of work conditions, so they were all fed in the cells. The other, less-serious offenders had the privilege of some communication with other humans. They were given an almost-inedible serving of porridge. Extremely unattractive, the thick, lumpy, indigestible sludge was heaped onto a tray. Ally choked it down regardless, because she needed the sustenance it provided.

After breakfast, the prisoners were taken to the facility's manufacturing plants. Here they made various items for the U.R.S.C., ranging from clothing to electronics to furniture, as well as uniforms and helmets for the military. The distances between the places were extensive, and they were forced to march there in the pre-dawn cold, stopping to perform exercises to ready them for the task. Ally would be so disoriented that her senses would lag behind, her eyes assaulted by a network of dots and shapes. From then on, the temperature would only grow more insufferable. Other prisoners would be forced into doing the mining work at one of the sites throughout the grounds. This was done on a rotating roster. They would work twelve hours, until six p.m., ceasing only briefly throughout the day for their water and food rations, so meagre that they couldn't support them for the strenuous work they undertook. It left them fatigued and broken.

In the death-row section, they were immediately taken back to their cells. They were forbidden from talking to other inmates and were blindfolded when they were escorted to prevent them from familiarising themselves with the building's layout. Unlike the day, by this time, the temperature was falling, and there seemed to be no escape from the nocturnal chills. They were given an evening meal consisting of bland, flavourless soup and often stale bread. Ally and Osiris would be so famished by the evening that they would eat the disgusting food with a raring enthusiasm.

The night sky around them was vast and starry, with no light pollution around to hide its indescribable beauty. It was the only thing that gave Ally any sort of hope or positivity. Looking from her cell window into its endless wonder and depth, she felt so miniscule, and she wondered what the rest of the country was doing. All of the different stories from the expansive nation, so many interactions and polar opposites, stories playing out while they were all stuck here, caged, so removed from everything. Ally refused to let this place break her spirit, even though she had been repeatedly beaten by the guards and was subject to the solitary confinement cells for misbehaviour, which were searing boxes at the far reaches of the camp. The temperature in there was so hot she would go delirious. She had been taken to the infirmary ward of the prison several times for severe dehydration and heatstroke. She would be hallucinating, and it would take a heavy toll on her body. Her vision was distorted and blurry; the colours were like an impressionist painting. Her mouth and throat were so dry, she could barely move her tongue. With severe headaches, she tried to limit her movement, as it caused nauseating attacks of dizziness. On some occasions, she was given an intravenous injection that delivered water, vitamins, and minerals to rehydrate her. It would take her many days to recover.

She tried to monitor her actions and limit any behaviours that would result in her being sent to the solitary confinement boxes, but she was sent there, anyway, for seemingly inconsistent reasons. She had done some of the same things she'd seen others do, and *they* hadn't received any punishment. There was no standard to the discipline and how the rules were enforced. It seemed like she was being punished for whatever they decided and when. They did this to breed animosity amongst the prisoners. If they saw others being treated differently, it would make them resentful. The idea was to distract the inmates' attention and focus it on rivalries and disputes, but mostly it had the opposite effect. The prisoners saw through this thinly veiled scheme and harboured resentment towards the facility and the system rather than the other enslaved individuals.

She didn't dream very often, but, when she did, they were morbid and malicious, with red and pink entrails oozing through the night, piles of rotting limbs, being chased, running through the endless desert plains of bodies, with people being mutilated or trying to murder her. She couldn't even get reprieve during sleep—which, in her previous lifestyle, had always been an escape for her. There was no escaping the desensitising horrors of this new life—even the minor escape and freedom of sleep was impossible in this soul-crushing place. This disturbed her immensely, making her mental state extremely fragile and dangerous. She could get absolutely no rest—in waking life *or* sleep! She feared for everything—nothing was sacred. Homicidal thoughts dominated her thought processes, and she could feel her mental stability beginning to disintegrate. Her sanity was so strained, her mind so unstable, under such stress, she thought she would snap and descend into madness—*like she was being deleted*! In her cell, she laughed hysterically at the thought.

Ally and Osiris were conforming to their new surroundings, adjusting to the new terms. They remained uninformed of anything that was happening outside of their new environment. The ever-present thought of their execution hung over them and plagued them with constant fear and worry—the *uncertainty* of it all was what dismayed them the most. They were in a state of limbo, unaware of what had been decided for their lives. They tried—without success—to turn it into a positive, by taking each extra day as another opportunity for their situation to change. But each new day was also a reminder that they were truly living on borrowed time.

But, so was everybody else. The coup had been the precursor to an uprising, and now they were facing the upheaval and anarchy caused by their trials and subsequent mistreatment. They knew there was a battle still to be fought, a war to be waged. They were being kept ignorant of the facts in the facility; there was no exposure to the outside world that wasn't carefully chosen or censored. The facility wanted to disengage them from that—it was another form of punishment. It felt bizarre to suddenly be cut off, severed from the world, and so quickly removed. People attempted to contact them. Ally knew she had not been discarded and forgotten about, consigned to the ash heap of history. What kept her strong was the people on the outside who would still continue to campaign for her, who were still thinking of her, strangers and companions alike.

On the outside, there were fears that the entire U.R.S.C. society was going to collapse; the new land-seizure laws were escalating the mayhem. It was like a catch-22: The U.R.S.C. wanted to reclaim land to pay for the country's mounting debt and damage, but, in order to do so, they had to increase the amount of fighting they undertook. Their enemies' strength and victories were mounting. From their perspective, the situation had already moved past the point of repairing the relationships. It had all the elements of another civil-war-in-the-making but wasn't being acknowledged as such. The sheer number of problems the government was trying to combat was proving to be their undoing; the rising tide of defiance was palpable. Senior ministers and those close to the president were reading the reports and advice they were getting; they were hoping to repair their relations with the population. But it was too late; the damage had been done.

CHAPTER TWENTY-FIVE

For many, the government had overstepped its boundaries and had blurred the lines between a democratic society and a totalitarian state. The biggest threat was from factions that had splintered off from the Naught-For Resistance. These new groups had taken deadly measures against all those who were deemed their enemies—anyone who had helped the regime or was complicit in its crimes became a target. However, assassination was disavowed by many other Resistance members who wanted a less-violent revolution. In turn, the government and law enforcement agencies fought the Resistance fiercely.

Konstantinos was going through a frustrating ordeal appealing Ally's sentence. Much of the focus had shifted to the storming of Palisades—one of the places spared, so far, from the escalating calamity. The highest institutions of democracy were being swarmed. The country's finances were being depleted, and resources were running out. Tariffs and embargos placed on the country were disruptive;

banks were defaulting; the currency was rapidly being devalued; the economy was spiralling out of control. Government departments were operating with skeleton staff; most were closed completely, leaving citizens without essential services such as refuse collection. All of this was having an impact globally and was hindering Konstantinos from starting Ally's appeal.

So, he decided to contact the Justice Department by telephone, but all of his calls would go unanswered. He felt he was getting nowhere. Finally, someone actually picked up his call.

"Hello. My name is Mihalis Konstantinos, registered barrister and owner of an independent firm. I'm calling regarding a client I'm representing who is currently incarcerated. I was enquiring as to whether you have received the lodgement for a sentencing appeal that I filed?"

After his identity had been confirmed, the conversation continued.

A female voice asked, "Could you please provide the inmate number for your client?"

"Certainly." He read Ally's inmate number, and she was identified in their system.

"I can assist you with that enquiry. Could you tell me what case number it was assigned in the court system?"

"It is pertaining to case number nine-zero-one-two-five. I want to ascertain the status of my appeal—whether it's been assessed yet or approved."

"I'll just have a look through our system . . . do you have the number that was assigned to the appeal when you lodged it?"

"Yes, I have it here." He read it to her. She entered the number and was silent for a moment while she looked through their system. "I apologise, sir, but we don't appear to have it in our system. I searched your appeal number, and I can't find anything."

"I don't understand why. Are you certain you got the number down correctly?"

"Yes, sir." She read it back to him, and it was correct.

"I lodged that appeal weeks ago. I filed it the day my client was sentenced. Can you check again, please?"

"I'm sorry, sir, but we're operating on minimal staffing capacity, and the cases we are currently processing are backlogged. I'm unable to do any further searching for your appeal application. You can lodge another application through the Department of Justice's Board of Appeals. Would you like me to connect you directly to them?"

"Yes, please," Konstantinos said, trying not to lose his temper at the woman, although he knew it was not her fault. He was placed on hold; the sound of Debussy's "Claire De Lune" came through the telephone receiver as he became more impatient. He got the impression they were deliberately prolonging the appeal to impede the case and Ally's chances for an alternative sentence or transfer. He filed another appeal, but he was told it could take months—even years—before it was processed.

Ally had been imprisoned now for twelve weeks without hearing anything from the outside world. With the vile conditions and inhumane treatment she had been suffering, it felt like much longer. She had enquired numerous times to the guards but was starting to become more agitated. She grew skilful in determining which guards would even listen to her and which guards could be manipulated.

"I have been here for three months without contact from anyone outside. I need to contact my barrister regarding the status of my case. You can't just completely shut us off from those we are trying to connect with. There are many matters in my case that I still need to attend to. I know I'm incarcerated, but I still have certain rights," she said to a guard.

"Any rights you had, you surrendered when you committed the acts that led you here."

"I was unjustly put here. Under normal conditions, I never would have been found guilty or imprisoned like this. I need to contact my barrister, who's working to remove me from here. There are people out there who have not forgotten about me. They will not go away despite your effort to keep us segregated."

"Any grievances or complaints about contact or visitation have to be taken up with the warden," was the usual response she received.

"That's the same response I always receive. Is there any way I can actually schedule an appointment with him?"

"I'm not sure. You would have to ask the warden," was the guard's snide response.

Konstantinos was also having difficulty establishing direct contact with Ally through the Executive Office and officials from Skyline Outpost. He was also sending her letters, and those just seemed to disappear. Engaging with people from the National Postal Service was of no use whatsoever.

At last, Ally was able to contact Konstantinos by telephone. Before the call was connected, a robotic-sounding female voice informed her that the call was being monitored by the Corrections Department, which made her nervous. Legal representatives were allowed to visit prisoners in Skyline Outpost, which she knew would be more discreet, though the journey was so long, it prevented most from attending. "Hello, Mihalis."

"Miss Rose, I'm so sorry about everything. I hope you are well, but I can't imagine the conditions there would allow for that. How are you doing?"

"It is terrible beyond description. I despise everything about it—the heat, the dehydration, the violence, the forced labour, the assaults from the staff. I need you to get me out of here, Mihalis. We have to be careful about what we say, but how is the appeal process for a lighter sentence going?"

Konstantinos exhaled slowly, reluctant to tell her.

"I can already tell it's not going to be good," she added before he spoke.

"I'm going to be honest with you, Miss Rose. It isn't going too well. It appears they're trying to obstruct us and slow everything down to keep it in their favour. Apparently, they couldn't find our original appeal and couldn't process it. So I had to lodge another one, which is going to draw out our struggle. I'm sorry to say it could take months or years to process, due to all the unrest around the country. We've become victims of our own notoriety."

This made Ally feel so deflated, so powerless and insignificant. "I'm trying not to allow the words you just spoke to break my spirit. I'm not losing hope. Do you have *any* good news for me at all about the application for transfer? You have to get me out of here, Mihalis. I don't want to leave here in a box. I won't last until my execution."

"The transfer seems to be much more likely, given our situation. I'm organising to, hopefully, get you relocated to a facility much closer to here, without the desert temperatures and rugged conditions. It's still high security, but it should be much better for you and our plea. If you get moved closer, I can have more direct contact, and we can work at full capacity on getting you released without interruption or diversion. While you're confined out there, we're forced to rely on the government to be the conduit for our communication. We don't have the best chance possible to beat this—hence, my already limited powers are reduced even further. That's why they want you out of the equation. Please don't think I have just forgotten about you or that I haven't tried. I've been trying to keep you updated about everything my colleagues and I have been doing for you through letters. But they keep mysteriously and conveniently vanishing in transit. Just like the appeal, there is such a backlog of cases; most governmental departments are understaffed—they're even reducing their services to save money. We've been inadvertently hampered by what we set in motion—the rioting that this case started. Still, I believe that the prospect of a transfer could be possible. I don't want to say anything definite and give you false hope. I'm merely saying . . ."

"I understand. Thank you, Mihalis; that alleviates a bit of the stress and worry that I was experiencing. What about a retrial? Have you heard anything about that?"

"Because you're incarcerated, I don't expect you to have heard anything, but it's getting more dire out here. It's deteriorating; there are widespread food shortages, water scarcity, power outages, massive economic loss. Thousands are dead. With the way things are going, a retrial is not an option—it's out of the question. Besides, you could get a similar sentence if they bring new indictments against you. Ally, unless you want to go through all of that stress and anxiety again and have your life dredged up for the nation to see, it is much better if we pursue trying to get your sentence reduced or you transferred somewhere less oppressive. You're a strong woman, Miss Rose. We will get through this."

"I don't really want to ask, but have you heard anything about the execution? Any details whatsoever?"

"I haven't been given a date or anything. Prisoners usually have a long time to lodge plea hearings before they're put to death. There's no way to determine how long a particular person will spend on death row, but it's usually a substantial period of time."

"What if it's all for naught? Do we still have other alternatives?" Remembering they were being monitored, Mihalis knew what Ally was suggesting without her saying it.

"I think we should be all right. It won't be for naught; if these options fail, I'm ensuring that there are contingency plans in place." With that, Ally had confirmation from the outside that Konstantinos was still working toward making a deal by any means necessary.

"Thank you, Mihalis. That makes me feel a little less despondent about this new reality I've become enslaved to, but, hopefully, with your help, it won't last for much longer. I'm not sure when I'll be able to speak to you again."

"Hang in there, Miss Rose. We're doing everything we can to get you released. Farewell."

"Farewell. Thank you for everything you've done."

Konstantinos still had no clarity or answers. The mystery surrounding her only grew. He turned to the media to keep public awareness centred around the mistrial and getting justice. He appeared on a string of televised interviews, speaking on news programmes with journalists who had large viewing audiences. He said he'd been receiving warnings to back away from the media spotlight and not publicise the matter so doggedly. He ignored these warnings and continued to keep attention focused and debate raging. He was drawing the ire of many. He appeared to be inciting those in the country with a predisposition toward violence, provoking them into unlawful actions, which was seen as very undesirable.

To the government, Konstantinos was becoming a problem.

The correspondence between Konstantinos and Ally became very limited. When they could reach each other, Konstantinos relayed what Ally was telling him about the conditions, revealing it to the outside world. They were shocked and dismayed to learn the truth about the deplorable conditions at Skyline Outpost and similar institutions. Konstantinos' persistent focus on this issue revealed the country's dark side. He appeared at protests and spoke at rallies, gathering large crowds and gaining support from people harbouring the same passion as his ideas and his words, infusing them with energy and strengthening their determination. The country had advocated and sanctioned other nations who had done exactly what they were doing. Thus, their hypocrisy was now out in the open.

There was no repairing the cracks that had formed within the current leadership. The more-fanatical groups within the Resistance began to launch large-scale attacks, which were seen largely as unnecessary and disturbing. Groups of terrorists were initiating long sieges, negotiating over hostages and rights. Groups from the Townships came into larger cities and sieged commercial establishments, government buildings, and theatres. This unorthodox behavior alienated many people who had been part of the Resistance from the beginning. A statement was issued refusing to give in to any terrorist demands, and, so, the people were stuck in an unenviable stalemate. Most of the sieges ended in bloodshed and huge casualties. No place seemed safe from the possibility of attack; it forced more struggling businesses and institutions to close. The U.R.S.C. was not going forwards or backwards—it was cannibalising itself. Hordes of people tried to flee the place once heralded as a paradise that had morphed into something irretrievable.

The true nature of places like Skyline Outpost had been hidden, and their practices had long since been outlawed. Now, reports of slavery and forced labour were worrying the public. Many people were fearful of what would happen; the government kept their actions shrouded in uncertainty. Among the people, the general consensus was that, if it were possible to be taken to a labour camp, then *anything* was possible. In the government-sanctioned media, many pundits denounced Konstantinos as a liberal demagogue—a traitor and terrorist sympathiser who was causing anarchy, dismantling the nation he hated, aiding and abetting enemies of the nation.

The work that prisoners were forced to undertake around the Skyline Outpost was tiring and arduous, and filled with safety violations. The factory buildings where they manufactured items were not maintained, and there were hazards and harmful substances. Accidents and deaths were commonplace. The majority of the murders that took place in those buildings were ruled to be accidents. It was the perfect way to cover up the act. They worked in a dangerous industrial setting, for which they were unqualified. They'd received minimal training and were clearly out of their depth. Ally regularly saw other women lose their arms feeding sheet metal into large presses. She'd had close encounters herself; one time, her sleeve was almost caught on a machine she was using.

They were forced to sift through debris from opal and gold mines, and the machines were treacherous and woefully outdated. The prisoners were rigorously searched every hour just in case they'd tried to keep some gemstones or minerals for themselves. They didn't have proper ventilation equipment, and the environment was contaminated. Outside, it was an effort to breathe. The inescapable dust was blinding and would sting. Ally had to cover her face with a cloth, but others didn't have that luxury. They were given only a scarce amount of water for their dusty mouths. Shade, protective clothing, and accessories were minimal. It seemed like they were on another planet, marooned, with no hope of rescue.

The areas they were working in had no fences or towers and only very few guards. Often, Ally had the urge to run, to escape into the desert, but she knew she wouldn't get far. Sometimes she thought about running out there and succumbing to the elements, but she was too fatigued. There were regular beatings from the guards, who were unsympathetic to the prisoners' plight and eager to hand out punishments.

She would end the day absolutely exhausted; her lips were cracked; her skin was blistered and scorched, making it uncomfortable even to rest. The ceaseless sleep deprivation, thirst, undernourishment, danger, and discomfort were making her psychotic. She became numb in order to cope—robotic and unfeeling, an inhuman shadow of who she was, all the while trying to keep her frayed mind from snapping. This perpetual mental battle raged for nineteen months, though she had little perception of how much time had passed. Everything was homogenous and blended together; Ally had struggled every minute, and it had seemed torturously longer. She worried she may not live to see her release from this trauma, no longer believing it would happen. Death was better than this; suicide became a more freeing alternative, which is exactly what her captors wanted to happen. The suicide rate there was disturbingly high. The lifestyle there was unbearable, including unforgettable acts of violence, gory murders, sexual assaults, and stabbings. Prisoners would mutilate themselves in protest of the conditions at the prison—especially fatal accidents and suicides with machinery. Ally was traumatised by the brutality and sheer number of things she saw; she saw them even when she closed her eyes.

Osiris was having an equally traumatic experience, compounded by the agonising lack of correspondence between him and his legal team. The thought of his execution and the uncertainty around the date were making it impossible for him to rest; it was taking over every aspect of his life. He felt forgotten and was desperate for interaction with those who had overseen his case and for some resolution to this whole ordeal that had come in and altered his and Ally's lives like a massive swing of The Pendulum, resetting everything. If Ally's philosophy was right, and if they had hope and surrendered a bit of control, then the universe would balance itself out, and the right sequence of events would unfold at the appropriate time, like some pervasive plan that crosses in and out of life. At other times, however, he would feel the complete opposite—nihilistic and defeated. Like Ally, he was trying not to let Skyline Outpost and reality get the better of him and crush his spirit, but it was a difficult attitude to maintain.

CHAPTER TWENTY-SIX

The people of Delphi Township were having a disastrous time in the wake of the ruling in favour of the government. They wanted to move in and finalise the eviction of the people, their relocation, and the dismantling of the slums and decrepit housing. Due to their campaign against the regime, there was already a large military presence in the area. Certain citizens were going to fight before leaving, and they were being sent weapons and ammunition in support. The military could be seen on the sweeping plains around them, hovering in the distance. While the appeals were being heard in the nation's capital, there was a stalemate. The military could do nothing while the matter was still being contested in court. They were still unwelcome; the soldiers symbolised the end of their home, their way of life—their very existence.

When morning patrols found soldiers mutilated, burned, or placed on stakes, it escalated the conflict. In retaliation, soldiers shot several young male protestors who were peacefully displaying banners and messages near the defensive perimeter established outside the Township. When they shot and mutilated the bodies of the unarmed young protestors, it made news across the country. Their deaths were caught on camera, and it was seen as a disgrace—the military exerting such force over unarmed young people who were still only children. This type of behaviour was not going to be tolerated by the public; many people didn't want to live in a nation that acted so barbarically. If they could turn weapons on people so young, then any one of them could be a target.

Portia had been trying to leave the Township. She had helped them all she could. She was trying to make it back to Italy, to anywhere outside of this imploding country that felt like a failed experiment. She no longer knew how to handle this. She knew there would be consequences for attacking the mines and seizing them from those in command, but she thought they would be protected by the land rights. She had no idea the government would pass a new land-reclamation law; it caught them all by surprise how they had disregarded the previous laws and rulings so brazenly to fulfill their agenda. She had attempted to leave on more than one occasion. The security around the area was too extensive, and her efforts angered many people on the Council and other important citizens. They accused her of leaving them when they needed her—she was departing at the worst possible time. They believed her duty to them was not over. She had assisted with the trial, but this was not sufficient; the legal battle had caused a myriad of new problems more dire than they had feared. She argued that she couldn't have foreseen this happening. There wasn't anything they could do out there in the Townships, and any victory for them would have to come from the capital. Out there, all they could do was defend, as opposed to the city, where they could attack.

She had heard that Europe was experiencing a resurgence of crisis and an elevated sense of chaos—sweeping disease, terrorism, environmental disasters, economic ruin, and conflicts across the continent. She came to a realisation that, perhaps, she was being selfish and unfair towards the people; she herself had set a lot of this in motion. To run away now because of the mounting chaos would be a cowardly act, she told herself. Besides, if she returned home to Europe, she would face the same adversities. So she caved in to others' pleas for her to stay and be accountable for what she had done and chose to fight the battle that she was familiar with.

Everyone in the Township was receiving a daily ration of rice and water. There were extensive lines and much fighting over access; everyone had been reduced to a dependent in a growing line, no matter their status in the community. There were some who tried to bribe others, but money and jewels were useless to those dying from starvation. The people realised they had to cooperate and pull together—that this was what the military and others wanted: the people's attention diverted onto surviving or fighting between themselves. The rest of the country's populace was on their side. People tried donating food, but much of it was seized by the army; there were air drops of food, water, and medicine over the town that salvaged them from the breaking point and surrendering. The besieged town was surrounded, in the government's hopes they could starve them into submission. But, a similar problem was encountered by the military, who couldn't be properly re-equipped, as supplies of important resources were diminishing and being stretched so thinly. This tactic backfiring signalled that *everyone* was being deprived.

Konstantinos had been invited to speak at a rally in Palisade, in the enormous Capital Square. The centre of the city's scenic, orderly political district was normally filled with tourists and the country's most important decision-makers. He was on the stage that had been erected in Liberty Park, an historically significant place that saw a record turnout of people. There were so many people that they poured out onto the main Avenue of Palisade, which estimates now put at more than 200,000, compacted shoulder to shoulder. There were so many bright-eyed young people with their future in their hands chanting for change. Konstantinos, who was beginning to be seen as a hero of the Resistance, was giving a rousing speech. Extensive marches through the streets took place with an emphasis on non-violent activity, though armed groups supporting both sides were present—and becoming more unsettled and edgy. There was a growing sensation, a fear, that tensions would inevitably turn into disaster. Humidity appeared to be aggravating tensions, the air palpable with the emotion of a crowd so anguished. Any short periods of peace were fragile.

Spread out all around them were the façades, domes, and towering marble columns of government buildings, including Palisade Lodge, containing the president's office and living quarters. It was overly extravagant, the perfect backdrop to remind the crowd—who were responding raucously to Konstantinos' speech—what was at stake. He had spent a great deal of time preparing, wanting to strike the right balance. He knew sections would be taken out of context by his detractors; they would say he was the instigator of insurrection against the regime. The stage was guarded by a large, private-security presence which Konstantinos had hired now that he was so prevalent of a personality.

He addressed this in the speech; he said he straddled the line between celebrity and campaigner for rights but not out of vanity. He did not enjoy the fame he had received and saw himself as a legal professional rather than a public figure. If it was necessary to get the message out to people who, like those in the crowd, were conscious of such issues, then he would make that transition. He largely condemned the non-peaceful practices that had been adopted. He wanted to deter people away from that trap.

There were television cameras focused on him, filming his highly anticipated speech, archiving the moments in this period of historic significance, so that others in the future could admire and connect to these pivotal moments in the new nation's history. While he was talking, he looked around the scene, alive with people and energy, the ardent faces in the crowd so enthusiastic about what was going on around them and passionately listening to his words.

He was the keynote speaker at the event. A number of organisers and activists spoke before him, and they shared stories of experiences from regular people who had been struck down under the might of the U.R.S.C. in this unforgettable period of time they were stumbling through. He was aware, while he was talking, of the security presence, which were interspersed throughout the spacious park and surrounds, keeping order throughout the crowd. Helicopters sliced through the air; military personnel, crowd-control vehicles, and fencing were placed throughout to separate the rival groups. There was shouting between them and items being thrown, and it deteriorated from there. Konstantinos could sense and see the hostilities growing in the crowds, but the mood had shifted entirely. He would stop his speech to plead with the crowd for calm. It was a delicate situation that he was trying to keep civilised.

He concluded to huge applause and cheers; he had passionately captured their struggle through his words. After thanking the crowd, he stepped away from the microphone and lectern to be led away by his security. He was walking across the stage waving as a man manoeuvred his way through the throng of people, his gaze set on Konstantinos as he moved aggressively to the front of the crowd. He pulled a revolver from his waistband and took aim. Konstantinos saw the muzzle flashes; he heard the sounds and confusion. It had happened quickly and unexpectedly; in bewilderment, he was on his back, bleeding, in a semi-conscious state of pain and shock. Gasping as everything around him faded and warped, he felt the afternoon sun on his face weakening. He blinked; the sky seemed to be blurring and seeping. He closed his eyes; all his senses were diminishing.

Before he was shot, the conclusion of his speech was about peace, love, and harmony. The gunman, trying to flee the park in the panic, was immediately swarmed by a mass of people and detained. Konstantinos' security entourage pinned him down. A total of five bullets had pierced his body in his torso area, and the people around him were frenetically seeking medical assistance and talking to him, hoping to comfort him, but it was not registering. He never responded to their calls. Everywhere around the park, people rushed for safety. Capital Square had turned into a shooting gallery, the sound of gunfire erupting through the air.

Paramedics who were on the scene made their way through the dispersing crowd. They immediately began treating Konstantinos while he was being rushed to hospital, in and out of consciousness. He would see hazy flashes of the ambulance interior and the paramedics standing over him with blood-stained gloves, but, to his ear, the sounds were muffled and felt distant. Their frantic journey was being interrupted by protestors and blockades on the road. The hospitals in the city and around the country were at a breaking point—they had been inundated with casualties and were struggling to cope. Emergency rooms were filling with casualties from the fighting.

The Palisade-Guardian hospital was already overcrowded, with patients in the corridors, their screams and crying echoing hauntingly as he was transferred from the ambulance and taken inside. His condition had worsened in the ambulance, and now, they were working to stop his massive blood loss, feverishly rushing to get him into surgery. The hospital was one of many that had been handed a mass allotment of casualties from the Liberty Park shootout, and a surging influx of injured patients overwhelmed it. He was operated on immediately by surgeons, who worked incredibly hard to save his life, but he had lost too much blood. He was pronounced dead on the operating table before they rushed in the next ballistic trauma patient; the line of wounded people extended down the hall, dying while they waited.

The news of his death spread fast, and it shocked many in the nation. His assassination was one of many killings that had been caught on camera in the U.R.S.C., and footage of it was shown across the country, to the horror of many who thought it was insensitive and disrespectful to show so scandalously. Konstantinos had somehow sensed his assassination was coming, and that, when it did, it would cause huge controversy. A massive outpouring of grief accompanied his passing. There was an enormous candlelight vigil, and floral tributes were placed in the park where he was murdered, which became the "official" site for mourning. He was another victim, another affront in the long list the government had compiled. There was a large public funeral service held in his honour, which was attended by hundreds of thousands who marched in the streets. As had been anticipated, it turned into a volatile affair; savage clashes between groups who supported or opposed him and law enforcement seemed unavoidable.

Many questions began to be asked about the gunman, a seemingly rogue assassin who harboured a hatred for Konstantinos and what he represented, and wanted to murder him to gain notoriety. Little was known about him; apparently, he was an unhinged loner who was being watched by law enforcement agencies, yet he appeared to be more of a puppet, like a Manchurian candidate. In interviews following his arrest, he had little memory of the assassination and appeared confused. There were a lot of people speculating it was a deliberate act by the government to remove the irritating presence of a man who had been so prevalent in the spotlight. Despite the fact they were part of the plot, the regime maintained publicly that they couldn't confirm or deny anything to do with Konstantinos' death.

It was a significant amount of time after he had died and his funeral service when Ally finally received the word about the grim development. She had been imprisoned now for more than three years; another barrister who worked in the law firm contacted Ally to tell her.

She had been patiently waiting for contact from Konstantinos, which had become very sporadic, an ongoing problem. Ally felt the chances of getting out of there were becoming weaker as time passed. She had ceased thinking about the outside world, and Skyline Outpost had become her universe. She received a telephone call; she was expecting it to be Konstantinos, but she heard a different person's voice—a man she recognised as one of the people on her legal counsel. She sensed something was amiss even before asking what was happening. He informed her of the depressing news, and Ally stared straight ahead, unprepared for the stunning surprise.

A suite of thoughts flashed through her mind. She processed the news as quickly as she was able, but all it did was throw everything into a tangle of uncertainty. If he was deceased, it meant Ally was alone now and that she had nobody on the outside who was crusading for her rights and for her release. He had kept her image, her plight, in the hearts and minds of the people. He'd kept the attention on it all, campaigning on behalf of someone who had become invisible. Now that he was not there to help her, she believed it was inevitable that she would be relegated to this fate, this inhumane imprisonment.

The caller told Ally that they would be continuing Konstantinos' work to free her and fix the justice system; Konstantinos, the caller said, had left extensive instructions to follow in the event of his death. They were being carried out by his team, but Ally was doubtful. They didn't have the same conviction, status, or connections that Kostantinos did, amassing a collection of allies within the country and its domains. Over his accomplished career, an aura of distinction and prestige had formed around him, a paragon of stature and repute. He could circumvent their rules to gain what he wanted—the type of reputation Ally thought they couldn't live up to. She was fearful that nobody would be able to free or transfer her away from the barbaric desert labour camp. It occurred to her that Agent Blaze was now one of the only people who could help her, but Konstaninos had been her link on the outside to him. All of the letters she had been writing and sending out to different addresses were not arriving, and the prisoners' ability to use the telephone was tightly monitored and restricted.

She gave the first directive she wanted the team to carry out: She asked them to establish contact with Agent Blaze to restart negotiations about a plea deal. She had to be careful what she was saying; she didn't want to divulge too much to those who were listening. The appeals process had largely broken down. Konstantinos had been struggling through hearings and had exhausted almost all avenues, though, from what he had told her, it was a deliberate effort to stop the appeal from going through. As before, she was left to wait and suffer in the horrid conditions to which she had been forsaken.

Skyline Outpost had changed since she'd arrived, and the terms of their imprisonment had changed. The situation across the country and its effects had found their way to a place so detached. They were kept in constant fear; the shortage of resources meant that minimal rations could be allocated to the prison system. The prisoners at Skyline Outpost were amongst the country's three million detainees and prisoners to feed, and the rations were being quickly depleted. As much as possible was diverted away from the prison system to fix the massive deficits across the U.R.S.C. It had wreaked havoc with the staffing; the number of guards and other contracted workers in the prison had been reduced due to funding cutbacks. Now redundant, they went on strike and left Skyline Outpost.

CHAPTER TWENTY-SEVEN

Those who remained were in a deepening crisis. There was the possibility they would be completely cut off from the world—stranded out there and left to die. The crucial deliveries of supplies were becoming less frequent, sometimes not arriving at all, putting more pressure on everyone. The morale there had fallen even further, and conflict erupted over the access to food and water. A murderous competition for survival began. The guards had largely stopped enforcing the rules, and they no longer cared about performing their standard duties, meaning the prisoners were running rampant and enforcing order among themselves—it had become pandemonium. The warden made an appearance and told them they would no longer be housed inside. A huge reduction in the vital supplies they were receiving meant it was becoming too expensive and inefficient to keep them there. The warden told them that the facility was using far too many utilities and that they had to adapt to the exceptional set of circumstances and make sacrifices—which was little comfort to them.

He made another announcement that executions there would also be temporarily suspended, which made Ally and the others relieved; it didn't ease their minds completely, as the inevitability of execution still plagued them. Ally had not received a date for her impending demise, and the fatigue of waiting had made her depressed and neurotic. With the knowledge that they were temporarily safe from execution for the foreseeable future, the people on death row were moved out into the general population. With the need to conserve what little they were now given, the forced manual labour could no longer continue at the Outpost, which consumed the majority of the prison's overall energy and water usage.

The people on death row were taken out of the building. Ally was dreading being moved outside and being made susceptible to the elements. She was shown to the designated tent, which she would be sharing with thirty other women, some of whom were in the tent when she arrived. Others were off somewhere in the vast expanse of space they had to move around in. There were rows of the tents set up spaciously and dispersed over the site. It was unbearably hot within the tent, and the shade it provided was little respite. A few of the women came and introduced themselves to Ally. "I would ask how the fuck you ended up here, but we already know—we've been following your case, and we heard they treated you like shit, so you're a hero here and an inspiration to us."

"I don't know why I'm being celebrated; I was just unlucky enough to be a victim they made an example of. I'm nothing special. I know you have many questions, which I'll answer, but, first, I need to rest," she replied.

Ally was assigned a bed which was unsuitable for a woman of her height. It was uncomfortable, and her legs dangled off the end. She immediately became a product of the environment and confronted one of the other women in the tent. "I'm trading beds with you," Ally said. When the woman protested, Ally viciously assaulted her and took her bunk bed while she bled on the ground, lying unconscious while the others went about their business. Nothing happened to Ally for the assault.

Out there, the primal instinct to survive overtook them. Ally had lost a lot of weight from malnourishment. It had left her weakened and more vulnerable. A woman tried to assault her with a sharpened piece of metal and steal her rations. Ally struggled with the woman; she wrenched the piece of metal from the woman's hand and repeatedly plunged it deep into her neck. The woman gurgled as long streams of blood squirted onto the dust; it even came from her eyes. She fell to the ground and writhed around with her mouth wide open, gasping and choking until the life left her body. There was little reaction to her death, and Ally faced no consequences. There were no guards watching them at the time. Under standard protocol, Ally would be indicted for that murder and appear before a disciplinary tribunal within the Outpost to receive additional sentencing. Since she had been sentenced to execution, there were few additional punishments to impose upon her. Some of the prisoners went through the pockets of the dead woman's bloodied jumpsuit, and her body stayed there for three more days, decaying in the desert sun, before someone moved it.

The bodies of the dead were burned in pits on the outskirts of the Outpost. There was a morgue building, but it had been closed. It seemed there were fires burning nonstop now. Ally had not been told the exact number of prisoners held there, but she had heard that, with the males and females combined, there were 2,000, and that number seemed to be plummeting. The ration line was where the most incidents began, and they would turn into large-scale brawls with weapons. Ally avoided them when she could but was unwillingly drawn into them; she had to be careful. There were some harrowing injuries being inflicted, and, without the infirmary working at full capacity, people were going untreated and dying of their wounds.

The men's section was also brutal, a machismo world with a complex hierarchy that thrived on violence, respect, and status. Osiris had affirmed his position as a higher competitor in the hierarchy; he had been in numerous altercations and fights when people tried disrespecting or taking from him. His criminal notoriety had made him well respected. He couldn't show any weakness. Everything happening to him was causing him to fall apart. He could recognise he was transforming into the violent version of himself, one that he strived to deny but could sense it lurking under the surface. It was a requirement of this new atmosphere. It was like he'd been broken by the system—these walls and the inhumane treatment that had become his daily routine.

At first, the ceasing of work had been a joy to the prisoners. But the compounding of unseen problems and the effects of problems far away had caused them to become more inflamed. They were all being further disadvantaged from a situation they were being told nothing about and had no voice in. Their complaints were dismissed, as everyone in the nation was suffering. Deaths from starvation and drinking contaminated water were widespread, and there were reports about people on the outside resorting to cannibalism to survive and the military using chemical weapons to clear out civilians.

In complete opposition to the daytime, the temperature at night was bitterly cold, and they could do nothing but shiver in their tents, with very sparse extra clothing and bedding provided. In the starlight, Ally would find a secluded spot to look up at the sky. She would contemplate everything—how her life had changed forever in a matter of days. She couldn't stop going over the events in her mind, constantly replaying them. She lamented incessantly over what she had suffered, even though, she regretfully reminded herself, it was all a result of her own heinous conduct.

Before his death, Konstantinos had been in a contentious dispute with Agent Blaze. They'd been fighting since the trial had concluded over the dissemination of files containing the truth of what happened during the proceedings. They wanted to release what they respectively had but were in a predicament. Both knew the truth could ruin them, so they were stuck in a mutually undesirable standoff. They'd had many secret meetings about how they could help each other go undetected and both get what they needed, without being discovered and the ensuing consequences. Now that Konstantinos had been removed from the equation, Agent Blaze thought that he could seize everything he wanted for himself without having to mediate with an adversary. What he hadn't expected was for Konstantinos to leave the intelligence he had amassed, with detailed instructions for his team to carry on his work. They had all of the files, and there were even more files coming from hackers in the Resistance who suggested Agent Blaze and others from the Prosecution were involved in Konstantinos' death, which they wanted to avenge.

Other barristers from the team continued interacting and meeting with Agent Blaze to further their efforts to help Ally. The appeals had been denied or blocked; Agent Blaze had been one of the figures ensuring that the appeal process was being unnecessarily extended. Ally's legal team had extensive meetings with him, discussing how they needed his compliance in helping Ally—or else, they would release what they had and ruin his life. He wanted to help her, but for his own selfish reasons, she had become the unwanted obstacle in his path. Without saying it, he needed her out of the way before he could continue his plans.

The hackers in the Resistance had been escalating their actions in the fight against the government, and, like others in the Resistance, they were frustrated. It had now been four years since the Coup Trials; and nothing had changed. The government had made promises and targets they vowed to reach, yet had not achieved any of them. The government had lied to ease the pressure, and there was a brief period when the chaos around the country looked like it was going to stop, which is what the citizens of the republic wanted. But, they, too, were unwilling to be part of a prolonged campaign for rights that were indispensable to them and future generations. The Resistance were resorting to more radical options to dismantle the current government, but president Saige Rico appeared to be impossible to depose. He had a lot of enemies in the political sphere who were competing against him for leadership of the country, but he'd poisoned or assassinated the majority of them.

The Rico dictatorship was facing an election and were trying everything and anything to push it back as long as they could; it seemed they knew their defeat was certain. Resistance hackers had been publishing revealing intelligence about politicians and the massive taxpayer-funded expenditures, including the real statistics that the government had changed, revealing the vulgar depths of their deception. There was talk in the international community about doing something to curtail the rogue state and stop their crimes against the civilian population.

A document was printed with parts redacted, showing how the regime had resorted to using chlorine and saran gas on protestors who had seized cities. The administration denied this; a government spokesperson said it was untrue and that they had never used chemical weapons or nerve gases. The outrage that followed was universal. Now that their atrocities had caught the attention of the international community, tariffs and sanctions were placed on the goods that they exported, another critical blow to the country and its struggling finances. Emerging candidates rallied in the support from the people, promising to replace the regime that had turned so corrupt. These candidates wanted to make a revolution through peaceful ways and end the destruction of the country, by legitimately invoking a new era of the country's governance. This idea and the candidates were largely embraced, as people had become desensitised from the violence; they knew these events would take many arduous years to recover from. They were used to dealing with misery and dauntingly long periods of uncertainty. For some, the scars would never heal.

It seemed nothing the hackers did was working, until a few of them began to formulate a plan that they thought would be the end—a blow from which the regime couldn't recover, and they would be forced to give in to their demands and step down. They developed a bold, last-resort plan for a cyber-attack to take control of the country's power grid, water supplies, fuel reserves, financial institutions, and defence systems, stealing secrets and holding the country ransom. It would be impossible for the government to continue if all of these assets were taken from them.

It started in the early hours of the morning. People working across the U.R.S.C. in all different sectors—as well as the military's intelligence sector—noticed alarming anomalies. Locations around the country desperately tried to contact the Military and Defence headquarters or the Presidential Office in Palisades, and, conversely, the personnel in those sectors tried to contact them—but all of their communication systems were down. They fell back on their emergency networks, which utilised various frequencies to still send encrypted messages and intelligence without interference, but, without the exchange, they would be helpless. It was vital for the regime to stay informed and able to relay messages, orders, and updates from Palisades to different cities and bases around the country. The military and its defence installations went into a state of panic: The U.R.S.C. was under assault, but they didn't know from whom.

In a huge coordinated attack, the Resistance's cyberterrorists, from different parts of the country, simultaneously hacked into different organisations and entities. They seized control of the national power grid which meant they had hijacked every important infrastructure network. Every major road network, government building, shipping port, airport, train station, and freight route had been shut down, rendered useless.

The country could no longer send or receive supplies domestically or internationally without the Resistance's authorisation. They gained access to spy- and intelligence-agency databases and stole classified secrets to hold for ransom. They released the names of every undercover government spy in the U.R.S.C., causing some to have their cover blown and then be assassinated. They took over certain nationally owned computer and broadcasting networks so that they could play propaganda and classified footage on repeat—footage the government wanted suppressed, which showed military aircraft opening fire on civilians, to footage taken by health workers in hospitals of the aftermath of chemical-weapon attacks. Many citizens were unaware of the existence of secrets like these, and they were incredulous to discover that this regime was like the ones in other countries it publicly disavowed and even interfered with. Now it was being played on repeat for everyone to see.

Masked Resistance figures would appear on camera and read sinister messages taking responsibility for the cyberattacks, listing their demands, and explaining why they had been forced to do something so ambitious. They were very unpopular to many; the Resistance knew that, if this failed, then almost everyone in the country faced certain death. They took to defending their decisions and were not going to back down or give in to pressure. They were realistic, too, fearful that the government wouldn't back down, either.

They shut off all the electricity to Palisades and plunged much of the country into darkness. The Resistance had control over everything people needed in order to live. They prioritised the delivery of food and water to the Townships, refugee camps, and remote communities, where, in some places, eighty percent of the population had died.

Saige Rico and his advisers could do nothing. Relying on their emergency-power generators and their emergency networks, they used their own analysts and hackers to fight back. They had lost control of their ludicrously expensive supercomputer defence system, used to gather data from the military and agencies to engage security threats around the U.R.S.C., which they madly tried to reclaim. They won back the majority of control over the defence grid, but it was a struggle to keep it from fully falling to the Resistance. An embargo on fuel meant the transport industry had stopped entirely; vehicles were left stuck, unable to deliver their essential service. The number of analysts, technicians, and resources the government could use was dwindling; law enforcement could do nothing. The modern world they had constructed was so fragile that all the analysts could do was scramble to regain whatever they could of the U.R.S.C.

A mere fifty hours after the attack had begun, the government were already on the brink of total annihilation. They couldn't reclaim everything that had been taken from them. They utilised the emergency network to dispatch military aircraft, launching airstrikes on known Resistance locations, killing a small fraction of its members, but they were unable to locate the others, who had mostly fled underground. Their lifeline was the emergency communication networks, a last-resort defence mechanism, without which they could never recover from these attacks.

Saige Rico and the military's top advisers and most trusted people were coming under increasing pressure to reach an agreement with the Resistance. Initially, they had denied that the situation was critical. They insisted that they were not going to give in to terrorist demands, but as time progressed, the attacks grew and morphed, like a living entity. They couldn't avoid engaging with them to end it. A fleet of ships were stuck just off the coast, unable to unload their cargo and restock the whole country's completely empty stores. The farming produce that was available couldn't be transported. The struggling farmers were on the brink of ruin; most of the farm goods had been stolen by thieves who were starving, determined to get sustenance at any cost.

Murder and conflict were inescapable. Scenes of humanity's evil side were on display for all, the cities thrown back into the Dark Ages. The only illumination came from the fires they started, and from the old regime burning down. Everything had halted now; the people had wanted to stop the world—and they had. The administration tried everything to resolve the attack without actually having to be punished for what they had done, but time was running out. Teams of people were working on it. They had been given an ultimatum by the Resistance that said if they didn't step down from their political roles in office and face punishment for their crimes, the attacks would continue. If they failed to make, at least, some attempt at mediation before the attack's one hundredth hour, they would continue for another one hundred hours and shut off all of the major dams.

But The Pendulum would still, again, and finally, rule the day.

The Resistance started experiencing the full gamut of the citizens' rage and hatred. All of these cyberwar tactics had caused so many unnecessary deaths. The tide of death had risen steeply since the start of the cyber meltdown. These hackers had shown themselves to be the unlikely architects of the country's disintegration. People were torn, declaring the Resistance attack as the final nail in the coffin of the U.R.S.C. It was a plan too bold, too ambitious, to succeed. The idea to use the people as pawns was one destined for failure. The Resistance had become subverted and had disturbing similarities to the enemy they were labouring to eradicate. The citizens wanted the government out, but not by embarking on a mission to bring wholesale cataclysm to the nation.

The standoff had entered its ninety-sixth hour. In Saige Rico's political bunker beneath the Palisade House of Government, there was a rush of activity. Analysts were on computers, using the emergency frequencies to communicate with others around the country. Telephones were all ringing simultaneously, and people ran around, stepping past each other in the crowded walkways. There was great difficulty hearing over all the yelling; people tried to talk over one another and give constant updates, which blended together discordantly. Everyone there— members of the party, the top-ranking officials, defence personnel, and expert analysts—were pleading with Saige Rico and his entourage to give in to the demands and accept that they had lost. The most trusted allies within his entourage began mirroring the same sentiment. Saige Rico's advisers begged him to adopt the strategy that personnel at the Government Emergency Management System—GEMS—a body that dealt with imminent catastrophe to the whole country, were ready to relieve the party of their official duties and take over the emergency network, the handling of the attack, negotiations, and relaying messages to the Resistance. It appeared the endgame had arrived; the government was, essentially, conceding defeat. They could no longer fight when they were so disadvantaged. There were going to be only remnants left if they proceeded to march toward a mass suicide. There would be no U.R.S.C. to inherit; they would become the rulers and government of a corpse pile, nothing but an empty space.

CHAPTER TWENTY-EIGHT

At Skyline Outpost, the inmates were wondering why everything had stopped. They had no way of knowing about the Resistance's cyberattack offensive. They knew something major had happened; what little amount of electricity they had left to power the lights and their communication lifeline was now completely gone. There were fears and rumours going around that this was the end, that the U.R.S.C. outside the prison had collapsed. There were some reports from the guards, who had received word from the outside world. The Naught-For Resistance had committed a cyberattack, taking the whole country hostage. The prisoners were worried.

Many, including Ally, considered trying to escape. She sensed that their chances for success had dramatically improved. People tried hoarding enough rations to escape into the desert, as the guards were no longer concerned about the inmates. The inmates had been left to completely run free throughout the facility grounds; they could do whatever without repercussion or discipline. The guards had their own section of the prison, where their living quarters were located. It was an isolated area of the facility. They resorted to barricading themselves in the quarters behind the security fencing and were concerned only about ensuring their own safety and survival. They had taken to shooting any inmates who tried to break in or got too close.

There was a lot of talk that the guards were keeping food and water from the prisoners and giving them much less than they required. Many of the inmates wanted to storm the place for the weapons and ammunition. They went around trying to recruit people; they talked to Ally about being part of it. "That's a suicide mission," she responded. Most of the guards left them alone; the inmates weren't worried about them, either. Currently, other inmates were more likely to murder them. Although she didn't like it, Ally fought, stabbed, and assaulted people to get their meagre ration of water. They were given only four half-litre cups per day. She did whatever it took to get that clear elixir of life.

She knew it would be a considerable amount of time before she was ready to move on and accept everything that had happened. She knew that the responsibility lay with her. She accepted that, as she had made the choices, the conscious decisions to do what she did. She felt, however, that she was examining this issue with the clarity of hindsight. She knew a lot of people were planning to escape. She thought it may be better in a group of people—there would be more rations. She asked certain women about escaping and found them equally as torn—between whether to die here or in the desert. Some of them were talking about making their way to a mining camp, restocking what they could, and then making the pilgrimage to one of the Townships or even the Lawless Zone. Both of those destinations were at least 1,000 kilometres away.

Then a debate arose around the fact that they were probably going to die here anyway. They weren't sure about what they had been told by the guards, but they didn't fully believe them about the cyberattack, as some guards were known to be untrustworthy. Some people were convinced they were being lied to again and that the U.R.S.C. had collapsed, so it was inevitable that they would die out here. Some didn't want to wait for that and wanted to take their chances escaping.

In the early morning, before most of the others were awake, Ally and a group of other women broke into the administration offices in the main building of the facility. They were looking mainly for any valuable parts to use but were also going about causing random destruction. They had resorted to their ingenuity and craftsmanship to engineer smart solutions to get them out of this crisis. They had begun digging in parts of the prison for water and were constructing makeshift machines to cook, fixing electronics, crafting deadly traps, storing and boiling water, committing murder, or anything else they could think of.

In an eerily still room that had quickly been abandoned, Ally pried open a filing cabinet. She was throwing handfuls of papers over her shoulders with joy when a folder marked "Declassified" caught her attention. She flipped through the index, reading over documents, and, when she was finished, she stood there, shocked. Wondering if she had comprehended what she read, she called out to the others to urgently come and look. They found her in the room and wondered what the fuss was about. "Read this—you have to read this."

Ally pushed a single page toward the other women; in the low light, they all stood very close to each other and read the report. Ally was watching their emotions change as they reacted to the note: "In the event of a catastrophic disaster, one which either directly or in conjunction with other events and factors causes the complete and irretrievable breakdown of the U.R.S.C. society, the Government Emergency Management System—or GEMS—under Section Six, Clause Three of the Emergency and Disaster Response Act, in subsequent reports titled

'Strategies for Managing Wide-Scale Disasters and Crisis Management within the U.R.S.C., Increments One and Two.' This system is for maintaining vital supplies at a safe level, to mitigate the possibility of increased crime rate and widespread dispersion of offenders. It is designated in Increment Two that all prisoners currently incarcerated in labour camps are expendable and will not be subject to rescue or assistance. In this event, GEMS or its acting organisations and bodies will not be obligated to supply any of the survival means necessary for inmates to remain in their incarceration." They were as shocked as her.

"Expendable," one of them repeated. "Fuck, they're going to leave us here to die—it was true. I didn't believe the people who were saying it. How can they do that?"

"We can't stay here, then; we have to escape now," the second woman said.

"How? We've got minimal rations; the closest thing to here is a two-week walk, at least. Even if we stockpile what we need, we won't make that. If civilisation has broken down, then our rations are going to run out soon, and then they'll disappear completely," a third woman added.

"We have to escape in a group, get more people if we need to, and salvage whatever we can from in here for the journey. Get material for shelter, containers to carry water, something to make a fire with," the second woman continued.

"It's not going to work. Even if we do bring materials and prepare what we need, it won't be possible. I think we should stay, use what we have, and try to survive. We have a better chance; if we go out into the desert, the risk of dying's much higher," Ally reasoned.

"You're just going to stay here? I think we're dead either way, so I'm going to take my chances escaping," the first woman replied.

"Where're you going to go? We don't even know what happened out there. If society has truly suffered a breakdown, we could be in the same situation if we travel somewhere and discover it's deserted and ruined. I don't believe what some of the others have been saying lately. Something major is going on, but I think it's the government being taken over. I reckon this'll all be resolved," Ally said.

"Then what? It's all resolved, things return to normal, we're not expendable, and then so what? We're still stuck here, we're still suffering in this fucking dreadful place, so let's leave now before we have to return to being caged and treated like dirt," the first woman argued.

"She has a point there. If we do escape, and there's carnage out there, then, good. There's no more fucking police or law enforcement to rearrest us. We can walk around with freedom and own this country. We can go wherever we want—everywhere will be the Lawless Zone now. We can live the rest of our lives without fear of coming back to this shit-hole. If there are no laws out there, then we'll fit in just fine—it might even be better. A broken-down society couldn't be any worse than here; besides, we won't be on the bottom; we won't just be inmates anymore; we can be something now," the second woman declared.

Days later, the women decided to escape, leaving just before sundown, Ally decided against it; she wanted to take her chances where she was, although some of what the women had said made her question the choice. What if everything was restored and they went straight back to the unbearable conditions? What if there was nobody left to help them, and they were doomed to remain there? On the morning of the seventh day after the escape, there was a fuss that caught Ally's attention. She was walking around during her new morning routine of talking and trading with the other prisoners when she noticed a group of them standing still, looking into the distance, their hands and arms on their foreheads, shielding the sun. Of the thirty women who'd left in a group, Ally saw only one woman limping back toward the prison, dehydrated, her skin blistered and scorched red. She collapsed when she came back. When she regained consciousness, they stood around her as she told a truly terrifying story of their ordeal, which made Ally lose hope. She told of how the desert was an endless expanse; even with navigation skills, it just kept appearing as an abyss; for every horizon they got to, there was another infinite stretch of impassable terrain. They walked at dusk and through until the morning, setting up shelter during the oppressing midday heat. At night, they would freeze in the plummeting temperature; they had to huddle together when resting, staying close to keep warm in the terminal darkness. Her shoes had filled with blood from walking so far and for such long periods. She and ten others made the heartbreaking choice to turn back, which was one of the hardest things she ever had to do. They never made it back, and the remaining women were dying of dehydration. They were drinking their own urine and resorting to cannibalising bodies to survive. Uncertain of how many were still alive, she said the women out there faced certain death. They were so unwilling to turn back, they would rather die in the desert, under their own terms.

The woman's account was incredibly chilling in its detail; after the haunting narrative, she warned against anyone else trying to escape. "The warden was right," she said with a raspy murmur. "There's no escape, the desert goes on forever, and we'll be here forever—to be forgotten about and erased from history. The world has forgotten about us; we've been forsaken, marooned here to remain forever, and our spirits after that." She had become delirious and was hallucinating. She said that her mother was standing next to Ally, and she slowly raised her arm. "There's nobody standing here," Ally responded, and the woman lowered her arm in defeat.

"You have to end my life, Ally—you have to do it,"

"What? You've *survived* this horrible pilgrimage. Why do you want to die?"

"You call *this* survival? I may as well have died out there. This isn't *survival*, this is *existence*—no living, no future, no growth, no reason . . .

"There *is* a reason—a reason to survive, to endure, to not let them win. There's a reason to keep going and endure all of the hardship and suffering. I'm hoping that The Pendulum will swing through and reset these dismal circumstances. I'll admit that it has gotten to me at times and that I've come close to admitting defeat. I don't keep a record of all the times I've fallen, but I do keep a record of how many times I have gotten back up. You must keep going!"

"Look around, Ally—they've won. They've won! We're nothing but rats in the cage. They've beaten us. If you don't end this suffering—if you don't end my life—then I'll do it myself or find someone who will." She again pleaded with Ally to end her life. "There are many others who'd be happy to do it." Ally granted her wish by smothering her with a large piece of cloth.

People everywhere were waiting anxiously; they collectively held their breaths as the final minutes ticked away. The crushing cyber-attack had entered its one-hundredth hour and no resolution had been arrived at. Instead of dealing with the attack and what would inevitably happen to them once it was concluded, Saige Rico and other members of government who had not yet been caught or killed fled the capital and went into hiding. They simply abandoned their roles and disappeared. A statement was released saying the party would be resigning from office and dissolving—yet nothing else. No other critical issues were addressed. There was nothing about the cyberattack, the Resistance, or what was to happen now that they had forfeited their political roles. The political figures used planes from their own fleet and private airstrips to take off from, escaping their accountability, leaving behind a shattered country. Some fled to different countries in Europe, while others went to North America. Other people who couldn't fly out of the country took to secret properties and shelters; it was a wholly unsatisfactory, hollow type of victory. They had fled so abruptly that many citizens felt cheated—robbed of everything they had crusaded for—and now those responsible were escaping justice.

It wasn't the scenario they'd wanted, but the Resistance had finally gotten the megalomaniacal Rico government out of power and office. They weren't even sure if they'd been successful, as they couldn't contact anyone. There was total silence on the other end of governmental phone lines. It was a few more hours before citizens even knew what had happened, as the governing political figues had left so hurriedly. This sparked a massive hunt for them—they were not going to just let them go away without punishment. People were screaming for vengeance; ordinary citizens dedicated their time and effort to locating them, mobilising huge search parties and researching into where they might be.

Other Resistance members and revolutionaries were now putting the pieces back together after the devastating attack had crippled the nation and brought it startlingly close to ruin. Power was restored to the country, which gradually came back to life. The numbers of deaths were revealed with the restoration of power—and those numbers didn't include the severely traumatised. Many were haunted by the visions of the gruesome acts they had been forced to witness and perpetrate in order to continue living. It had taken five years to bring an end to their despotic governance; unchecked by restraint or justice, it had collapsed under the weight of its own evil, its own folly. They had campaigned on the promise that they were going to change the U.R.S.C., and, actually, that was the only promise they'd kept—they had changed it for the worse, turning it into something alien and detestable.

A massive void had now been created. Despite the country's resumption of "normal," many services had nobody to manage or perform them. Sanitation services were being neglected, and massive piles of festering rubbish lay in the streets across the towns and cities. Water and electricity outages were not being repaired, and transport was still not fully back on the roads, on the rails, or in the air. Businesses were not able to pay their workers, who had nothing to support them. Essential services like hospitals were forced to continue but were receiving nothing in return; they had lurched into stagnation. There were those who thought that the country would never get back to its previous state, its previous glory. The vacuum that had been created needed to be filled; without support services for its citizens, the country couldn't convalesce or heal from the trauma it had gone through.

Political parties began to organise from the shattered ranks, heeding the call to rise up and represent the people. The parties were made up of politicians from different walks of life, and to get a sense of the diverse range of people they were serving, every party was monitored under rigorously performed checks. People took it upon themselves to abide by strict criteria, since there was nobody to enact it into law. They wanted the same careful screening of the new candidates running for office, in order to avoid anything similar to the previous regime getting in. There was a much greater level of transparency from the new candidates who rallied across the country on the campaign trail; voters were understandably weary. The candidates had been extremely busy, spawning a cavalcade of political rivalry as more serious contenders emerged. The race developed over the course of a year, which meant that Ally and Osiris had now been imprisoned for six years. They were uninformed about what they were battling against—they had not been sure for years now. Neither of them had spoken to anyone on the outside for months.

CHAPTER TWENTY-NINE

Now that a tenuous order had been restored, there were deliveries and other supplies coming back to Skyline Outpost, its vital supply chain having been re-established. It was a crazy period for everyone there; the whole thing didn't seem real—like a feverish hallucination, a heat-stricken, blood-smeared delusion. It was not back to normal at Skyline by any means; many of the guards had not returned or had died during the breakdown. The inmates were still living outside, suffering and being fed on rations. The whole feeling in there had shifted after what had happened in the rest of the country; delayed reports were filtering through about the evolving competition to win the new election. They had heard uplifting reports about lenient new governments getting in and promising to address the violations to human rights. There were others who wanted to outlaw labour camps again, which had been allowed under the Rico administration. This filled them with hope. The military tried to move in and temporarily govern, but their bid was unsuccessful.

A normal election campaign would last more than nine months, and, after the campaigning came the voting by the citizens. There were unfortunate supporters among the candidates who had been left behind by the Rico administration to face all of the questions and bear the ire of the public's fury. To some degree, these people were simply unknowing sacrifices, thrown into the gears as the procession stopped. People got so distracted with going after them that they weren't seeing the blatant contempt of the wider deception that they'd suffered under.

The political election became more serious as different groups emerged. There were those with the dangerous goal of reimposing the former type of regime if they won the ultimate prize of governance. It wasn't difficult to see that there were other parties with the potential to morph back into the same entity they had tried to get rid of. The Rico dictatorship had left the country fractured and disconnected from the realities of those they were opposed to, sometimes only on the basis of nothing more than unfounded hatred and fear.

Electioneers with different interests began returning to their political tactic of choice—assassinations. Nobody seemed to be immune: Sophia Bettencourt had been the victim of a bombing; members from the Prosecution Department; barristers helping Ally from the Konstantinos law firm. Agent Blaze, who had become unpopular as a hated symbol and sycophant for the Rico regime, became the target of a particularly sinister Resistance betrayal. They fooled him into thinking he was receiving a secret file, intercepted by one of his trusted sources. They had contaminated the letter with anthrax. When Agent Blaze opened the envelope in his office, he didn't anticipate the plume of spores dispersing into the air in front of him. He inhaled the deadly substance into his body and immediately raised the alarm to the other agents. But the course of the damage couldn't be stopped, and his death was inevitable. He was rushed from the Federal Complex to hospital but died only days later.

Some candidates in the running had been murdered. Those who weren't became much more sheltered, withdrawing from public rallies and events, broadcasting from secret locations. It all felt very sanitised, but there *were* candidates who gained support by taking the risk and getting out to the people. They proved to be much more in touch, which was represented in early polls.

The majority supported emerging-candidate-and-soon-to-be-clear-favourite Maia Alvarez. She was a young woman who had immigrated from Central America, fleeing drug-fuelled conflicts. She was fiercely protected, as there were fears that anyone the people chose would become the next target. Originally, some people wanted Konstantinos to run, though he supported Maia Alvarez. Passing over him, the people picked the vocal and well-known campaigner throughout the "Years of Revolt," as it was now being referred to. She had a political education from a prestigious university but was short on political experience. She was the leader of a small independent liberal party, pushing for social rights and reform. They had never held much power in the Houses of Government. Any bills they promoted were rejected or voted against.

Recently, however, she had embodied the spirit of the struggle, had well-developed policies, and was exceptionally popular. She risked her life going around to campaign; when the safety concern was elevated, she would visually record messages and appear on programs through a video link or via telephone. She was criticised for this, though she quickly became the highest bounty in the country. Many Facilitators and other people wanted to assassinate her and collect the $100 million bounty being offered by criminal entities, who were frightened of the deep reform she wanted to implement, which would virtually paralyse them. There was an incident in which she'd been poisoned by spies with a nerve agent, but she survived and was hospitalised. This made her popularity skyrocket. She was still looking pale and weakened, appearing from her hospital bed on state television saying that she was firm in her will to continue undeterred and that the incident had made her only more intent on victory.

There was a consensus among people that she would prevail in a remarkable victory, though there was some doubt and conjecture growing. The population turned out in record numbers, as compared to previous elections. This time, many of the younger generation voted. They had been born in the U.R.S.C., and they had seen it come to the precipice of oblivion, almost going off a cliff onto the jagged rocks of ruin. They wanted to make sure they could do something to contribute to changing the system under Alvarez's leadership.

There was a huge repair-and-cleanup effort underway; the detritus and wreckage from the seven years of conflict were still painfully evident and in view—the barricades and the graffiti were reminders of what it had cost. They would never forget that millions of people had died over the entire course of the revolution. It took much longer than usual to transport and count all of the votes. The nation held on, in an elated sense of anticipation. It was announced that Maia Alvarez and her party had won the most seats in all of the voting regions they needed to take the House of Federal Government.

It had been a close race, and, towards the end, it seemed like her competitors were riding that old "Pendulum Effect," but the numbers proved otherwise. People voted for her in overwhelming numbers, and, for the first time in so long, happy, joyous people, elated that their candidate had won after so much unease and attempts on her life, filled the streets, cheering and laughing as opposed to screaming and crying. Around the U.R.S.C., the same streets that had been the scenes for horrid sights and tragedy, where so much misery had been perpetuated, were now filled with celebrating crowds. Detracting, however, from this partying and revelry was the claim, right after the announcement of her victory, that there had been massive fraud and that the votes had not been counted properly. It overshadowed Alvarez's victory and further delayed her party from getting into office. The people weren't too excited about this development. They saw it as the opposition doing whatever they could to slow the process and try and get a recount. They saw all of their hard work being erased in baseless claims and false evidence.

It evolved into three more months of court hearings and enquiries. The new President Alvarez and others were called before tribunals made up of the few people who were left and qualified to make up an emergency leadership and make decisions in the interim before a new party was inducted. These reports came through to Ally, Osiris, and the others on the long list of people incarcerated. They had been intently following the developments of the election, mainly because Maia Alvarez had pledged to outlaw labour camps.

She promised to reverse the laws on journalistic freedom and reporting, to overturn the convictions and executions of those prosecuted by the former regime, and to give them a pardon. Though it was revealed that some people who were released would be extradited to their home country, or, failing that, another country with which they had an agreement.

This news was amazing to Ally. She began to believe she would never get out, that she was doomed after Agent Blaze had died. Now the very real prospect of getting out filled them with vigour that they hadn't felt since before their arrest, though the slow pace of it all made them anxious. They could feel their freedom so near, but it kept slipping away. In the seven and a half years they had been imprisoned, they had never been so uplifted. There was still so many things Ally had to do with her legal team to certify that the process could happen without some technicality getting in the way of her freedom.

Her team was looking at everything—especially all of the laws that banned forced-labour camps. Skyline Outpost would be shut down permanently and all of its staff and inmates relocated. The prisoners were forced to work very hard in the twilight hours of their imprison-ment, while they could still be forced. They had to prepare the prison to be closed. They dismantled all of the equipment around the prison and packed it away; they took apart the machinery and manufactur-ing equipment, the last symbol of their slavery being relocated to be scrapped. It was a perfect metaphor for dismantling the old system and a new machine coming to take over.

During the period when there was no supervision or enforcement, they destroyed almost all of the machinery and factories, as it was already dead, and they were just hammering in the final nails. The warden addressed them all and told them about what would be happening. He was opposed to the labour camps closing; he thought this whole thing would be the real beginning of the country's decline. The population of the prison was vastly reduced; approximately three quarters of the inmates had died during the "Blackout"—or the "Reckoning," as they called it. It was evident by the small numbers of the crowd gathered in the massive yard where they were forced to line up every morning and night for counting.

Ally and Osiris had to be patient and wait for their convictions to be overturned; they were worried when people in the political opposi-tion spoke out against it, stopping the motion by taking the matter to court—the new court that had been established under President Alvarez's order. Nuisance appeals and lawsuits stopped not only them from being released but also others. They argued that the arrests were justified to protect the peace.

It was at the beginning of the eighth year of their incarceration when the push to keep them interned was defeated in court and thrown out. One of the first actions pursued by the new government was to immediately suspend all prisoner executions until further notice. When Ally was told over the phone, it was the happiest she had been for a long time, and the relief was intoxicating. She dreaded the decision being overturned and facing execution. Until receiving that news, the thought of it had been devouring her. When they were in the worst of the shutdown, the prison was not focused on executing people; the main priority was survival. The thought had never subsided or left Ally; when it was overtaken by the battle to live, she knew it was only a matter of time before she would think about dying again. Unable to relax or have peace not knowing when she would be put to death, she had spent years on edge because of it. It was the first concern gripping her when she awoke and her last thought before falling asleep or apart.

What was left to do now was wait to see what the new administration would do. They had embarked on a major reshuffling and changing of the departments that had existed before. Ally was told this would take some time. Only after this was done could they see what the new departments were like, what their constraints were, or what they could do. These were completely different entities they were dealing with, which left them in a tough place; they had tangled with the previous departments and knew them well. Her team couldn't guarantee Ally that everything was going to turn out to plan. All of the work they had done before, in the last regime, was useless. That was before most of her lawyers had died as well; some of her team remained, but others were dead.

Another event everyone was excitedly waiting for was when they would leave Skyline Outpost. A fleet of buses came to transport the people to all the different locations they were going. Ally and Osiris were being sent to different prisons, but they knew where the other one was going, and they were located close together. On the ride, Ally fantasised about their life outside; the women watched the prison, far behind them, growing smaller. It had seemed so sinister on approach, and now they were cheering and raucously shouting as it disappeared. They assumed they would be there forever, and now they were never going to see it again.

CHAPTER TWENTY-NINE

"Farewell, bitch."

"Good riddance, cunt."

"I never want to see you again, fucker!"

These were some of the elated shouts the inmates made; the experience was behind them now. Her romance with Osiris had been blooming just before all of the unpleasantness made its way into their lives. In a way, she felt it had made their feelings stronger; it had strengthened their resolve. These events had united them and brought them closer. They were changed people, and this experience had made them take another look at how they felt about each other and life. She wanted to take a different path now, no longer in the criminal world. She had wanted to leave that life through almost her whole career as a Facilitator, but this had made her determined. Osiris felt the same way. This had been their clarion call to depart from that world.

This had made him think about what was special. Their romance and relationship had been so crucial to him. It had, sadly, been put on hiatus just as it was starting to blossom into a beautiful, enduring love. Previously, they had talked about what they were going to do. Before their arrest, they agreed to make their relationship more serious, sharing a deeper bond than their previous arrangement. Where they weren't sure of the extent of their commitments or boundaries. Ally had been single long before her incarceration—in fact, she had been alone most of her life, and she felt nothing would be different now. She had become used to being by herself; she had always done everything by herself, the only one she could rely on. She had come full circle, as now she was alone again, adrift in an ocean filled with deadly creatures. She did not want to draw a person into her world and have them become vulnerable to her enemies. In her earlier life, she had dated a mixture of women and men. She had not been looking for a relationship, but now her outlook and opinion had shifted.

Prior to their arrest, she had found herself becoming more attracted to Osiris as they spent time together, growing more intimate and acquainted as they learnt more about one another. When they had first met, there was an air of mystery surrounding them, but lurking were the usual hostilities that came with both of them working in the same industry. There was an implied rivalry and competition that quickly dissolved when they finally spoke to each other. She wanted to leave this whole part of her life here in the U.R.S.C., leave that anathema and concentrate on a more holistic life. She wanted to buy an isolated property and live off the grid, more simply and wholesomely. To feel the breeze on her face, read old books, grow her own food, breathe the clean air, fornicate, and bask in nature; she knew that the best pleasures in life were those that are free.

The status of what would happen to them was still being hotly contested. Ally was informed that there were appeals and motions aimed at trying to keep her in the U.R.S.C. once released. Though she did not want to stay, even if she was allowed, she was resolute in wanting to leave. She wanted to return to the Seychelles, though it was looking like they would be forced to stay in the U.R.S.C. until another country agreed to take them. They were unsure whether that meant them being transferred, yet again, to an immigration holding facility. She hoped she would be able to be reunited with Osiris and that they could plan something together, though she had her doubts. She didn't know if she would be able to contact him. She planned on sending letters and contacting him via telephone; the intermediate prison's conditions she was going to couldn't be any stricter than Skyline Outpost.

CHAPTER THIRTY

S he asked her legal team to get in touch with Osiris's team so they could exchange details about where they ultimately ended up. They did promise to talk again and put all of the mistakes of the past behind them; they wanted to grow and flourish together. The prison she was going to was located in the hinterland region outside of Sheernova, an inland city 2,000 kilometres southeast from Skyline Outpost. It was an area with rugged natural beauty and very little infrastructure, situated in a lush, remote valley. A much more standard setup than Skyline Outpost, it didn't look overly threatening. *This appears oddly comfortable*, Ally pondered, considering where she had come from. Osiris was taken to a prison roughly 600 kilometres further to the town of Viento-A-Favor, near the South Coast. It was now an anxious wait to see what the new government would decide about their fate. Ally assumed they would be released immediately if their convictions were overturned, but, ostensibly, they had to wait while the system was being rebuilt. The new government wanted to get it right, which Ally understood, but that was scarce comfort when she was still without her freedom.

The new prison was easier to acclimate to than Skyline Outpost. Ally was relieved that she was no longer on death row, though that meant she would be placed in the general population. That was more treacherous for her, because she was so recognisable that some couldn't help approaching her. The people at her table were fascinated by her; they bombarded her with questions about herself until she became annoyed. "I don't know what I've done to deserve your admiration, but I can assure you it's ill founded. I'm not some hero, nor do I want to be. I don't know why you have idolised me; there are people more deserving of your respect and veneration. Please, just leave me alone. I don't want to recount why I'm in this soul-destroying place."

"It's just that we've never had someone like you here amongst us; nothing ever happens around here, so, when someone like you arrives, it's exciting," a woman responded.

The people were complaining about the conditions, but, to Ally, there was no comparison: This place was much better than where she had been, and she told whoever complained to be grateful about their situation, because someone out there had it worse. Here, they weren't forced to work. This prison offered great educational and vocational courses, and Ally enrolled in all of the classes that she could. The prison offered a class about reintegrating back into society. They had a great support network outside and tried to keep recidivism and reoffending levels low. It had been one of the most successful programs in the U.R.S.C. In her daily life there, she attended courses, so she was excused from performing chores or manufacturing work.

The prisoners also helped rehabilitate injured animals, which filled Ally with a joy she didn't know she was capable of feeling anymore. She felt really humbled taking care of a four-year-old female Golden Retriever named "Angie." The animals, with their purity and unconditional love, made her realise that she had been rather self-centred on the outside before her arrest, caring only about herself. She rediscovered the joy of helping others. She had been living in such violence and hatred that she had begun to become that person, but now she had a responsibility. She had a reason to get up in the morning—she had a friend who was relying on her to provide. Ally became so attached to her she would kill any person who would hurt Angie. She had been neglected, and, when she was trained more and rehabilitated, she would go out into society to become an assistance dog for citizens and war veterans experiencing trauma. Ally was heartbroken on the day the dogs graduated from the program. She couldn't bear to see her new friend depart. The love she felt for her was so pure that it was refreshing and made her feel alive after becoming so dead inside.

For all of the things that were different, it was still a prison. There were assaults, murders, intimidation, and a thriving black market in the prison.

Ally and Osiris were not allowed to communicate whatsoever. Both her and Osiris's legal teams on the outside had been secretly delivering letters between them. She wrote to him saying that, if they were separated, he should meet her in the Seychelles. Ally managed to acquire a cellular telephone off another inmate. Once she did, she regained contact with her legal team. She asked them to pass on her contact details to Osiris so they could speak without being so closely monitored. Ally got rigorously involved in the black market of the prison, and, because the legal team were depositing a generous per diem into her prison account, she could buy whatever she wanted. She traded food items from the prison canteen for alcohol, drugs, cigarettes, weapons, currency—anything she could trade and make a profit on, she did.

She spent most of her days intoxicated on drugs to block out the horrible milieu around her. She quickly became the go-to person for contraband, much to the chagrin of the former prevalent players. They approached her and told her to stop what she was doing. In Skyline Outpost, she would have assaulted or murdered them, though she was told she could be charged again for any offence while she was waiting for release, so she had to be well behaved. Even getting caught for selling the contraband would be a serious charge that could force her to stay here longer. She hoped Osiris was doing the same and trying not to reoffend, but she understood it wasn't easy. She was bribing whichever guards she could to keep quiet and provide her with contraband smuggled from the outside. The guards made measly salaries, so the incentive to make extra money loomed large for some of the guards.

Osiris's experience was much like hers: He was surprised by how easy this prison seemed to be, compared with where they had just been. Because his reputation had preceded him, he had to fend off many challengers who wanted to beat him in a fight for the credibility it would grant them. Osiris was an adept fighter, but some of the inmates were more vicious and determined than him. Considering his defeats, Osiris still had a high status and effortlessly commanded respect. He was very good with electronics and quickly became the person to see to repair them. He made a number of ingenious makeshift tools in his cell from implements he found.

If this was to be her life, well, Ally had been institutionalised, and she was used to the regimen, being on edge, and vigilant of assaults— the code that they all lived under. It was a different mentality, ruled by respect, reputation, and conflict, where emotions were hidden and weakness was preyed upon, unlike how society functioned. Ally tried not to concern herself with the outside world; the country was still trying to find a new normality, longing to get back elements of the way the country was before the upheaval, yet finding a new peace in transitioning to a different future. In the time she was there, she began exercising again and eating all she could. She had become so gaunt and frail from the famished state she'd lived in at Skyline Outpost. With nothing but time on her hands, she got back the toned, athletic body she had when she was a Facilitator and regularly exercised.

All of the exposure to the sun had taken a huge toll on her skin. Sometimes she felt she had left her old self there at the Outpost, dead and burned. The experience had changed her life in some ways that were irreparable, as she suffered ongoing health problems. Her brain had changed, and she was becoming unsure of whether she could return and integrate back into the wider world. The ways of violence, emotional disengagement, and reputation had become so normalised in her, such an indispensable part of her daily existence. She was anxious about being unable to let that go.

Now firmly inducted, the new party set about reversing the decrees made against all the Townships, including Delphi Township. It was reopened with its mining permits and rights fully restored. The military presence was gone, and people started to come back, no longer in fear of the hostile presence intruding on their lives. Their already impoverished homes had been ruined in the melee; the place showed the scars from everything that had happened. It was painfully evident how much was still in ruins; some places were already just piles of discarded materials. There was a tangle of former houses and businesses, stacks of metal, beams of wood, and rubbish in mounds. It had taken a Herculean effort to clear the wreckage, though the community was more than willing to help, and they cleared it all. The Alvarez government signed all new deals and enacted new policies that would see services and infrastructure around there improve greatly. There was a pledge for more useful resources like education, better-quality housing, and medical and water access. There had been many painful lessons learned.

Now content that she had helped the people, having served her purpose there and no longer needing to stay, Portia knew it was time to depart and move on. She was celebrated by the Council, and they held a magnificent farewell party for her. With dancing, singing, and fireworks, it was a grand way to exit. It was what was needed by many people to forget about the recent terrors that had befallen them, and they had come back to a bleak prospect, a crushing new reality. They forgot about their troubles temporarily in the festivities. There were many people sad to see her depart; some pleaded for her to stay, saying she was what was needed to help this place prosper. She declined, saying the people already had the determination to do it. She was sad to leave, but that was only a stop along the way in her wider plan—she had to continue on her path. She was reminded of Ally's Pendulum theory as she moved to the next stage of her life. She had done all she could for the Township, and now their future rested with them, the Council, the inhabitants, the young and old who strolled its twisting streets.

She travelled back to Paloma Ferry and boarded a plane bound for Rome. She was leaving this place behind her; like the United Republic had done for Ally, this place had given rise to many of her aspirations and dreams. It was a double-edged sword that had also given way to despair and the worst parts of herself. She was leaving somewhat embittered and jaded.

It was another six months of repairing in the country for it to take shape. By the end of the year, it was promised that all the people unjustly convicted, imprisoned, or sentenced to execution during the previous administration would have their cases reviewed and overturned. There had been thousands of people stripped of their freedoms and placed into prisons. They were eagerly awaiting something like this, and it was met with high acclaim. A cohort of extra staff had been placed in the new Justice and Legal Departments to handle the huge volume of cases that they were going to receive.

It also had a service for people incarcerated before the revolt who wanted to see if their conviction was incorrect and could be overturned. Their system was, expectedly, swamped with appeals; they were worked through as efficiently as the new system could cope. Each individual case was to be inspected because of the circumstances, for everyone differed. Certain people needed to be deported or released into the outside world, while there were actual criminals who needed to remain. There were calls for them to release everyone, though they didn't want to put every person into the public without reviewing what they had done. A host of crimes and depraved acts went unchecked during those long years of metamorphosis. This was a balancing act the new government were performing, and they had been given a very unenviable position upon coming into office. Ally had been hearing small pieces of information through the radio; when there was an update, she listened intently.

As did others she had talked to who had been unjustly detained and deprived of their liberties and freedom by the Rico government, people had stories of being taken away from their homes unexpectedly in the middle of the night. They were snatched away from their families and sent to slave-labour camps, like her, with no idea about when they were getting out, what would be their fate, or what they had done to deserve their fate. A lot of those people were not there to have their story heard or their freedom reimposed. There were people in there who had shared information about the "Coup Trials," as they were now referenced. Those trials had found their way into mythical status as one of the most critical events to herald change in the history of the country.

This release program had become a debated issue. The new party's opposition and critics, which contained some sympathisers with the previous party, labelled the program as ". . . freeing all of the heretics and those who compromised the nation's security—merely letting them go . . ." The hard work done by their predecessors to remove these offenders from the wider public had been erased by left-leaning idealist traitors, with their liberal policies betraying the country's safety and ideals.

Before their case was heard by the new Department of Justice, it was a hugely publicised spectacle, televised and closely followed because it had become so eminent. People from all over the world who had an interest in the case listened or watched. These cases, which were of such monumental importance, were heard in the upper Federal Chamber of Parliament, where the new top politicians and Department of Justice ministers who drafted the legislation sat. On the third day of deliberations and arguments from both sides, their convictions were overturned.

Maia Alvarez appeared in the Chamber and gave a celebrated and moving speech. She apologised to everyone who had been victimised. She apologised for how they were treated, speaking for three hours. With unflinching candour, she recounted the gruesome account of the past few years and everything that had led to this new era. Having lost her own father, she imparted commiseration to those who had lost people. She sympathised with those who lost their homes, businesses, and everything else. She spoke directly from the heart and to those who had their life shattered or were unfairly imprisoned.

She vowed to redress all the destruction inflicted at the hands of her predecessors. Her emotion broke through her solemn deliverance, showing her human side, the emotional aspect of the suffering that had been caused. She said, "It has taken much more from us than simply economic loss and a decline in business. It has caused suffering that is intangible and cannot be seen. That does not mean it is not there. We are entering into a time of healing, a time for rejuvenation, regrowth, and renewal. I thank all of the citizens who believed in our party and our ideologies; there are opposers, but that is necessary for a democratic, equitable society. For now, we are grieving over the mistakes and wounds of the past, yet let us also look to the future with hope."

Under her decree, their sentences were commuted; it was officially confirmed that they would no longer be executed at the hands of the U.R.S.C. The new judges and ministers in the Department officially denounced the actions of the last government, and they vowed to put an end to forced-labour camps once again. While this was mostly positive for those imprisoned, however, not everything they said or decided upon was in their favour. It was deemed that some of their actions were questionable, but no further indictments would be pursued. They would no longer remain imprisoned but wouldn't be released to the wider society. A portion of their accounts had been confiscated to pay for damages, but they were eligible to be moved to an immigration facility for deportation to another country.

When the hearing was dismissed, morale was growing as people exited with high spirits, ready to enact the new decrees. Her law team rushed out of the public gallery to notify her. "Ally, we have excellent news from the capital. We've just gotten out of the last hearing held at the Federal Chamber of Parliament. Your conviction has been overturned; your sentence has been changed. The administration has confirmed that you will not be subject to execution; they have reversed that decision. Another great victory for us is that they have also ruled that you'll no longer be in prison. You're going to be taken to an immigration facility and deported; you will finally be able to leave the U.R.S.C."

"Are you sure?"

"Yes. You're going to be ferried out of this country. You'll no longer have to serve any more time there. You will have to go to an immigration holding facility until you leave. You are not allowed to wait for your deportation while free in society. Additionally, you will have to fund it, and they garnished some of the money from your accounts to pay for damages. But there is still a significant amount of money left, enough to accommodate your life in another country. Now that the hearing has been concluded, we are working straightaway on getting a deal signed for your departure. We're going to contact the French government or one of their territories, and we're going to do everything we can to get it completed for you as soon as we're able, so you don't have to spend months or years waiting in immigration holding. The government should be helping us now; they've formed a great network of support that we can use, but it's going to be a difficult diplomatic issue to resolve. We don't want this to become an international incident. The chaos here was widely followed and watched by the world, but we want to be able to get you home, or wherever we can, without postponement."

"I don't even know what to say. This has been such a long time coming; this feels so surreal."

"Yes. Congratulations, Ally. It has been long overdue. We no longer have to worry about that; we can look now towards working on getting you a safe departure from this country. We will contact you in the next few days to inform you of where we're at with the next stage and if anything changes."

"Thank you so much! This means *everything* to me. I am so glad that you have all been so ready to continue Mihalis's work. He was my link to the world, and, when he died, I was afraid that link had died with him." After she received that call, she was elated. She would be leaving this place and the U.R.S.C.

Osiris had heard small sections of the hearing and the subsequent media coverage. When their convictions were overturned, he was also given the word by his team, though his case was a little less straightforward. He couldn't apply for deportation and asylum in Australia. "If I'm not allowed to apply for relocation to Australia, then what do I do? I'm stateless."

"We're doing absolutely everything we can. We are in talks with the Australian government to try to get you sent back there. We believe we may have found a legal technicality, a loophole in international law that might allow you to travel back there. Presently, they are largely opposed to the notion of accepting you. The Australian government has taken a hardline approach to its citizens committing terrorist acts and crimes in foreign countries. It says it doesn't want to take these people back to reintegrate them into society. We are arguing that they are legally obliged to accept you under their Constitution."

"None of that sounds very certain. You said that might allow me to travel back there. I'm hugely thankful for what you're doing—all of you. You're the only ones who extended a hand in the all-consuming darkness of my worst hour, but I've got to be honest with you: What you've just recounted to me doesn't fill me with a lot of hope or excitement. Perhaps we should focus our effort elsewhere if that's not going to come to fruition. We're wasting our energy."

"We're trying to apply for your asylum in another country as a refugee. We've been able to get you classified as a refugee fleeing persecution from the U.R.S.C. At this stage, we haven't been able to make a deal with any country. We're hoping to change this, though it may be difficult with your indelible profile that's been created. There may be some countries that are unwilling to accept a notorious person and the attention and publicity it entails. We're in talks with the Egyptian government, and it's looking promising that they may accept you—the most promising so far. If not, however, we are in talks with other governments and diplomats around the world. You may have to fund your journey there, but we can provide some financial support."

"How long is this going to take?"

"It could be a considerable wait. These are very sensitive discussions we are having, and on a very contentious issue. In some nations, you have been denounced as a thug and a terrorist, a danger to their citizens and interests, but other nations have celebrated you as some type of anti-hero idol. There are some places who prize that rebellious nature. So we have lots of options, Mr. Jackson."

Their disrupted new life of relocations, restraints, corridors, and prisoner-transport practices went on. It had become routine; everything was ephemeral. They were used to this from their previous lifestyles outside, so there were no surprises. They had dealt with the transient way of existing. For them as Facilitators, it had become a part of the profession; they weren't worried. Ally had lived out of her suitcase, in her younger days transiently drifting between different hostels and accommodations. She'd stayed at a host of momentary lodgings amidst the gritty backdrop of the U.R.S.C.: Fierce drug dens, deranged flop-houses, upscale inner-city lofts, and decadent luxury hotels. It had all become merged into a single, wild montage in her mind. For her whole life, she had been on the move, never staying in one location. She felt the compulsion for wanderlust, to move around and satisfy her spirit.

CHAPTER THIRTY-ONE

Without any trouble, Ally was taken away from the prison. The Desiderata Immigration Centre was in the outer suburbs of the country's second largest city. A highly controversial place, many disliked its mere existence, believing it was more than what the criminal immigrants deserved. It had a less-sinister, less-stifling atmosphere than the other places Ally had experienced. This was a holding facility and the last stop for criminal deportees. There was reduced security and more open space, which was conducive to less fear. It was structured less like a prison. The rooms where they stayed were very spacious, more like a hospital room. They were more receptive to a person's needs. The energy of the place was much different; the interior wasn't so depressing or drab. The walls were painted in vibrant colours, accompanied by bright sky tones, radiating an airy, relieving vibe as natural light streamed in from high windows.

Osiris was taken north to a centre for males closer to where he was imprisoned; there were only a few such centres around the country, and they had high volumes of people to send away. There was no worrying about violence or inhumane living within the centre. Most of their days consisted of sorting out their affairs before they left; everyone was focused on their own dilemmas and didn't want to do anything that would earn them more punishment and keep them from leaving.

Ally had to transfer accounts, fill out paperwork about her situation, and apply for all new identity papers. She was busy and afraid she wouldn't accomplish everything with the deadline for her departure fast-approaching. Ally had talked to other foreign women who'd had their cases reviewed and overturned. They were also being returned to their countries, and there was a sense of excitement amongst them to be returning home. The deadline set for their departure was three months hence, which gave them little time to prepare for their new realities—regardless of whether they were prepared, *they would be leaving*.

Ally thought that seemed like a generous amount of time, but she realised how much there was to do before it was upon them. The woman who ran the facility said she didn't want to punish people. She wanted to make the transition as smooth as possible for the deportees; she had just been appointed to the role and wanted to do it ethically and professionally. Ally was growing nervous; she had not been in France since she'd been a teenager. The date for her exit was edging closer, and she had family there but was unsure what had happened to them or anyone else she knew. Turmoil, famine, and war around Europe had been raging on and off for many years. She didn't know how she would suddenly fit back into life on the outside so rapidly, transitioning so quickly. It made it especially stressful because she had no support network if she failed. She was given the details for different social and legal services to help her if she experienced problems upon arrival and settling. She was cynical and expected no actual help.

The programs the centre provided helped them make their transition. Ally was assessed and assigned a caseworker named Zuri Nakshatra, an Indian woman who was helping her organise what she would need. They were doing whatever they could to ensure her life there would be established, preventing her from slipping into reoffending out of necessity. It was made very clear that wasn't going to be tolerated. She became friends with Zuri and very close to her. Zuri was genuinely interested in helping Ally however she could. "I just got off the phone with the airline company. I'm much closer to getting a flight booked for you."

"Thank you for being so willing to help me. I couldn't have done this alone."

"You think the outside world has ignored you, turned its back on you. There are those who care. I was in your position. I was where you are, and I was going to be deported back to India, where there's war and genocide, to face prosecution and death from the government, because of my religion and for speaking out against ethnic cleansing. I was a successful activist and journalist, and suddenly I had nothing. My career, my home, my loved ones. I was nobody, and I had nobody; I know the fear you are hiding. You are inspiring to me, a role model the world sorely needs."

"I'm not hiding fear. I'll openly admit that I'm fearful. I'll admit that everyone thinks I'm some icon, which I've come to embrace, but I don't fully understand. I'm just a woman who has lived her life and made some ill-informed moves. I have not grasped that people want to respect and venerate me for my life and what this has all represented. If it brings them hope and inspiration, perhaps encourages them to make a difference in their life, then that is worth striving for. I want to focus my life on mending."

"Yes. I see it, in your bones, in your voice: You are afraid—afraid of what you can't see in front of you. You must listen and look inside yourself. That is where the answer lies. I can see within you that you have an understanding of your destiny. You need to believe in the plan that has been decided by the universe. Though you must still have initiative in your life to manifest it into existence with your actions."

"The Pendulum," Ally whispered.

"Pardon?" she responded.

"You were supposed to come into my life, supposed to cross paths with me, to help me believe that this is the right thing, that it's meant to happen. You were meant to swing through my life to remind me that The Pendulum will set me on a renewed path if I let it . . . without excessive intervening. I must enhance it with my conduct and not be inactive. I have to remember that, no matter how far back you swing the Pendulum, it takes the same amount of time to return."

"That is why I took this job when they offered it to me. After the old government was gone, I was allowed to stay here, to help others out of the same things I went through. Now this country's my paradise because I'm free. Now, I'm using that second chance; I'm using it to help others, like you must now do. You must now go and help, not destroy, not kill but help."

"That's what I've been thinking of lately—changing who I am, changing what I do, living more altruistically and generously. Now you're here, confirming what I've been thinking and ruminating on. I had the answers all along; they were inside of myself. I only needed to block out the background discourse, reflect, and look inside. I can't silence the nagging sensation inside that I don't deserve this leniency. I feel so unworthy and unmerited to receive another lease on life. I ask, *Why me?* Why not someone who is no longer here because of this tempestuous epoch, anyone more deserving. Yet I live."

"It is normal for you to have these emotions, to have self-doubt and loathing, to have unresolved issues and feeling that you are not good enough. Like you told me before, you have grown from this terrible part of your life. This is important after what you have gone through—that you are still on a path of growth and self-improvement. It is a treacherous path to walk."

"I just needed some reassurance that I was making the right decision. You have inspired me to extract the utmost from this advantage. I aspire to do something with this priceless treasure I've been gifted. May I please hug you, Zuri?"

"Yes, yes. You may."

"You have shown me the goodness that sleeps within people. You have shown me the side of people—of the world—I had forgotten about: That I can change my life and strive to create happiness, warmth, and positivity. I had focused on and thought about only the evil, hence, that's what my life became. It ruled my reality, and now I've cleansed myself of that curse. Those shackles are gone."

She talked to representatives from the French government about what her options were upon returning and where she would go. They weren't in a great position to help her, but she was a citizen, and so they agreed. There was much deliberation and talk about where she would be placed in the country. The government were considering placing her in the country's south near the Pyrenees Mountains or the Alps in the east. There were shelters in those areas that housed repatriated criminals and helped them until they could go back into the community on their own. They had also been considering housing her in a detention-centre-style initiative to reintegrate people back into their society. Zuri had been trying to get her employment for when she arrived there, but she was finding it difficult. There was factory and seasonal work she could perform, but Zuri was trying to get her more lucrative work, where she could utilise her business and financial experience. Though many companies were unwilling to employ a criminal like her, despite her being fluent in French and well qualified, this made her feel disheartened, like she was worthless. A burden passed around as an unwanted gift. Many places wouldn't even give her a chance. They simply dismissed her as a liability, a pariah that no entity wanted to be associated with.

She had strange feelings about leaving the U.R.S.C. and starting anew. It had been the place that had given life to her dreams; it had also been the cause for misery and life-changing experience. Ultimately, she wished she had never come. She wished she had never been swindled by the promises and pulled in by its magnetism. For all the wallowing she found herself in, she understood that it was all part of her destiny, her grand journey, and that it had contributed to the person she was—her experiences and the platform of knowledge she carried. For everything that had happened, it had forged her into the person she was, like Osiris. He was now thirty-eight years old and she was thirty-six; a lot wiser from all she had endured, beholding the insurmountable will to survive. She had made up her mind; she had millions in offshore accounts. Between them was amassed some of the money she had made from crime to avoid taxation in the U.R.S.C. She planned to withdraw the money when she settled overseas. She was set on abandoning any program or placement to go rogue, funding a new life for herself. It was a closely guarded secret she shared with nobody.

She had been staying in touch with Osiris, now that it was permitted. She was closely following how his bid for deportation was faring. She had been very upset to learn that his application for asylum in France had been denied by their government, not because of his status or what he had done, but because he was not a citizen. Osiris and his caseworker, with the help of his legal team, appealed the decision, though they kept their options open. Talks with other countries were going much better. It appeared as though the Egyptian government would take Osiris, the only country relatively close to her. His bid was not ratified; foreign relations had been damaged, and many nations were still hostile toward the U.R.S.C., perceived as an unpredictable, impulsive nation, making his plight harder.

At the end of their eighth year of imprisonment, all the arrangements were made for Ally. She was finally going to depart for her birthplace. It had been such a long time coming, she didn't know what to expect upon returning. She couldn't picture how her life there would turn out; on the day she was told, she did not react how she expected she would upon hearing the news she was existing to hear. Osiris had still not found any country that would take him. In some countries it would take years for his approval. Ally did not want to leave if it meant abandoning Osiris without his freedom. She asked if she could remain until Osiris and his team knew definitively where he was going and what would happen to him. She'd never imagined herself asking to stay any length of time longer. She was told it would still take some time before all of the diplomatic work was finished, but she couldn't stay in the country. They explained to her the new government had been very lenient on her and co-conspirators—when they all should have been retried and spent time in prison for certain crimes, but they were willing to excuse that. In exchange, the former prisoners had to depart from U.R.S.C. shores; the government were firm about that.

It had taken away some of the ecstasy she'd had about regaining her freedom; in the correspondence she expressed this. Osiris replied, "Dear Ally . . . it has come to my attention through my legal counsel that you have expressed to them your desire to remain here until I have secured a deportation accord with another country. . . . I must explicitly ask that you do not stay here because of me. I'm still alive; go out there and be someone. Pursue the amazing feats that I know you're capable of. It's my fault that we're here, that this happened. That's why I want you to leave and get out of this place. Don't worry about me. I'll be fine. It wouldn't be right for you to wait around for a fool like me! Spread those wings, and go make a difference, live, and breathe a new life.

"I wish you hadn't suffered because of what I got you into. I should have gone overseas with you when we had the chance. I can understand if you no longer want to know me. I've made a few mistakes in my time, but hurting you stands out as my most haunting regret. Of all the things I've done, the fact that I destroyed your life also will be a regret I will carry to my final day . . . please know that. The times I experienced with you will crystalise in my mind as the fondest memories of my life. I was afforded the pleasure of knowing you, and I threw it away chasing some utopian dream. You're an amazing, insightful, and fiercely intelligent woman—much more intelligent than I am. You deserve to start afresh without someone like me there to ruin it. I hope you fulfil all the ambitions you told me about. . . .

It's looking as though I may never get out; the extradition game isn't going too well. What can I say? Go figure. I try not to think about the outside world very much. . . . If I must stay here, then so be it. *Que sera.* It's not so bad here—it's a resort compared to Skyline Outpost. Unfortunately, you, of all people, could attest to that. . . . I've been sober for six months now. I hope you're doing well in your struggles with substance abuse. I know in previous letters you said you were fighting addiction, but they have some beneficial programs you can engage in that will help, immensely. . . . I did, and I haven't looked back. Regretfully, now I have to conclude this letter. Rest assured that I am eagerly awaiting your reply. Receiving it is the only thing that brings me any even-remote semblance of happiness. I can't wait to hear from you.

"Love . . . Memphis 'Osiris' Jackson."

"I love you, Osiris," she whispered, clutching the forbidden letter close to her chest. "You did not ruin my life. . . . I made the choice."

They made the beginnings of plans to reunite when they were both free. For Osiris, his release could be any time in the future; exactly how long he remained became more ambiguous. Ironically, with their love blossoming, they were being separated. As their romance was flowering, they were being driven apart; Ally feared it may be forever. Though they had a vital line of contact between them, their respective legal counsels made a commitment to keeping them connected, regardless of where they ended up. Ally was relieved to have that in place, a romantic failsafe. She was afraid they would still somehow lose contact and be unable to relocate each other, never to reunite in the vastness of the world.

She was planning to move to the Seychelles as soon as she could, even if she had to flee from France once again. It was decided for her that she would be put into a detention centre outside of Paris on her arrival, participating in an initiative to help deportees convicted of crimes return into the community. At the end of a tiring endeavour, she had not managed to gain any employment. She was confident a suitable position or opportunity would arise exactly at the right time. She couldn't reinitiate correspondence with anyone she knew from before, or the little family she had left, yet she had come to terms with it being a completely fresh start.

The red-letter day had arrived when Ally would make her grand exit from the stage that was the U.R.S.C. In an immigration vehicle, she was taken from the Desiderata Centre and conveyed to the airport. She had waited so long and was doubtful about whether she was prepared—ironically, because she had so much to do it seemed to expire exceptionally fast. She had a sense the process had been rushed; there were still some facets of her supposed new life she was not even certain about. There were plans still unmade, and she was disheartened that Osiris couldn't be with her when they arrived, so that they would waste no time in forming a new existence. He was no closer to leaving or reuniting with her. She overcame this by vowing to welcome whatever the next part of her journey would bring through the craziness of life—even if it was unsure to her. Through all the trauma and triumph imprinted onto her during the experience, through all the images that would remain with her, there was a guilt she harboured that she hadn't escaped justice. So much had been taken from her life because of a few irrational choices she made in the moment. Invariably it had changed the trajectory of her path, and if she had resumed her way of life, she wouldn't have stopped, like she wanted to. She was grateful to be so fortunate. There was no great or aspiring conclusion to the life she was leading. She would have continued until she died or something terrible happened. Now she had gone through such sheer terror. This was her swan song to her former identity, drawing the final curtain.

She was being accompanied through the bustling terminal by two immigration officials walking on either side of her, holding onto her handcuffs. They would hand her to the French Police when the flight arrived in Paris. The disapproving and judgemental looks she received from people did nothing to dampen her spirit. She had been freed, departing as a rare outcome. She felt as though she was facing some type of repercussion for her past. There was still a piece of her that believed she emerged on the other side with less punishment than she deserved. There were others who were dead due to the unfolding events of the previous years. Though everything happened for a reason, the reason still eluded her. It was the grand plan for them all as the Pendulum swung through their lives, gathering energy and momentum to set them on a new course. It was an interplay of the uncanny threads in the tapestry of life and the world. She believed this had not happened by accident and was interwoven into her destiny, to swing through her life and ricochet her onto a different direction, a different path.

She thought about all of this as she laid eyes on the aircraft taxiing on the runway. The sight gave her the first genuine relief she could remember. The early-spring morning bloomed with a softness while they walked toward the plane. An enlivening fresh morning breeze swirled around them; it was almost curative. Hurtling down the runway, the chartered aircraft took to the skies, spiriting her away. She had gone to the U.R.S.C. in search of glory and was leaving in disgrace. Those thoughts dissipated into her mind. Sapped of energy, she watched as the plane cruised above the metropolises, with so many lives and stories interconnecting. The cities faded away over the barren desert plains; the shadows of clouds dappled the empty landscape below. The mood in the cabin was very relaxed. Upon reaching the coastline, they glided smoothly along as the coast gave way to open ocean. She was going home. *"Au Revoir,"* she said quietly before she fell asleep, peacefully and uninterrupted for the first time in years.

www.ingramcontent.com/pod-product-compliance
Lightning Source LLC
Chambersburg PA
CBHW020347120726
47904CB00002B/494